Watch Your Step at the Wishing Well

A Novel

By

Lisa Mottola Hudon

Cover design by Kevin McShane. Visit Kevin's website at: www.kevinmcshane.org

Library of Congress Cataloging-in-Publication Data
Hudon, Lisa
Watch Your Step at the Wishing Well: a novel / Lisa Mottola Hudon. ---- 1st ed.
p. cm.

ISBN: 978-0-557-35378-1

Printed in the United States of America by Lulu.com
Set in Cambria

Visit the author's website at: www.lisamottolahudon.com

To order additional copies of *Watch Your Step at the Wishing Well* or the sequels,
Just Another Shitty Day In Paradise and If It All Blows Up And Goes To Hell visit:
http://www.lulu.com/spotlight/lisamottolahudon

For James William Buffett, an inspiration . . . for my story . . . for my life. May we meet one day on the far side of the world.

Lisa Mottola Hudon
Tacoma, Washington
October 14, 2008

"In writing, I shall always confine myself strictly to the truth, except when it is attended with inconvenience."

-- Mark Twain

A special thank you to Rick . . . for your continual love

To Jessica, Shelby & River . . . for your patience

To Mom & Dad . . . for your encouragement

To Amy & Carol . . . for your enthusiasm

Chapter 1

Tired of That Same Old Same

Have you seen those parking lot partiers dressed in hula skirts, coconut-shell bras, and flowers around their necks, carrying portable blenders and sporting shark fin hats?

I have . . .

My first encounter took place four summers ago, driving home from college, the ink barely dry on my diploma. To say that I was cruising is to put it mildly. My 2000 Mazda MX6 couldn't move fast enough to erase the stress and headaches this former student of architecture had endured.

Having grown up the daughter of a traveling salesman, I know the back roads of Illinois as well as any John Deere tractor-driving farmer. And it was on one of those country roads that I unknowingly came face to face with my future. Actually, I almost collided with it.

Like the corn that's grown there, farm roads in Illinois typically stretch straight and true for tens of miles. (Let's call that my excuse for exceeding the speed limit.) I just happened to be racing down the one and only road containing a set of blind hills. —Up and over the first one. *Whoa!* My heart was in my throat. *Okay, that woke me up.* (Cornfields are hypnotizing.) Before I had a chance to slow down, I flew over the second hill—four tires, mid-air. That's when I saw it all: a new outdoor amphitheater off in the distance, a sea of cars in the parking lot, and directly in front of me, a mile long, bumper to bumper traffic jam! Four tires hit the ground. I slammed on the brakes, closed my eyes, and braced for the inevitable. Brakes screeched, rubber melted, my car fishtailed, and I came within inches (I kid you not, *inches*) of the pick-up truck in front of me.

Now, this was no ordinary pick-up I'd almost careened into . . . the hot tub in the bed of the truck was my first clue . . . the three over-weight men in grass skirts at my window were the next.

Within moments, a colorful crowd of luau-laden fans had rescued my car from the ditch and set this wobbly-kneed graduate back on her way. Besides realizing how very lucky I was to be alive, I remember thinking, *Who on earth are these people? Why in God's name are they dressed this way? And who is capable of causing such a stir?* Surely it wasn't me. You see, I'm not much of a drinker and seldom, if ever, do I swear. Heck, a cigarette's never even touched these lips. I'm a straight A student of life. A Catholic schoolgirl at heart. *I* am your average Midwestern girl next door . . .

At least I *used* to be.

I know you're probably wondering what the heck I'm talking about, so let me start at the beginning:

Only a year ago I was your average 24 year old, living in a Chicago suburb, working as an architectural apprentice for a one-man show, and house-sitting for a friend. I was regretfully unattached with no plans for the future, career-wise and relationship-wise. I had no money to speak of and nary a guy knocking at my door. In other words, I was a typical 5'-5", brown-eyed, brown hair, half Italian, half German, Generation Xer, eking out a boring and mind-numbing existence at the end of the commuter line. (At least that was *my* window on the world.)

Well, I should at least explain how I got myself into such a situation. Let me start by saying that I'm not a city girl; I'll take rural over urban any day of the week. Not that I don't enjoy a bit of city-life on occasion, but you're more likely to find me ice-skating on Oakwood Shores Lake than lunching at The Pump Room. (I happen to find this particularly ironic, considering my formal education is in architecture; you know, building structures that keep people *inside*.)

Anyway . . . unlike many of my classmates, I never had visions of working for one of those big firms in Chicago. Yet, I had attended one of the top 3 Architecture schools in the nation, studied in France, chiseled my way into the highest 5% of my class, pulled all-nighters for years (blah, blah, blah . . . you get my point), so I figured I owed it to myself to become an architect. After all, it has a prestigious sound to it, doesn't it? "Architect" To the average person it's a mysterious profession, combining design and vision with a rare knowledge to create timeless structures where once stood nothing but dirt. How could I not get caught up in that? But if you really want to know the truth, being an architect was the way my *parents* perceived me; those were the plans that *they* had. I was just along for the ride. (Besides, who came up with the idea of making us choose a career at 18 anyway?)

Getting a job wasn't the hard part. I was known throughout Oakwood Shores as a well-liked hometown girl and had excellent references to boot. I figured I'd work close to home until I could make some money of my own, then move out and . . . Well, I wasn't quite sure what I would do beyond that.

So why did I despise my job so much, you ask? (After all, I was being mentored by a fabulous architect who became a steadfast friend.) It was the day to day tedium that drove me nearly insane . . . sitting behind a drawing board for 8 plus hours a day, often on my own, taking a break only to use the bathroom or eat a sack lunch in the conference room. I couldn't help but wonder if that's all there was to life. (I'd heard about this happening to people in their 40's, not their 20's!) What a let down. As an architect, hadn't I been taught to think big? Heck, I had studied abroad, experienced the European back-packing rite-of-passage, dreamed of adventure on the high seas!

But truly, my career disappointment wasn't the only thing that had me in the doldrums. In fact, probably just as bothersome (okay, more so) was the fact that I was lonely. Really, truly lonely. I needed some action, and I'm not talking the sexual kind, (okay, maybe a little). But I knew I seriously needed a change. Latitude, attitude, I didn't care—just a change.

Add to that the fact that I had been living at home with my oh so loving, but oft-times smothering parents ("Why don't you join a church group, Nichole . . . that's a great place to meet a boy.") and I was on the fast track to the mental institution.

Needless to say, I jumped at the chance to housesit at my friend Mia Lundstrom's parent's house. Going through an unexpected divorce—unexpected to everyone but them—they wanted to sell their house and needed a neutral party (enter moi) to look after it while they got their issues in order. Yes, it was a change of pace for me, but 4 or 5 blocks down the road, I was still bored, lonely, and on the edge of insanity.

Chapter 2

My First Look

... O n the edge of insanity.
Come to think of it, that's exactly how I was feeling one fall day last year—a beautiful fall day. You know the kind I'm talking about: a brilliant blue sky, a strong scent of burning leaves in the air, the ideal chill for wearing your favorite wool sweater. I had just gotten home from work and was anxious to put my Monday boredom behind me. A good therapeutic run usually does the trick, so I put on my tunes and really burned off some steam. I ran through my neighborhood, a charming old-oak area of Oakwood Shores called Lakeland. I love running along the lake. In fact, it's the only place I've ever been able to run. Six miles, east to west and back . . . just long enough for those endorphins to wash away the monotony of my day. That evening, as the sun sank into the west end of the lake, I caught a glimpse of a good-looking guy getting out of a Jeep in front of one of my favorite houses. He seemed in no particular hurry as he smiled a wonderful dimpled smile at me and said, "Hey," before going inside. My curiosity was peaked. I knew that house on the corner had been for sale (it ranked on my top 5 list of the most picturesque homes along the lake), but I didn't know someone had bought it. I wondered who else

was attached with "Mr. Dimples." Surely such a big house couldn't belong to a bachelor.

I had nothing else to think about as I walked up and down the length of Lundstrom's street, waiting for my heart to catch up with my feet, so my little mind meandered . . . *okay, it's six o'clock and he wasn't dressed in a suit and tie, but in jeans and a flannel shirt . . . if he was married would he have smiled such a pleasant smile at me . . . not to mention, he had only one bag of groceries in his hand, not a family-sized grocery run.* (So goes the analytical mind of an architect.)

As you can imagine, sleep, in the master bedroom of the former Mr. and Mrs. Lundstrom, seldom came easy for me and that night was no exception. I tossed and turned more than usual under Granny Lundstrom's hand-made quilt as all sorts of questions regarding my mystery man floated around in my brain. Finally, as if to appease my weary mind, I decided I'd go for a run every day that week in hopes of finding some answers.

The first three nights, I saw his lights on inside, so I knew he was home. Then, on Friday night, I spotted his silhouette on the back deck as I jogged around the corner and I *swear* I saw his head turn. But still, I never saw anyone else at the house . . . and it was Friday night no less!

I decided to solicit the advice of one of my oldest, dearest friends, Sarah Lorenzo. Why Sarah? Well first of all, Sarah and I come from the exact same background: good Italian Catholic upbringing, same values, same insecurities, but more importantly, Sarah speaks to my rational mind. She's much more sensible than I am (if that's even possible) and at that point, I needed to know if my silly crush was simply that, silly.

Saturday, I convinced her to go for a walk with me through Lakeland.

"You say he's older?" Sarah asked. "How much older . . . a few years, or has he already RSVP'd to his 30 year reunion?" (Keep in mind, Sarah has a healthy appetite for skepticism.) "Remember what happened the last time you dated an older guy?"

"Well, if I'd have known he had a wife, I wouldn't have dated him, now would I?" She went on, "And what kind of guy in his 30's or

40's lives alone in a big house on the lake anyway? I'll tell you what kind of guy . . . a loser, or a guy with a lot of baggage, that's who."

Within moments, Sarah had slammed on the brakes of my inexistent love affair; although part of me knew she was right; maybe I *had* been acting a bit dreamy-eyed.

"I saw my cousin Anthony last weekend," she continued, "at my Nanna Rose's 75th birthday party."

Oh no, I thought, *not this again.*

"I hope you don't mind, I gave him your number."

I stopped walking and let out a big sigh. Okay, now I don't know about you, but I can't understand why people insist on doing this sort of thing, fancying themselves as matchmakers. I personally believe that if you're "set up" on a date, then all the excitement is taken out of that very first encounter. Let's face it, by the time you actually go out on the date you have all these preconceived notions and background stories that go along with the person. And God knows how many half-truths and lies *they've* been told about *you!* And since we're on the subject of taking all the excitement out of things (be patient, I'm on a roll), it reminds me of those people who are having a baby and before the baby is even born, they've told you the sex of the baby and the name of the baby and, thanks to malpractice suits and vacationing OB/GYNs, they've even told you the date and time the baby's going to be born! What's left to discuss? Heck, you can't even talk about the traumatic labor and delivery. Where has all the excitement gone? I figure, few things left in this life are genuine surprises anymore and meeting the potential man of my dreams should be one of them. —Sorry. I just had to get that out. Back to the story. . .

"Nikki, Anthony's been begging me for your number ever since you guys met at Angela's First Communion."

"Sarah," I started, but before I could object, which she knew I would emphatically do, she added, "He's really a funny guy, Nik." (Warning: beware of the "funny guy.")

"Funny is an understatement, Sarah. Believe me; I know what kind of a guy Anthony is. In fact, I have several cousin Anthonys in my family and there is definitely a reason none of them are married."

"Are you saying you won't even give Anthony a chance?"

The conversation volleyed back and forth like this as we rounded the corner of Gate 16, and quite frankly, we would have walked right past my mystery man if he hadn't raised his rake up in the air, smiled, and said, "Afternoon ladies. How y'all doin'?" in a soft Southern drawl. I somehow managed my best smile and said the nicest hello you've ever heard. It took all my composure to keep walking past his yard and not look back, but thank goodness Sarah did; she said he was watching us walk all the way around the corner!

Suddenly, Sarah was singing a different tune. "He *is* easy on the eyes; I'll give him that. And I didn't notice a wedding ring. And he doesn't look *that* much older than us."(Not quite a passionate approval but an approval, nonetheless.)

That night I poured over the questions that had been plaguing me and came to a few conclusions. 1.) He was definitely gorgeous . . . in a rustic, leading-man sort of way. Let's say a cross between a young Kevin Costner and a toga-wearing Russell Crowe. (I admit, I'm a face girl first, with body a close second. My college roommate can attest to that fact as I'd plastered the walls of our dorm room, floor to ceiling, with *G.Q.* ads. What can I say; we architects have an aesthetic eye.) 2.) He probably wasn't attached because no one was helping him rake that big yard, and 3.) I needed to meet him before I drove myself crazy!

I decided long ago that the saying "look before you leap" was meant for relationship-challenged people like me, so I spent the entire month of September keeping a low profile yet watching his every move. One particular weekday evening as I was cooling down from my run, I saw my mystery man, or "Mr. Dimples," as I'd come to refer to him, sitting out behind his house at the end of his pier. His feet dangled down above the water while off to the left the sun performed a spectacular grand finale. As was my habit, I turned off my music upon approach of his house. (Just in case I needed to hear him calling out to me. Ha Ha) Well, he wasn't calling my name, but I did hear him strumming a guitar and softly singing. I couldn't make out the words, but the melody was enchanting, and it made me literally stop in my tracks.

That's when a couple walked by and noticed me listening to his tune. "Some people pay a lot of money to hear him sing, and can you believe we get to hear him for free on our evening walk?"

It took me a moment to sort out what the man had just said, and before they walked away I quickly asked, "Is he someone I should know? A singer or something?"

"Sweetie," the woman said kindly, "that's *Garry LaForge*; you know, 'Tropicana Jam.'"

Chapter 3

It's as Big as It Seems

My mind had to race to catch up with myself. "Tropicana Jam!" My God, I didn't know a single soul who hadn't had that catchy tune stuck in their head at one time or another—me included.

> *"Oh no, you'll never understand*
> *My Tropicana Jam*
> *As I lounge my days away*
> *You're just a loner in LA . . ."*

So that's why he looked hauntingly familiar, I thought, *and that explains the Southern accent. But why Oakwood Shores? And why is there no visible woman in the picture?* And finally, and most importantly, *what the heck am I thinking? He's waaaaay out of my league.* I literally sprinted home and looked up "Garry LaForge" on the internet . . . humble beginnings in Alabama, gold records, sold-out summer concerts, magazine interviews, boats, planes, a life of parties at the beach. My God, I couldn't imagine living like that!

Now don't get me wrong. I was by no means a party girl, yet I wasn't exactly a wallflower either. My high school and college years were laden with enough pre-parties, post-parties, tail-gaits, and blind dates to last a lifetime. In fact, in the advent of my dating years I was the kind of girl asked out often by all types of guys from geeks to jocks. I realize now that I was nice . . . too nice, come to think of it. I went on many a date when I should have said no. The trouble was, the guys caught me off-guard and I wasn't quick enough on my feet to conjure up an excuse. But that all ended my senior year when I found who I *thought* was the perfect guy, my own personal Homecoming King. But, as is often the case, I was dethroned as Queen just days before going off to college. Following that important lesson in heartbreak (at least I was *told* it was an important lesson), I dated off and on throughout college, a well-intentioned guy here and there and a jerk thrown in for good measure. But as of late, I'd kept my heart guarded and my nose to the architectural grindstone . . . which led me to reaffirm, yet again, that Garry LaForge was waaaay out of my league.

As a result, I spent the rest of October trying to forget about my silly obsession with Mr. Rich and Famous. (Okay, so maybe I bought 1 or 2 or 30 of his songs.) But really, I did try to dive into other pursuits like helping my parents rake a payload of oak leaves in their yard, and getting together with girlfriends more often, and trying to figure out where I was going to live since Lundstrom's house had recently sold.

Chapter 4

Wondering How in the Hell I Got Here

O n Halloween night, another of my long-time friends, Jenny Ward, had asked me if I wanted to join her and her two toddlers as they trick-or-treated around Lakeland. I definitely didn't feel like staying home handing out candy all by myself, so I said yes and ... Well, I'll let you decide for yourself if I made the right choice.

* * *

"We can't go to that next house, Jen," I said as we approached Garry LaForge's place.

"What do you mean? The porch light's on."

"What I mean is that ... well, uh ... there's a guy living there that I've kinda sorta got a crush on ... And he's also kinda sorta famous."

Jen looked at me cross-eyed. "What do you mean, kinda sorta famous?"

"Do you know who Garry LaForge is?" I asked.

"*The* Garry LaForge—the singer?"

I nodded my head yes.

"Why would Garry LaForge be living in Oakwood Shores?" Jenny asked.

"That's exactly what I've been wondering."

"Did you meet him? Do you know him?" she asked.

I shook my head no.

"So, you've got a crush on him, huh?"

Uh oh, I knew I should have kept my mouth shut.

Now everyone who knows Jenny Coleman-Ward agrees she's not known for her predictability; therefore, I held my breath as she marched her kids right up to the front door.

With a big smile on her face, Jenny said to her daughter, "Go ahead, sweetie, ring the bell. Let's kinda sorta see if Mr. LaForge is at home."

My heart pounded as she rang the bell. A guy in his 30's or 40's answered, wearing a Captain Hook hat and holding a huge bowl of candy. It wasn't Garry LaForge, but I could see and hear several people inside having a party. He wished us a Happy Halloween and as we turned to go, someone else called from inside the house, "Hey y'all hold on a minute!" I turned around and saw that it was, in fact, Garry LaForge—with a pirate's bandana on and an eye-patch. My heart was in my throat!

"I haven't seen you around lately." He came to the door, took off the eye-patch, and looked straight at me with piercing brown eyes and the longest lashes I'd ever seen. —Then he noticed the kids. "I didn't realize you had kids."

"No, they're not mine; they belong to my friend, Jenny."

My response was met with charming dimples. A sign of relief, perhaps?

"Do y'all wanna join us inside? I've got some friends visiting."

I looked at Jenny, who had a stunned look on her face. "Go ahead," she said, "the kids are ready to head back to my Dad's anyway."

I hesitated just a moment, not wanting to blow off my 17-year friendship with Jenny for a fleeting brush with fame.

(Sorry to interrupt, but I think it's an appropriate moment to point out that I'm an extremely loyal friend. My girlfriends always come first—hey, wait a minute, that's probably half the reason there was no man in my life! Anyway, what I'm trying to say is that I've never been one of those women who act differently around men. I can't stand women who are bitchy and self-righteous around other women, but the moment a guy enters the conversation they're all sugar and spice and everybody's girlfriend.)

"Really, I mean it. Go ahead, Nik. I'll talk with you tomorrow," Jenny said, and she actually gave me a nudge.

"What d'ya say, *Nik*?" Garry imitated.

"Are you sure you don't mind, Jen?"

"Go," Jenny looked at me wide-eyed as if to say, *Are you crazy? Garry LaForge, the world famous singer, is inviting you inside his house and you're concerned about trick-or treating with me and my kids?*

* * *

Just between you and me, I've never been a truly confident person. I have only *appeared* to be. I'm far too analytical to be that sure of myself. I learned very early on, though, that outward appearances are everything. I don't mean that in a shallow way of course, but clearly, confidence is a visual art: a simple turnout of the hip, a tilt of the chin, a laugh at just the right moment. As I walked through that door with Garry LaForge, I summoned every ounce of outward "coolness" that I possessed. (In other words, I may have *looked* calm on the outside, but I was a frickin' basket case on the inside!)

Garry closed the door and turned to me with an inviting smile. "I'm glad you said yes. I've been wantin' to know who you are, and like I said, I haven't seen you around lately. You used to go runnin' nearly every day past my house . . . and then you just disappeared. I'm Garry, by the way. Garry LaForge."

Wow, talk about a bizarre twist! Did I just hear what I thought I heard? He had noticed me? He wants to know who I am? I knew I shouldn't have worn my hair in this damn ponytail!

I had to force the words out of my mouth, "Hi Garry, I'm Nichole—Bocelli."

He shook his head, stumped. "Did you say Bocelli? As in Andrea? As in musical genius?"

"I did," I replied with a smile and then quickly added, "a distant relative."

"Ah ha. Well then, Nichole Bocelli, let me introduce you to my fellow buccaneers."

Garry introduced me to four of his friends from various places: Josh and Smittie from Florida, Ryden from Georgia, and Tyler from Tennessee. They all made me feel welcome, especially when Josh, who'd had a bit much to drink, said, "So you're the mystery woman who keeps running past Garry's house in the dark of the night."

Garry gave Josh a shocked look of disbelief. *Oh my God,* I thought, *He's been talking about me to his friends! What kind of things had he said? Sweet things? Endearing things? What do guys talk about amongst themselves?* (Riotous, raunchy, naked things, that's what!) I looked at Garry with raised eyebrows. I'd be lying if I said I wasn't just a bit giddy inside to hear such a thing. He put his arm around me and asked if I'd also like something to drink, "Although you'll obviously never catch up with Josh."

Once the trick-or-treaters finally died out, Garry turned off the porch light and started the fireplace out on the back deck. Then, just to add to my anxiety, he said, "Your musical choice tonight, Nichole."

"You're joking, right?" I asked.

Talk about unsettling: five pairs of eyes starring at me, not to mention deafening silence.

"Why do I feel uncomfortable selecting the music of the evening?"

"It's a test, Nichole," Josh said with a laugh. "Garry wants to know if you two are compatible."

Garry shot Josh another evil eye. (They interacted like two pesty siblings.)

"I better not pick any Garry LaForge music, then," I joked.

The flirting came easy, spurred on by a couple of glasses of wine. Garry led me into the living room and set me in front of an overwhelming music selection while he went to get more wine. When he came back from the kitchen I handed him a Jackson Browne CD. He knelt beside me and winked. "Perfect choice." The sexual chemistry between us felt palpable, and I thank God he took me by the hand and led me outside again or I would have melted right there on the spot.

"Who picked this piece of crap?" Tyler called out as we approached.

"Hey!" I said

"He's kiddin'," Garry assured me. "Tyler happens to be the godfather of Jackson's son, Ryan."

What am I doing here? That's all that kept running through my head.

Chapter 5

No Intention of Becoming a Star

G arry and I rocked leisurely on the glider. Frost was working its way across the back lawn, and although the fire raged, he spread a warm blanket over us. Basically, we spent a couple of hours just talking. Garry and the others asked me questions about myself, and I found out about their lives. They're all part of the Garry LaForge conglomerate in some way. Josh and Smittie play in Garry's band, Ryden heads up the road crew, and Tyler is Garry's tour manager. I also learned that Garry was renting the house through a friend of a friend of a sailor he knew with the intention of spending some time far from all the commotion in Key West. But what I found most interesting of everything told that evening was the fact that they were all such down-to-earth guys, each and every one of them . . . even Garry, especially Garry. I don't mean for that to sound like my expectations were low. On the contrary. For the past two months, I'd created, in my mind, such a wonderful trumped-up image of "Garry LaForge," that I figured, if I ever *did* meet him, I'd surely be disappointed.

Somewhere past dark-thirty Josh staggered in to crash on the sofa, and Smittie, Ryden, and Tyler got the crazy notion to take the boat out for a spin. Garry went inside and put on "Dark Side of the Moon."

"You're going to throw me over the edge," I said while he refilled my glass of wine and cozied up even closer.

"Would that be so bad?" he asked.

I smiled a mischievous smile as he put his arm around me.

Normally I would have been a bundle of insecurities at that point, questioning everything from my hair to my posture to the words spilling out of my mouth (I mean, how often does one get the chance to sit thigh to thigh with a rock star on his back deck on Halloween night?), but thank goodness the wine had kicked in.

"So tell me more about yourself," I asked. "I mean, what's it like to be Garry LaForge? Is it what you imagined life as a rock star would be like? Have you become jaded by fame? Are you constantly hiding from paparazzi? Are all the ladies at your beckon call?" (Okay, so I have a tendency to babble when I'm nervous.)

"Whoa, hold on there, Missy," Garry said, looking me right in the eye. "First of all, darlin', I am by no means a 'rock star' per say, and I never really envisioned myself as one. I know this may sound funny, but it just sort of happened somewhere along the way. I always thought I'd become a journalist—write for the *Mobile Register* or maybe even *The Times-Picayune* if I were really good. But durin' my first year at 'Bama I discovered the guitar and started playin' with a group at some bars on campus to earn some extra money . . . and it didn't hurt one bit in the female department, if you know what I mean."

Garry flashed the most charismatic schoolboy grin. There were those dimples again!

He went on, "It took me five years, but I finally did graduate with a degree in Journalism and a minor in History. I stopped home just long enough to stuff that diploma in the top drawer of my dresser and pack a duffel bag for The Big Easy. Well, one thing led to another and I started playin' more and more clubs along the Gulf Coast. Eventually, I met a friend, Jimmy, who lived down in Key West and invited me to hang out there for a while—play a little, drink a little, fish a little—you get the idea. Anyway, for some bizarre reason I developed a sort of cultish following in the venues up and down the Florida coast. —Now, my lifestyle at that point suited me just fine and I really had no intention of takin' it any further until the Miami radio stations got a hold of 'Tropicana Jam.' 'An overnight sensation,' they called it. And

everything just went haywire. It's been that way for the past 12 years, and I must confess, I could use some rest. So here I am in Oakwood Shores, *Illinois*, of all places, lookin' for some peace and quiet so I can pursue my
latest dream."

"Which is?" I asked.

"Meetin' you, of course." He squeezed me tighter. "Nah really, it's to write a book. Fiction/non-fiction. A little of both I guess."

There was silence. I longed for him to go on. I was hypnotized by his Southern drawl, not to mention, taking intense pleasure in studying every feature of his godly face.

"And what about all the ladies at your beckon call?" I asked (half seriously).

"Ahh, the ladies." He looked up at the sky as if in reverie. He wasn't going to answer, and I got the point.

"Enough of this borin' talk about me," he said. "You really shouldn't let an old man ramble on."

"Old?" I said flirtatiously.

"Old-ER. Enough to make me very, very nervous. Or as we say in the South, as nervous as a long-tailed cat in a room full of rockin' chairs."

I couldn't help but laugh. I was reminded of my college friend, Trevor Morgan, Southern Illinois' Junior Roping Champion. In fact, roping is how I met Trevor. He had a habit of roping unsuspecting girls as they stepped off the elevator in the dorm. Anyway, every morning at breakfast he'd come up with a new way to greet me: "Mornin' Miss Nichole, you look purtier than a pig's tail today." Or "You're lookin' hotter than a June bride in a featherbed." I tell you, we Midwesterners got nothin' on those Southerners and their colorful expressions.

"Should I be?" he asked.

"Should you be what?" I said.

"Nervous?"

"Most definitely," I said with a smile.

I thought it was a good answer (if I do say so myself) and waited for what could potentially happen next when, BANG! went the end of the pier. Alas, the boating sojourn had come to an end. (Warning: beware of a man's friends.)

Garry stood up, "Hey, it's gettin' late. Why don't I give you a ride home? I assume it's not far from here?"

"Drive *or* walk. It's not far at all, just down Gate 18 on the other side of Lake Avenue."

He pulled me to my feet and whispered in my ear, "Let's walk."

I said my goodbyes to the guys who were leaving the next day, and Garry grabbed his coat. He slid his big warm hand into mine, hooked my pinky around his, and said, "Now don't you try to get away; I got ya hooked like a billfish on a fly." (FYI: I love a man who holds hands!)

A more gorgeous night did not exist. Above us, a crisp, clear sky sparkled with every constellation imaginable, while back on earth, Garry's cold breath mingled intimately with mine. Except for the gas coach lights at each corner, we were completely in the dark. Garry held my hand in his coat pocket and we walked, in silence, most of the way, but odd as it may seem, it wasn't an awkward silence at all. In fact, it was rather sensual. That's the only word that truly describes that walk back home.

Now, no one hates first date good nights more than I do, and my normal strategy goes something like this: talk, talk, and just keep talking. If he's second date material, he'll surely find a way to make me stop. If he's not, he'll give up easily enough and allow me to breathe a sigh of relief on the safe side of the door. BUT, that night was no ordinary night. I had been captivated by Garry LaForge's Southern drawl, charmed by his Southern expressions, and had talked endlessly with him about every topic imaginable. Those past four hours with Garry left me wanting more. Or to be more specific, those past four hours with Garry left me . . . *wanting.* As we stood there at my door, I knew that leisurely chitchat would *not* be a workable strategy. So, with all the courage I could muster and trying not to sound desperate, I whispered in his ear, "Wanna come in?"

Garry closed his eyes and bit his lip, as if he had to think about it. "Nichole, with all my heart I'd like to come in. I truly would. But I don't want to mess this up, alright?

"I really want to see you again. Will you be home tomorrow?"

The next day was Sunday. "Yeah, I will." I tried not to sound too disappointed.

"Good. I'll drop by."

My mind filled with questions again. *Is he just trying to find a way out? Maybe he thinks I'm too young. And what does he think I'm going to do, sit at home all day Sunday waiting for him to stop by?* (You bet I would!) *I knew it was too good to be true. After all, I'm just an average girl, leading a tiresome little life in the suburbs. Why would Garry LaForge be interested in me?* I tried not to appear as disappointed as I felt, although I must have been looking down at the ground because I clearly remember Garry lifting my chin and giving me one more wonderful dimpled smile before pulling me toward him. It was the perfect first kiss—warm and gentle, sweet and lingering—no tongue jammed down my throat (listen up, Ray Zimbowski, if you're out there) and a small soft kiss at the end. Let's just say, after that goodnight kiss, all my doubts flew right out the window.

And you guessed it—I couldn't sleep that night.

* * *

At this point, Garry feels the need to interject, which, with eager curiosity, I am compelled to permit.

She caught my attention the very moment I stepped out of the Jeep, a long brown ponytail bobbin' up and down to some mysterious tune in her headphones. (My music, I'm sure.) Her stride was effortless, and in my opinion, her participation in the sport had absolutely nothin' to do with weight control.

I was relatively new in town, and in keepin' with the friendly Midwestern spirit into which I'd been indoctrinated, she and I greeted one another in syncopation. And although I closed the door behind me that evenin', I must confess, I watched her delightful departure through my front room window.

My immediate thought was, What the hell are ya doin' LaForge? *First of all, she looks younger than a dogwood saplin' in spring. And second of all,* didn't you come here to get away from all the distractions?

It wasn't easy, but I kept remindin' myself that every evenin' as I searched for her out the front room window.

I caught sight of her bouncin' by several days later. I stood out on the deck grillin' up some ribs and just happened to turn my head as she rounded the corner. I can't say why in particular, but I was intrigued. I guess sittin' at the computer all day long, recountin' past adventures has a way of makin' me antsy.

So, imagine my good fortune when, lo and behold, there she was that very next afternoon, walkin' right by my house! Her auburn hair hung down past her shoulders and she was dressed in perfect fittin' jeans and a jacket, but there was no mistakin' that easy motion or that beautiful smile.

Our eyes locked instantly as if we'd previously met. The only problem was, we hadn't . . . and I needed to figure out how to rectify that as soon as possible.

So what's my normal remedy when such a problem arises? Why, write a song, of course. (Screw my publisher! That New Year's deadline was asinine anyway.) I spent hours, no, days, pourin' out my soul with the point of my pen. I realized I was crazy for wantin' another woman in my life. Hell, Brooke Walker's call had just about done me in the week before.

I glimpsed my joggin' beauty only once or twice after that, and barrin' runnin' after her down the street, I had no idea how she and I were ever goin' ta meet. By the end of the month, I tell ya, I was one hurtin' fella. Thank God Josh, Smittie, Ryden, and Tyler were headin' to town. I knew they'd be able to snap me out of it. There's nothin' like a weekend of oblivion to set the mind straight again.

I actually almost missed her. It was Halloween night. I was on my way to the kitchen to drown my sorrows in yet another bottle of Merlot when I saw her walkin' down the porch steps. I would have recognized that backside anywhere.

Now I'm not a bettin' man, but you can be sure I wasn't about to let such an opportunity pass me by.

I think it's fair to say I'm a confident, take-charge kind of guy (although I wasn't always that way, havin' spent the first eighteen years of my life tryin' to get by as a quiet and shy Catholic schoolboy), yet the moment I came face to face with Nichole, I became, once again, an awkward teenage boy with an enormous crush on the girl next door.

I'm sure Nikki's enlightened you with all the finer details of our meetin', but I'd like to add my two cents here by sayin' 1.) She looked young 2.) I knew she was a keeper by the way she held her own with the likes of us flawed individuals and 3.) Did I mention she was young?

And by the way, for y'all's information, it took every ounce of energy in these hormone-driven bones not to go inside with Nichole that first night.

Chapter 6

Raking Mom's Backyard

I sprang out of bed in a panicky state. I forgot that I promised my parents I'd finish raking with them that afternoon. Over three cups of strong coffee, I hemmed and hawed about not helping out, and finally, after talking with Jenny (who'd called at 7:45 am!), I decided to keep my promise to my parents. I left a note for Garry on Lundstrom's door *if* he should in fact stop by.

> Garry, I completely forgot I promised
> my parents I'd help rake their yard today.
> Sorry I missed you. Give me a call. The
> number is 489-1919.
>   Nik

Now, it may be no big deal to most folks, but it's everything to me, signing my name "Nik." You see, if I don't know you or if I've just met you (or if you're my freshman college roommate and I can't stand you) then the name is *Nichole*, thank you very much. Only my closest family and friends call me Nik or Nikki. Whether or not Garry knew it, signing my name "Nik" was my way of inviting him into my personal world.

Oh, and in case you're wondering, it *had* occurred to me, more than once, that Garry might not take me up on my offer. After all, he'd had an entire night and half the morning to come to his senses. I don't mean to sound cynical, but let's face it, I wasn't an up-and-coming Hollywood starlet, or a lanky runway goddess, or even an all-American sun-bleached beauty . . . any of which I assumed one had to be to attract the attentions of a "rock-star."

And this I mused, crawling on my hands and knees under the evergreens in search of musty leaves. I was in pretty deep when my phone rang from the patio.

"Hello?" I said, out of breath.

"Afternoon darlin'. How's my billfish doin' today? I just stopped by your house and got your note. By the way, I couldn't help but notice a big ol' *Sold* sign out front today. Did I scare you off already? Or are you just smarter than I think?"

I could almost see the dimples of his big smile. "Yes, Garry, you frightened me so much last night I've decided to move away and join the convent."

"Now don't tell me you're a good Catholic girl, Miss Bocelli."

"Numerous years of Catholic education, Mr. LaForge."

"Lordy, lordy. What *are* you doin' to me girl?"

"Seriously, now, when can I see you again?"

"If you feel like raking, you can come see me in two minutes," I joked.

"I sure could use a good rake. Don't mind if I do. Just tell me where your parents live and I'll be over, lickety split."

"I was joking, Garry," I said. "You don't have to spend your afternoon raking a half-acre of leaves."

"Who's jokin'? I'd love to help out. If it means spendin' the afternoon with you, then it'd be my pleasure. That is, if Mom and Dad would approve." (That's another thing I've noticed about Southerners. They always speak as if your relatives are theirs and visa versa.)

"Garry, really," I protested.

"Are you gonna give me the directions or do I have to drive around Lakeland lookin' for you?"

After I hung up I made a B-line for the bathroom to evaluate the situation. —Wait, back up a minute. After I hung up, I immediately turned off my phone. All I needed was for Garry to hear my new "Tropicana Jam" ring tone! Anyway, back to the bathroom situation: ratty hair, dingy clothes, absolutely no make-up. "Shit," I said to the mirror. I tried to fix myself, but figured he'd have to take me as I was. Then I found my mom and told her, "I just got off the phone with someone I met last night and believe it or not, he's on his way over to help rake."

"Oh, I think I like him already," she said. "So tell me about him. What's his name? What does he do? How did you meet him?" (My mom is a born listener, an Iowan—slow talkers, good listeners. Or as my dad, a New Englander, says, "Iowa, where they grow beautiful corn and tall women.")

I'm not one for details, especially when discussing men with my mother; and besides, the countdown had begun. "His name is Garry. He's a musician. He's renting that big white house on the lake at Gate 16 that was for sale. We met last night officially when Jenny Coleman and I were trick-or-treating with her kids. I know that sounds strange, but our paths had been crossing several times before that. Let's see, what else? He's older than I am. A lot older."

"How much older?" she asked, purely out of curiosity I'm sure, because she and my dad's 10 year age difference has always made age a non-issue in our house.

"Well, I don't know exactly; although I'm sure it's at least 10 years, maybe 15?" (Are you kidding? Of course I knew how much older he was! Fourteen and a half years, to be exact, but I felt the need to be flippant about our "relationship"—or whatever one might have called it at that point.)

She simply raised her eyebrows. That's when I saw Garry's Jeep driving down the street.

"Here he is now."

Reminding myself to breathe, I walked around front, past my dad on the rider mower with his headphones on. When Garry pulled in the drive, my heart came alive.

Correct me if I'm wrong, but I'm sure most of you have experienced the same feeling I was having at that moment: sometimes when you meet someone, especially at an evening function where alcohol is involved, you wake up the next morning with all sorts of amnesic episodes and insecurities . . . nothing is as it seems . . . or is it? Therefore, it's always reassuring to have a second meeting during the sober, daylight hours just to make sure the thoughts and feelings were real, not alcohol induced. In that case, Garry's dimpled smile as he stepped out of the car was a good start. The hug was even better.

"So this is where it all began," he said as he looked over the house and yard.

"This is it, my humble beginnings."

That's when my dad realized we had a visitor and pulled up loudly with the mower. He cut the engine and detangled himself from his deafening headphones. (That's my dad, living life full volume and full speed ahead. In fact, he gained popularity at my high school as that parent up in the stands ringing the 10-pound cowbell and yelling at the referees.)

"Dad, I'd like you to meet Garry LaForge. (I didn't think the name would strike a bell with him). Garry, this is my dad, Gino."

They exchanged pleasantries and Garry jumped right in, "Looks like you're all set with your ridin' mower and tunes. Can't get much better than that."

"Oh, maybe with a beer in hand the job would go quicker."

"So what is it you listen to while you cut the grass?"

"Let's see, a little jazz usually; some Benny Goodman today."

Garry looked at me. "I think we're gonna get along just fine."

The funny thing is, it's the first guy who came over to the house that I hadn't had a chance to give the run-down on my parents, especially my dad. I knew I'd just have to let Garry wing it and figure it out by himself. I thought it'd be interesting.

"Well, Mr. Bocelli, I have come armed and ready to work. Your lovely daughter here insists I don't help out, but I'm sure y'all could use an extra hand. Am I right?"

Garry opened the back of the Jeep and pulled out all sorts of yard implements: rake, trimmer, hedger, etc. He spoke loudly from the car, "Now, just because I'm a musician doesn't mean I can't get dirty with the best of 'em. Just point me in a direction and I'll serve my time well."

"Oh, a fellow musician?" my dad said. Garry had unknowingly ignited my dad's interest.

Garry looked at me, then my dad. "You're kiddin' me, right?"

"Northwestern School of Music . . ." My dad went on to give his never ending laundry list of music credentials, and to my surprise, Garry listened intently. "And what line of music are you in?" he asked Garry.

I couldn't have been more curious to hear his answer. "Yes, Garry, *do* tell us what you do in the music industry," I teased.

"Oh, I'm just a refugee from a rock 'n roll band, Gino. —I sing, I write, I play . . ." He didn't get to finish because my mom joined us, rake in hand.

"Garry, this is my mom, Mary Alice. Mom, this is Garry LaForge." I wasn't sure if she knew of "Garry LaForge," but with my mom one never knows. She's often aware of things that surprise me: neighborhood gossip, fashion trends, what time I *really* got in on Prom night.

They shook hands.

"Garry was just telling me that he's a fellow musician. Did you say you play an instrument?" My dad asked.

"My dad sells instruments," I added.

A big smile spread across Garry's face. "I play, or I should say, I pick at the guitar, and I'm not half bad at keyboard, and I can bang a mean drum if I have to, but mostly I love the guitar—acoustical."

They continued to discuss instruments a bit, and I'm sure Garry's answers led my dad to discover that not only does Garry know his axial-flow valve from his spit valve, but he also knows his music—from Gillespie to Gershwin to Genesis.

Soon enough, Garry was off and hedging. In all honesty, he was a great help and didn't follow me around asking what to do; he really pitched in and did a little of everything. *Hmmm. A take-charge kind of guy. Gotta like that.* Finally, as Garry manned the burn pile out back, my dad's verdict had come in: two ice cold beers—one for himself and one for Garry.

Meanwhile, I stood again at the bathroom mirror, desperately trying to fix my hair.

My mom called from the kitchen, "Do you think Garry'd like to stay for pizza? I'm assuming you'd be okay with that?"

"*I'm* okay with that," I called down the hall, then turned to the mirror and quietly said to myself, "I just hope *he's* okay with that."

I quickly gave up on the whole looking good idea and joined the men out back. "Y'all don't have to go to any trouble, really," Garry said.

"No trouble at all, Garry," my dad answered. "Mary Alice probably has it started already. Stay and have a few beers with us. You put in a hard day's work."

"Only if Nichole can put up with me a while longer," he said, hanging his arm across my shoulder.

"I definitely can. Definitely."

We spent the evening eating and drinking in the kitchen and talking up a storm. My dad gave Garry the nickel tour of the house while I tagged along. You might find it a bit odd, giving a tour of the house, but you'd have to know my dad and how exceedingly proud he is of the unique house he'd help build. I realize, now, that it was a rather presumptuous thing to do, but at the time it seemed like a normal course of events, and crazy as it may be, to this day, I find myself giving unasked-for house tours during dinner parties. —See what our parents do to us!

Anyway, as we meandered from room to room, I wondered what Garry's parents were like and what his childhood home looked like. I wondered if I'd ever get to meet *his* family. (But wait a minute; it's thinking like that, that ruined more than one relationship for me.)

The deeper subject of Garry's occupation never really came up, and as I said before, I just didn't want to go there yet. Garry, ever the humble guy, would never have brought it up unless I did first. (*Humility. Another likeable quality.*)

It was nearly 10 o'clock when Garry thanked my parents for a great evening and they, in turn, thanked him over and over again for helping out with the yard. They walked him to the door, and I walked outside with him to his car. The funny thing is, my dad had one of those motion detector lights installed right down the driveway, so as we walked to the car, we were suddenly in the spotlight.

"Makes you feel like you're back on stage, huh?" I said laughing.

"Don't tell me you had to go through your high school years with that light?"

"No, thank God. It's fairly new, although I'm sure he's wishing he had one installed back then . . . especially for my older sister, Jane."

"I'm sure it wouldn't have mattered much for you, huh?" Garry joked.

"Let's just say I knew where to park and where *not* to park cars at night."

"I look forward to hearin' about that," he laughed.

We walked to the back of the Jeep and sat on the bumper.

"I really enjoyed myself today," Garry said. "Thanks for lettin' me come over to help and bend your parent's ears a bit."

"You? I didn't think my dad would stop talking. I didn't have a chance to warn you."

"Are you kiddin'? Your parents are superb people. And now I have more insight into who Nichole Bocelli really is. I have to admit, it's not exactly what I had in mind for a second date with you, though."

He came and stood in front of me, straddling my legs. "How 'bout supper—I mean dinner—with me tomorrow night?" He leaned in closer, and whispered in my ear, "Just you and me. Alone."

"Supper *or* dinner," I said. "And just you and me would be wonderful."

He kissed me softly and sweetly then looked up toward the front door. "I guess I better get a move on before Gino calls the police. How about 6, my house?"

"I'll be there."

He hooked my hand in his and we walked to his car door. We kissed once more, more passionately, and then I walked, in a dream world, back inside.

My mom and dad were gushing about Garry, and I have to admit, I was all smiles about him too. They did bring up the age difference though, which surprised me. And my mom said something like, "He must make good money if he's renting that big house on the lake."

I played dumb. "I guess so."

I still wasn't sure if I should tell them who he was. On one hand, I was dying to, but on the other hand, I wanted them to know him without fame and fortune attached to his name. Also, I know this may sound childish, but there was a part of me that didn't want to portray

Garry as "the perfect guy" to my parents. I was afraid it would ruin his appeal. (Even at 24, there's still something annoying about agreeing with your parents about a guy.)

I bid my parents good night and went back to Lundstrom's, exhausted from hours of yard work and plenty of thinking about Garry.

Chapter 7

Just You and Me. Alone

I bounced into the office the next morning with a brand new attitude on life. Not that I wasn't normally pleasant with Roger and Edie; after all, they were marvelous people who'd given me an amazing opportunity to test the waters of architecture, but on Mondays I'd been known to bribe myself with the promise of Ben & Jerry's just to get my behind into that office. I was sure Roger would notice the big Mardi Gras grin on my face. He said nothing—that is, until the flowers arrived! A stunning tropical bouquet that was difficult to overlook.

"Someone's either begging for forgiveness or you've got one hell of an admirer on your hands," Roger joked.

"Whoever they're from, I'd say he's a keeper," Edie added.

Roger went back to work while Edie held her wide-eyed gaze on me as I read the note to myself:

> Nichole, I'm looking forward to many more
> days raking Mom's backyard with you.
> See you tonight –
> Just you and me. Alone.
> Garry

An enormous smile spread across my face. "He's a definite keeper," I said.

"And who might *he* be?"

I shook my head. "You'd never believe me, Edie."

"Try me."

(Divulge my secret? I wasn't so sure.)

"Is it someone I know? —Nichole?"

"OK. But you have to promise you won't tell anybody."

Edie seemed thrilled to be let in on my secret and stepped closer with anticipation.

"You know who Garry LaForge is, don't you?"

"Of course. Roger and I listen to his music all the time on the boat." Edie waited for me to continue.

A moment of silence was followed by a dazed look of confusion.

"I told you, you wouldn't believe me," I said.

"Are you telling me that the singer, Garry LaForge, sent you these flowers?"

I nodded my head.

"Roger!" Edie called into his office. "You've *got* to come here."

And so I confessed. They somehow drug the truth out of me. The whole truth—well, almost all of it. They were downright shocked and just about as excited as I was.

All afternoon, I did my best to stay focused on my projects, but Roger, being the softhearted romantic that he is, looked at the clock at 4:30 and said, "Nichole, what the heck are you still doing here? You've got a dinner date with *Garry LaForge* and you're sitting around working on locker room layouts? You better take yourself and those flowers of yours and get out of here."

* * *

I was pretty anxious. Strike that . . . Anxiety seeped through the floorboards of my otherwise boring life! I spent a lot of time making myself look presentable. I remember trying on outfit after outfit finally deciding on a mix between "this is just another casual date" and "I'm not as young as you think." I also recall a sudden sense of panic at not finding any matching bras and underwear in my drawer. Don't forget, the only times Garry had seen me, up to that point, were when I was jogging, bundled up for trick-or-treating, or in dingy clothes doing yard work. That night I wanted to make sure he saw I could actually wear nice clothes, put on make-up, and do my hair on occasion. Lastly, I searched my wine reserves and came up short (A $7.00 bottle of Zinfandel wasn't going to cut it), so I made a mad dash to the store and hurried out carrying a $35 bottle of Chateau Saint Somebody with a strong endorsement from the manager.

Oh, one last thing I think you ought to know about me. Up until this point, I've probably led you to believe you're dealing with a nice, sweet, good Catholic girl; which, don't get me wrong, I am. But, I've been blessed (or cursed, depends how you look at it) with a streak of mischievousness that earned me the title "Nichole the Unpredictable" by my college friends. For the most part, I live my semi-normal existence, but every once in a while I get an itch in my brain to do something . . . let's say "a little less than holy."

That being said . . .

I arrived at Garry's in a rush; it was already 6:25.

"I was beginnin' to wonder if you'd had second thoughts," Garry said with a hug and a kiss on the forehead.

"Haven't you ever heard of fashionably late?" I presented the bottle of wine. "I didn't know the menu du jour, but figured, if anything, it'd go well with dessert."

"Oh, *Chateau Saint Chalon.* One of my favorites. Why thank you, Nichole Marie."

"How did you know my middle name was Marie?"

"Just a lucky guess."

"No, really, I don't remember telling you, did I?"

"Remember how you said your dad's a talker?" He smiled. "There are all sorts of things your parents told me about you. You didn't think your dad and I were just talkin' about the weather out at the leaf pile, now, did you?"

"Now you've sparked my curiosity," I said. "What else did they tell you?" (I hoped to God my dad hadn't bored Garry with some lame story from my childhood . . . how I got stitches in my knee from chasing a boy on the playground, or how I used to dance in the living room in my underwear. Once, while running behind schedule, I left my date alone with my dad for no more than 10 minutes. I was never told exactly what transpired between the two but darned if that boy didn't hold the car door open for me, change our plans from the beer bash to the ice-cream parlor, and have me home by 10 o'clock!)

"First of all," Garry said with a wink, "save the sparks for later, and second of all, that's between them and me."

I followed him into the candle-lit living room. "Why don't you select the music for the evenin' while I get supper on the table. I'm starvin'."

"You always put that pressure on me, don't you?" Once again, I waded through the vast array of CD's. "What mood are you in, Garry?" I called into the kitchen.

He brought me a glass of wine and kissed me, long, hard, and with complete confidence. "I hope that answers your question." And he walked away.

My knees nearly buckled and it was tough to focus. "Loud and clear," I called out.

Okay, I thought. *Something sultry and sexy.*

"Sade," Garry said, carrying out two plates of food. "She reads me well."

"I thought I'd go Italian tonight in your honor, so I made my famous clam sauce with angel hair pasta. Sorry I didn't make any hors d'oeuvres. Multi-tasking isn't my forte, but there's plenty to eat."

(I know what you're thinking. *What's with this guy? He's sexy, handsome, well educated* and *he cooks!* Hey, believe me, I was thinking that *exact* same thing. I was also thinking, *what's the catch?*)

"It looks great and smells even better," I said, even though I actually couldn't give a damn about the food and knew I'd have to force myself to focus on eating. (By the way, the man truly *can* cook!)

"Now, if I can just make it through this meal," Garry said under his breath.

I gave him a knowing grin. *My feelings exactly!*

"Hey, Mr. Romantic, you caused quite a stir in the office today."

"A good stir or a bad stir?"

"A good stir. And thank you, they were gorgeous."

"Gorgeous flowers for a gorgeous lady. And by the way, you do look spectacular tonight."

"You mean you weren't impressed with the ripped-jean and sweat-shirt look of yesterday?" I joked.

"Don't forget, Nichole, I'm just a down-home Southern boy at heart. Ripped jeans and a sweatshirt get me all hot 'n bothered."

"So were you all hot and bothered yesterday?" I asked with a smile.

"This poor boy had to come home and take a cold shower! — Speakin' of hot 'n bothered, is it an inferno in here or is it just me?" he said, stripping down to his t-shirt.

A warm tingling sensation overtook me (you women know the one I'm talking about). There's just something about a man in jeans and a white t-shirt . . . especially a sexy man sporting a November tan.

We ate and drank and flirted recklessly until we could stand it no longer. Garry took our wine and I followed him into the living room where he grabbed his guitar and sat on a chair. I hoped he would play me a serenade. I'd been wanting him to so badly, but of course I'd never have asked.

"It hasn't been my intention to write music while I'm here, but this song has been chasin' me around the block these past couple of months and I needed you to hear it. It's called, 'Been Tryin' To Catch Up With You.'"

He then mesmerized me with the most melodic ballad about distant love, secret desires, and a chance encounter. *Hey, wait a minute.* I thought. *That sounds familiar! Are you telling me he's been thinking about me these past couple of months without even knowing me? Here I am, jogging by his house every night, watching his every move when apparently he's been doing the same thing?*

"It's beautiful," I said. "I love it."

He set his guitar down on the floor and moved over next to me on the sofa. "Do you really? Because I wrote it for you."

Now, such a statement certainly warrants a response. After all, it's not every day someone tells you you're the inspiration for a song. But the fact of the matter is, that song, and all its implications, had impaired my normal mental function.

Garry leaned in and kissed me passionately, with fire in his eyes. "I hope I don't regret this," he said. "I'm a damn fool when it comes to love . . . always followin' my heart when I should be listenin' to my head."

I didn't say a word. I was entranced by his kiss.

"God help me Nik, I'm *14* years older than you."

The only sound was our beating hearts and I whispered in his ear, "Then take good care of me." And I kissed him passionately back.

"That I promise."

I'd be lying to you if I said I hadn't spent sleepless nights fantasizing about having sex with Garry, but you have to understand that my mother, and more importantly, my devoutly religious father, are quite possibly reading this, so I'm sorry to say that I'll have to leave all the juicy details to your libidinous imagination. Garry pulled me to my feet and led me up the stairs to his bedroom. It was the moment I'd been dreaming of for the past two months, and with each step I took up those stairs I was completely aware that those steamy sex scenes you're thinking of right now could possibly come true.

And come true they did. Sure, I never envisioned any of those awkward moments that go along with first-time lovemaking or the fact that the phone would ring two different times, or that Garry's hands would tremble ever so slightly when he undressed me, but I did imagine it to be as urgent and as intense as it proved to be. Now granted, I was only 24 years old, but I had never experienced such deeply passionate sex in my life.

(On a side note here, which you know I'm full of, I'd like to point out the one true advantage/pleasure of an older, more mature man: oft times—imagine this ladies, and listen up younger men—they consider the needs of the woman *before* their own!)

Afterward, as we lay tangled in the sheets, Garry pulled me close, kissed me and said, "I don't think you need a bit of takin' care of, my dear. You do just fine on your own. In fact, I'd like to know how a 24 year old like yourself knows just how to do what you do."

I must admit, I felt a certain satisfaction at hearing those words. I hope that doesn't come across sounding too smug, but think about it, I'd just had what I considered to be amazing sex with a handsome rock star and there *he* was singing *my* praises. I'm sure we can all assume that Garry's ventures in the sexual department far out-weighed my measly three experiences, one of which I hesitate to even count for the mere fact that it was more "experiment" than "experience," so any and all compliments went straight to my head.

Garry started the bedroom fireplace and asked what I wanted to listen to.

"Just your heartbeat," I replied.

To my surprise, he grabbed the remote and hit *Play*.

"Normally I wouldn't listen to my own music," he said. "But you asked to hear my heartbeat, so here it is, my latest labor of love. And I swear to you, every single organ of this body went into the makin' of this sucker."

Now, I happen to pledge allegiance to the church of post-sex lingering and as such, will *never* forget that moment, lying in bed sideways next to Garry, my head propped up on my elbow as he gently outlined with his fingers, each and every curve of my body; from my face, down to my feet and back up again, all the while, narrating the songs from his latest CD, telling me who wrote them and the meaning behind the words. I could have stayed there in his arms forever. I had never felt more comfortable in such an unlikely situation in my entire life.

BUT, I decided I realistically couldn't stay the night. I had work in the morning and knew Roger and Edie would find me out if I arrived late and in disarray. I made a move for my clothes on the floor.

Garry grabbed my arm, "Oh no you don't. You can't just run away, Nichole."

"How do you know I'm running away?" I asked.

"I can see it in your eyes."

"Garry, I've got work in the morning and . . ."

"And NOTHIN'," he finished.

I sat back down on the bed. *Is that a look of hurt or annoyance?* I wondered.

"I'm out on a long thin limb here, Nik, and I need to know you're smack dab beside me."

"I'm too rational, aren't I?" I admitted.

"Rational is good. It balances out my irrationality."

I smiled and knew that he really meant it.

"What can I do to have you stay? An early wake-up call? Breakfast in the mornin'? A quick trip to Lundstrom's to get your things?—We could do that."

So that's what we did, and I felt much better about it. Garry was ever the gentleman, helping me pack, carrying my bag, etc. He even set the alarm for me, got up when I did in the morning, and went down to make coffee and breakfast while I showered.

I walked into the kitchen that morning reeling from the carnal pleasures of the night before. "Boy, I could get used to this every day," I said, sitting down to scrambled eggs and toast.

"And every night?" he asked.

"Especially every night."

I'd like to be able to say it was a storybook ending as I trotted off to work that morning, but it wasn't. It was an awkward goodbye at the door—Garry the househusband with coffee in hand as I gathered my things. The right words didn't come to me as we parted, and the lack of reassuring words from Garry seemed to choke my throat. I reminded myself, *one night of passionate sex does not a relationship make.* All I knew was that I was in deep and if there's one thing I learned from that all-important lesson in heartbreak, it's that there's no free ride in this carnival world.

"Thanks for a wonderful dinner last night. And dessert," I said.

Garry winked and left me with only his dimpled smile to think about . . . and think about . . . and think about.

* * *

Hey, it's me again, Garry. I promise not to butt in too often, but I thought y'all might be interested in my perspective on things . . .

I was smitten, although I must confess, the fourteen-year age difference between us kept pokin' me in the eye. I mean think about it, I was buyin' school supplies for my first year at Holy Cross High on the day Nikki was born! In any event, that issue was pleasantly resolved on our first official date. It was then that I discovered age and maturity are not one in the same.

Chapter 8

Being Rich and Famous Seems to Have Its Ups and Downs

M y boredom at work that day was unfathomable. I truly tried to make the best of it, but worry as to why Garry hadn't mentioned getting together again consumed my every thought. Unfortunately, I was alone at the office all day and had nothing but my neurosis and Garry's music to keep me company. Roger arrived by 4:30, wanting to hear all the details of my evening. Of course I didn't give him *all* the details. I gave him the abridged version, although I'm sure my permanent smile gave me away. That's when there was a knock at the door. (I had a hunch it was Garry—no one ever knocks at our door). Roger opened it and there stood Garry, an apparition to my weary eyes.

"Somebody told me a lovely lady I know works here."

Roger welcomed Garry like a star-struck teenager. (I remember praying to God that he wouldn't ask for Garry's autograph.) Sometimes, at moments like that, it would dawn on me that Garry had this whole other life and persona that I had yet to come in contact with. And I'll let you in on a little secret, whenever I *did* think about it, I'd start to get nervous and doubt everything. I wasn't so sure at that point I wanted to know "the famous" Garry. I liked things just the way they were going along.

I gave Garry a brief tour of the office and my daily life, such as it was. And I have to say, the fact that he took a sincere interest in my work made an impression on me. Garry has a way of making people feel their lives are important, no matter who they are or what they do for a living.

As if on cue, one of Garry's songs began playing on the stereo. "I see y'all have great taste in music," Garry commented to Roger.

A moment later Edie burst into the office in her usual conspicuous and hurried manner. However, upon spotting Garry, she came to a complete and sudden halt. It was priceless to see her all gooseflesh and a-giggle as Garry turned on his schoolboy charm.

"Mind if I steal this lady away for the evenin'?" Garry asked.

"Just don't steal her away for good, young man. We'd be lost without her," Roger half joked.

"I'm thinkin' I might be too," Garry replied.

I smiled politely, but inside I jumped for joy.

Hand in hand, we ran through the rain to Garry's car. Once inside, he leaned over and kissed me. "I think I forgot to do that this mornin', didn't I? I've been waitin' all day to do that."

"And I've been waiting all day to hear that," I said, surprised by my own brazenness.

Garry smiled and kissed me again.

What happened next may seem of no major consequence, but I thought it significant enough to tell you in that it was my first real exposure to a life of celebrity and the prickly package in which it comes.

We went out to dinner; *The Feedbag* of all places—the most ordinary middle-class establishment in the Midwest. Can you imagine, sitting on a hay bale with Garry LaForge at *The Feedbag* in Oakwood Shores?

Somewhere in the middle of our fried mozzarella sticks, I noticed people starring at us. Flattering, yes, but also unnerving.

"Is it my imagination, Garry, or are people watching us?"

Garry leaned in close, "Don't let it bother you one bit. They're just admirin' that fancy saddle you're sittin' on, that's all."

But as Garry took the first bite of his cheeseburger, a man at the stall next to us rocked back on his saddle. "Hey, buddy," he said, "Has anyone ever told you you look like that singer, um, what's his name? You know the one . . . he sings that song "Tropicana Jam." He began humming a few bars. "Garry LaForge, honey," his wife chimed in. "I just love his music." Everyone in the "Cowpoke" stall concurred. Garry, of course, didn't let on and just laughed along. That is, until the waitress brought back his VISA.

"There you go, Mr. LaForge. You have a nice evening, now."

Seven flabbergasted faces and several handshakes later, we were out the door. But not before the entire restaurant had either gawked at us or asked to take a picture with Garry.

"It takes some gettin' used to," Garry said as we drove away.

"What does?"

"The realization that your life isn't your own anymore—that your every move is being analyzed. I can't complain too much though; people are basically nice about it, at least with me they've been. I have always said, I have the greatest fans in the business. But I know some people who fight it all the time and never come to terms with it."

"Like . . .?"

"Like Harrison. He's hell-bent on keepin' his privacy, even if it means livin' a thousand miles away from where he works."

"Harrison? George or Ford?"

Garry chuckled. "Ford. He's a real number. I meant to get out to Wyoming for a visit this fall, but I just didn't get a chance."

"Your life is so surreal to me, Garry. I mean, I have friends like Jenny, who works as an administrative assistant at Kraft Foods, and Amanda, who's an engineer for Chevron, and Jessica, who's a buyer for Macy's, and you have friends like Harrison Ford and Glenn Frye and James Taylor for God's sake!"

Garry just laughed and leaned over to kiss me. "I know, Nik. Don't think I don't find it surreal at times, too. That's why I love the relative anonymity of Oakwood Shores and why I don't go to all those celebrity events in Hollywood and why a weekend at my parents house in Camellia Bay is absolute heaven on earth for me. —You know, livin' in the briar patch ain't what it appears. More often than not, I'm workin' harder than a one-armed paperhanger. My life can be mighty hectic and my house has a tendency to become Grand Central Station. There's no way I could have accomplished any writin' there. Don't get me wrong, I have a boatload of great friends and band members. We're just with one another all the time and know a little too much about one another, if you know what I mean. Tourin' all summer long can really wear on relationships. That's why I'm takin' some time away."

Here's where I actually got up the nerve to ask a question I wasn't sure I wanted to hear the answer to:

"How long do you plan to be here?"

"That's a good question," was his reply. (Not quite the answer I was looking for.)

I wanted more out of him, of course. I wanted to hear him say he was rethinking his plans, that *I* was the reason he was going to stay longer than expected. I wanted him to tell me he'd never been so happy in his life, that I was occupying his every thought. For God's sake I wanted to hear him say that he was falling in love with me! (If you haven't guessed it by now, I'm a hopeless romantic. I also have a tendency to get way ahead of myself.)

I picked up my car, and Garry followed me over to Lundstrom's house.

I went to his window. "Aren't you coming in?"

"Thought you'd never ask."

To tell you the truth, I hadn't slept much lately and could have used a good night sleep, but my desire to be with Garry superseded any fatigue I had.

"How long have you been livin' here?" Garry asked as he poked around the house.

"It's been about three months now."

Garry noticed a stack of unopened mail on the counter. "You said the Lundstroms are goin' through a divorce, but don't you find it odd that all their things are still here?"

"Yes. It's very odd. It's like they woke up one morning, grabbed some necessities, and went their separate ways. All her jewelry is still here, the newspaper continues to be delivered every morning . . . there were even dirty dishes in the dishwasher when I arrived."

"Good thing they left behind this nice Baby Grand." He sat down and started playing scales.

"I didn't know you were a pianist," I said, sliding in next to him.

"Lessons," he rolled his eyes, "once a week, first through eighth grade. Mom insisted. How 'bout you?"

"I started in first grade too. But I lasted only a few years. Do you remember those beginning piano books where all the notes are numbered and each number corresponds to a finger? Well, instead of learning to actually read the music, I felt it would be infinitely easier and certainly faster if I just played by number. Well, within a year or two, I'd mastered all the beginner books and dutifully moved up to intermediate level. Those books, of course, contained no numbers, which basically meant I was screwed. My teacher was baffled as to why I could no longer play the piano and I was too embarrassed to tell her. So I quit. —I did learn a couple of classics, though."

Garry clapped politely for my performance of "Peter, Peter, Pumpkin Eater" and "Mary Had a Little Lamb" then proceeded to show off with a flawless rendition of "Swan Lake."

I pushed him off the bench. "No fair showin' off," I said. "Didn't your mamma teach you to let the girls win sometimes?"

Garry was on the floor laughing so hard he couldn't get up. "Believe me, baby. You're winnin'. You're definitely winnin'."

There were those hypnotic bedroom eyes again!

Speaking of the bedroom . . .

Have you ever slept with someone and experienced severe regret afterward? Or better yet, been in the throws of naked pleasure and known that something just wasn't right—he was far more attracted to you than you were to him? You were using him as a rebound? He was far too kinky for your tastes? I've come to the conclusion that making love with someone the first time is all about passion. Without a doubt, it involves explosive excitement and sexual tension; it's completely hormone driven and lacks any amount of rational thinking. *But*, making love with that person the second time around is all about purpose. It's a mental choice, a decision of acceptance and approval.

To put it simply, I was comfortable making love with Garry. No regrets. No remorse. No need for repentance. I felt as relaxed as a child gnawing on a pacifier (don't go there) . . . yet I realized, as every new parent does, that the use of a pacifier quickly becomes an addiction!

Admittedly, Garry and I *were* children that evening. We'd discovered where the Christmas gifts were hidden. We were giddy with excitement and just *had* to take another look. But that second time around we weren't as hurried about it, and we definitely took more pleasure in the exploration.

That night, Garry and I were the Magellan and Cortez of our time!

Chapter 9

Silver Wings

T he next morning Garry was in the shower when his cell phone rang. "Nichole? Can you get that?"

I wasn't sure it was a good idea, but oh well. "Hello."

"Oh hello." It was a woman. She sounded surprised that I'd answered. "I'm tryin' to reach Garry. Is he available?"

First, I wondered who the woman was and second, I wasn't sure what to say. "No, I'm sorry, he can't come to the phone right now. Can I take a message for him?"

"Could you have him call Susan? Tell him to call me straight away. It's extremely important." The woman had an accent like Garry's.

Just then, Garry came dripping out of the shower. I mouthed the word Susan.

He put his hand out for the phone. "Hey there sis," he said, winking at me.

That put me at rest, although the tone of the conversation suggested something was awry. Not wanting to intrude, I continued getting ready for work. (Of course I tried to listen to his every word.)

Garry walked downstairs, towel around his waist, still on the phone.

"It's rainin' pitchforks here, but I'll see if I can get out this afternoon. Don't y'all worry. —I won't. Just tell Dad I'll be there tonight. What about Sammi? —Alright. I'll call you in a bit. —Bye."

He sat down on a kitchen chair and I must say, in the short time I'd known Garry, I'd never seen him so distraught.

"It's Mom. She fell down this mornin', unconscious. Luckily, Susan was at the house. She and Dad called an ambulance. Looks like Mom's had a stroke."

"Oh my gosh, Garry. Is she okay?"

"She's in the hospital, doin' alright. They're runnin' all sorts of tests right now."

He was lost in thought, and rightly so. (Apparently I know nothing about Southern boys and their mothers. To say that Garry and Charlene are close is an understatement. Not that Garry and his father *aren't* close; it's just that I'd have a hard time explaining the subtleties of Garry's relationship with his father. Let's just say that Charles LaForge had had high naval expectations for his one and only son, whereas Charlene is much more forgiving.)

I sat down next to him. "I heard you say you're going this afternoon."

"I'll try to get out if the weather clears. It looks like it's gonna open up. I need to call the airport."

What I didn't realize was that Garry was flying *himself* down to Camellia Bay. I knew he was a pilot, but it hadn't occurred to me that he had his own plane at the Oakwood Shores airport.

"I think I can get out by noon. Can you come, Nik?"

"To the airport, or to Camellia Bay?"

"To Camellia Bay."

"You're kidding, right? You should go by yourself, Garry. I'm sure your family wouldn't appreciate me tagging along, especially at a time like this. Besides, I can't just leave work."

"My family would love you, by the way, but I understand what you're sayin'." He stood up and hugged me close. (Actually, I think it was Garry who needed the hug.) "I don't know how long I'll be gone. I'll call you, alright? And you've got my number. Call me any time, day or night. I mean it."

I went to work feeling lost, but ducked out to the airport at 11:30. I spotted Garry on the tarmac, checking his plane. He looked up, saw me in the window, and dashed inside with a huge smile on his face.

"Hey my love." (*My love???!!!*) "Tell me you've changed your mind."

"No, I haven't changed my mind, but I wanted to see you off."

"I'm so glad you came. I forgot to give you this." And he handed me a key. "Here's my house key and here's my parent's phone number. Will you keep an eye on the house? You can stay if you want to. I'd like that."

"Sure. I'll have lots of parties there while you're gone," I said with a sly smile.

"The only parties allowed there are private ones with me," he replied.

"I'll be waiting," I said.

He kissed me on the forehead. "Close your eyes and I'll be back real soon."

* * *

It was an awesome sight as Garry took off and headed south through a hole in the clouds.

Chapter 10

Big Blue Hole in the Middle of My Heart

A s for me, there was a hole in my heart that afternoon. I'm telling you, it took all of my being to keep working at Roger's that day. I would have thrown in the t-square right then and there to be with Garry. All I kept thinking was, *what the hell am I doing in this place?*

Let's see, that was Wednesday, only four days after we'd met, and the loss I felt at Garry's absence was profound. I know, I know, we'd only known each other *four days*, but my friends would be the first to tell you that when Nichole Bocelli falls, she falls fast, and she falls hard.

Pacification came with Garry's constant calls—from the airport in Camellia Bay that afternoon, the hospital that evening, and one more time before going to bed. By the end of the day he sounded wiped. His mom rested in intensive care, fragile, but coherent. The entire family held vigil—his oldest sister, Susan, who'd been visiting from Wyoming with her three kids, and her husband, (the director), Gregory Rosenberg, who'd arrived in the morning, and middle sister, Samantha and her husband, Colton Devereaux, who'd driven from New Orleans that afternoon. There were also various aunts and uncles and cousins living in town who were in and out of the house. We didn't talk long and as I said, I sensed Garry's exhaustion. He was staying at his parent's house and said he'd keep in touch. I felt so helpless and suddenly disconnected from this newfound person in my life. I couldn't help thinking there was still so much about Garry I didn't know.

As soon as I hung up with Garry, the phone rang again.

"Garry," I said, without looking at the screen, "I thought you were going to sleep."

"Nik? It's me, Sarah. Who did you think I was? —Wait a minute! Oh my God! You haven't met Garry LaForge, have you?" (Okay, I know I should have called her. But I'd been busy, alright.)

We talked into the wee hours of the night about the new course of events in my life. Finally, I had something to talk about. Usually it was Sarah who rambled on and on about her relationships, or should I say, relationship *troubles*. She was shocked about everything and skeptical, as usual. ("You haven't done anything irrational like sleep with him, have you? You know these celebrities . . . here today, gone tomorrow.")

That's why I decided to call Christi. Not only is Christi Delaney a night owl, but she and I are umbillically connected when it comes to the opposite sex. Without a doubt, I can count on Christi to swoon over any man I deem desirable, which was exactly what I needed after my conversation with Sarah.

"Hey Nichole," Christi answered. "You sure are calling me late. There must be a man involved. Am I right? Wait. Before you answer . . . I'm finishing up a report for work, but if you tell me the word orgasm is going to be part of our conversation, I'll gladly put it off 'til the morning."

(How I can have two such different friends is beyond me.)

Chapter 11

Predator Friends

I n an effort to breach the distance between us, I went over to Garry's house that afternoon, a cold and rainy November day. I snuggled into a cozy chair in his bedroom, overlooking the lake, and eagerly read some of his personal writings. But first, I'm going to admit to doing something that no one ever admits to doing . . . I snooped around Garry's house. (Don't tell me you wouldn't have done the same thing if you were in my position.) There was nothing of much importance, really. In the kitchen, a surprisingly full refrigerator, well-stocked cabinets, and a supply of hot sauces to last a lifetime. In the medicine cabinet:, a complete alphabet of vitamins, along with two different migraine prescriptions, sleeping pills, and muscle relaxers (*a little bit stressed, are we?*). Upstairs, well-organized closet and drawers (is that important only to me?), and finally, the nightstand, (I *am* thorough, aren't I?) Twain, Hemingway, Campbell, Chatwin, Jones, Wouk, to name but a few. But the reason of my true curiosity lay within the nightstand itself. There it was, one box of 12. A good sign. I would *not* have liked to find a jumbo stash in there. And I was certainly glad not to find some sort of girly magazine. I picked up the box, which promised "hours of extra pleasure," and instinctively looked around (I don't know why—hidden cameras?). I'm a bit embarrassed to tell you that I actually began to count... seven, eight, nine, ten. *Alleluia! Ten condoms left in the box.*

Curiosity satisfied.

I happily sat down to read Garry's latest manuscript entitled *Gospel From the Coast* (which, by the way, he had invited me to do). Within moments I was whisked away to the island of Mauritius, lounging topside aboard an age-old schooner with the smell of frangipani wafting on the breeze. Pages later Garry had me caught in a treacherous storm in Chile as I hiked with him up the mighty Aconcagua. I can tell you, it was a real treat to delve not only into the adventures of Garry LaForge but into the mind of Garry as well. His most heart-felt thoughts were right there, in 12 point courier, laid bare for me to see. After hours of reading, I came to realize that Garry, at the age of 38, could spin a tale like the most seasoned of explorers. In fact, I hadn't realized Garry had *done* so much exploring, and I'm not talking happy-go-lucky holiday traveling either. He'd lived in cities, walked through jungles. He'd witnessed storms and starvation. Heck, by the time I'd graduated from Middle School he'd already traveled half way around the planet.

Afterward, I crawled into his bed, under the covers, where I could breathe in his lingering scent, and fell asleep . . . until I was startled awake by the house phone.

"Hello," I said in a raspy voice.

"Oh hey, is Garry there?" . . . a male voice with yet another Southern accent.

"No, I'm sorry he's not. He's out of town. Can I take a message?"

"No, that's alright. I tried him on his cell, but he didn't answer. I just thought I might catch him there. You said he's out of town, huh?" I wasn't sure just how much information to give. If Garry led a normal life, I would have divulged more.

"Yeah he is. I don't know when he'll be back."

"This is Marty." I remembered Garry saying that Marty Anderson was his best friend and personal manager. They'd grown up in the same neighborhood in Camellia Bay and gone to the same Catholic grade school and high school together. He also said Marty was a smooth talker and a player, despite his 10 year marriage to "the sweetest Southern Belle this side of the Mississippi" *and* a baby on the way. "Everybody loves Marty," Garry had said, "but beware, he's the kind of person our parents warned us about."

"Hi Marty. Garry's mentioned your name several times."

"And who might you be with the pretty voice?"

"I'm a friend of Garry's. He had to go down to Camellia Bay on Wednesday. His mother's not well."

"Really? Is it somethin' serious?"

"She had a stroke."

"Charlene had a stroke? You're kiddin'? I'll call there straight away. —Well, it sure is nice of you to hold down the fort while he's gone."

"I'm not really holding down the fort, just checking in on things, that's all."

"So will I be meetin' you in the near future, Miss ...?"

"Miss?" I repeated, knowing full well he wanted more information about me.

"Miss mystery woman. Aren't you goin' to give me a name to go with this splendid conversation?"

"Nichole."

"Miss Nichole ...?"

He was persistent. "Bocelli," I reluctantly added.

"Bocelli? As in Andrea? (*If I've heard it once ...*) You've got to be jokin'. Bubba died and went to the suburbs and met up with a Bocelli? Well I'll be damned."

"We Bocellis get around, I guess."

"Well I hope you and I get around to meetin' one another real soon," he said ... as sweet as apple pie on Sunday afternoon (as Garry would say).

Chapter 12

Girls . . . Girls . . . Girls . . .

My dance card was empty that night, and as the sun went down, I felt especially lonely at Garry's house. I called Sarah and found out that she and the rest of the girls were meeting at *The Cabin*, a local hangout in Oakwood Shores. (Not quite as swank as *The Feedbag*, but a close second.) Lots of people I knew from high school were there, including my good friends, Christi, Amanda, Melanie, and Jessica.

Let me explain to you a little bit about my friends . . . I hang out with girlfriends—lots of them—almost all of them from high school. I know, they say your closest friends throughout life will be your college friends, but guess what, I'm the exception. There are about a dozen of us who keep in regular contact—a few seeking their fortunes in the wilds of the city and a few more already busy changing diapers and hosting backyard barbeques. The rest of us, those who remained in Oakwood Shores, were carefully weighing our options, waiting to make our big moves on the board game of life. Please, please, do not confuse us with those locals who have absolutely no intention of expanding their horizons beyond their yearly vacation to the Wisconsin Dells. Those are the locals that we refer to as "townies," as in, "You don't want to go out with him; he's a "townie." I know that sounds snobby, and to the townies, I'm sure my girlfriends and I are, but hey, I'm just here to tell the truth (as I see it anyway).

"Where is he?!" Amanda ran up to me and demanded to know. (Besides being a brain, Amanda is joyously excitable . . . *always* joyously excitable.)

"He who?" I replied innocently.

She went on, "Nik, you've got to tell us everything! Sarah and Christi said that Garry LaForge invited you to a party at his house on Halloween. Is it true? What happened? What's he like? Why is he living in Oakwood Shores?"

The five of them moved in for the kill.

"Let me get a beer first," I said.

When we sat down, I answered as best as I could. "Yes, Garry LaForge is renting a house in Oakwood Shores while writing a book. Yes, he did in fact invite me into his house on Halloween night. No, we weren't alone; he had four other friends there. We had a great time talking, drinking, listening to music . . ."

"And?" they asked.

"And—and we've had dinner a couple of times since then."

Everyone's eyes lit up.

"Come on, Nichole," Melanie said. "Dinner a couple of times? We don't want to hear about dinner. We want to hear about dessert!" (Melanie, a font of knowledge of all things sexual. Heck, in high school she was dating guys from towns we didn't even know how to get to!)

I just raised my eyebrows as if to say *maybe . . . maybe not. I'll never tell.*

"Where is he tonight?" Jessica asked. (Jessica: pretty, quiet., fashionably dressed, and always the first to be asked to dance.)

"He flew home to Alabama on Wednesday. His mom's sick."

Five women with nothing to say . . . impossible!

"You're not bringing him to Ellie's wedding next Saturday, are you?" Sarah asked.

"I'm not sure. I haven't asked him. I don't even know if he'll be back in town."

"You know Ellie and John are huge Garry LaForge fans, don't you?" Christi added.

"No. I didn't," I replied.

"It'd be so funny if you didn't tell Ellie and you showed up with him at the wedding. She would flip out," Amanda said.

Trying to sound very nonchalant, I added, "We've just had a few dates you guys. Don't get carried away here. And *please*, don't start telling people I'm dating Garry LaForge. I'll be really embarrassed if I'm dateless next weekend."

Just as I said that, "Tropicana Jam" sang out from my inside my purse. I looked at the number then did my best to stifle a smile. Everyone's eyes bugged out.

"It's him, isn't it?" Amanda whispered.

I nodded my head *yes* and walked to a quiet corner.

"Hello."

"Hey my love." (*There's that 'my love' again!*)

"Hello Mr. LaForge. How are you?"

"I'm goin' crazy. I was just lyin' here in bed thinkin' 'bout you and now I can't sleep."

"Go on, go on. Tell me more," I said.

"Well, if *you* were home in bed I would, but from the sounds of it, you're in a drinkin' establishment of some sort?"

"I must confess I am. I'm having an awful time without you, though."

"That's just what I like to hear."

"How's your mom, Garry?"

"Mom's doin' much better. As a matter of fact, she'll be comin' home tomorrow. I thought I'd stay a few days then I've got some business in Key West I need to take care of."

"Do you think you'll be back by next weekend?" I dared to ask.

"I sure could arrange that. Is there a special reason?"

"I have a wedding to go to. My friend Ellie's. I was wondering if you'd like to go with me. But before you answer, I have to tell you that Ellie and her fiancé are big fans of yours. They don't know that you and I are ... uh ..." (Talk about goin' up a glacier without a pick ax.)

"Hopelessly in love?" Garry chuckled.

Now that's what I like to hear. "Okay. Hopelessly in love. Either that or just hopeless," I said. "Anyway, I'll understand if you'd rather not go."

"Are you kiddin'? I'd go anywhere with you Nichole Marie. Just tell me where and when and I'll be there."

"I miss you so badly," I said. "The nights are especially long.

Chapter 13

Stick a Candle in the Window; I'm Comin' Home

I have an older brother named Luke. Luke lives in Minnesota with another of my high school girlfriends named Mia. "Don't you find that a bit awkward?" is the most common question I get asked in regards to Luke and Mia. And my answer is, *yes, at first I did, but not anymore.* It all started my junior year in college. No, I take that back. It started in high school. My brother Luke happens to be rather good looking in a dark haired, blue-eyed Italian way. Of course, *I* never saw him that way until my sophomore year when, every Friday afternoon, religiously, my girlfriends would ask me, "What's Luke doing this weekend?" Funny thing is, although Luke was voted "most desirable date," he never took an interest in dating. He and his friends were more involved with camping, target practice, and pick-up hockey games. Anyway, while I spent my junior year of college studying in Versailles, Mia spent hers in Norway. It took me about two seconds to figure it all out when Luke came to visit *me* in France, yet spent two weeks traveling through Norway. The awkward moments came in the beginning of their relationship when Mia would call the house and I'd answer. She and I would chat for a while, and because she was too polite, she wouldn't ask to speak with Luke, although I knew that's what she wanted, so I'd ask her if she'd like me to go get Luke and she'd say "oh sure," as if the thought had just dawned on her. They also had the habit of inviting me to go out with them, which was a bit too bizarre for me, so I'd come up with something pressing that needed my attention. Since then, Luke and Mia's relationship has become as ordinary as fireworks on the 4th of July. It was my *unordinary* relationship that I had yet to tell them about.

My parents had already gone to bed and we were discussing our plans for Ellie and John's wedding the following day.

"Garry LaForge! Are you flipping crazy?" Mia asked. "What do your parents think about you dating Garry LaForge?"

"They don't know who Garry is. I mean, they've met him, but they don't know *who* he is."

"I can't even believe it!" Mia said, shaking her head. "Your date to the wedding tomorrow is Garry LaForge? The multi-millionaire singer, Garry LaForge? —Luke. Can you believe this?"

Luke's mouth literally hung open. He was speechless, which is a lot to say for my brother who usually has plenty to say about everything.

The following morning couldn't come soon enough. I felt excited and anxious all at the same time. I had yet to share Garry with any of my friends, and I was nervous as to how it would play out. Luke and Mia begged to come along with me to the airport, and I couldn't really say no. Besides, I didn't know the exact time of Garry's arrival, so I figured they'd keep me company.

We sat together at the Five-Stool Lounge at the Oakwood Shores airport. (Yes, that truly is the name, and yes, you guessed it, there's only room for five.) Anxious for Garry's arrival, I found it increasingly difficult to focus on small talk. That is, until Luke turned to me and said, "I told Mom and Dad about Garry. I hope you don't mind." (Focus regained.)

"You told them *what*?" I said, hoping he didn't mean what I thought he meant.

"They were bound to figure it out sooner or later. But that's not why I told them." He paused to order some drinks.

"You see, I said Garry was arriving today and we were all going to meet him at the airport. They thought I meant O'Hare, of course (which is an hour away), and they were wondering how we'd make it to the wedding on time." Luke took a moment to tell the bartender he'd like an olive in his Martini.

He continued, "So I said Garry was flying his *own* jet and would be landing at the Oakwood Shores airport."

"Hey, that's not Garry is it?" he said, pointing to a Cessna oscillating terribly upon approach.

"No!" I snapped, somehow offended at the insinuation.

"Man, that guy's having a tough time," he mused.

"Luke, what happened next? With Mom and Dad?" Patience was not my virtue that afternoon.

"Well, one thing led to another and—well . . ." He took a sip of his drink. He put his hand to his mouth and whispered, "Remind me never to order another Martini here again."

I put my forehead down on the bar.

Mia jumped in. "For Christ's sake, Luke. Get to the point!"

"They're happy about it," he added. "They were stunned, of course, but completely okay with it. Mostly they wondered why you hadn't told them before."

"Actually," Mia said, "Gino thought that *Luke and I* had discovered Garry's secret identity and that *you* still didn't know who Garry was!"

We all got a good laugh out of that, and to be honest with you, although I wasn't pleased with Luke for butting into my personal business, I did feel somewhat relieved that the truth was out.

Well, that discussion took up much of my waiting time, which was a good thing because for some reason, I was a poster-child of insecurities again.

I scanned the southern skies once more then spotted her, *Celestial Explorer,* coming in, smooth and steady (of course).

"Oh, I think that's Garry."

The overhead speaker announced Garry's call letters. "Yup, that's him."

Within minutes, Garry executed a perfect landing then turned and taxied toward the building. I couldn't help but be proud.

A worker informed us that we were allowed out on the tarmac once the stairway was down. So we waited . . . and waited. I suppose there was a lot for Garry to arrange inside the plane, but I was on my last nerve by the time I saw him at the top of the stairs. We walked outside (okay, there may have been a little skip in my step) and Garry broke into a magical smile. I'm happy to report that he hustled down those stairs, dropped his bags, and gave me a sailor's welcome. It was wonderful, and I longed at that moment to be alone, but introductions were made and a quick peek inside the plane was essential. Garry, obviously in a wild mood, kept hugging me and wouldn't let go of my hand the entire time. I wished we didn't have a wedding to go to! But we did . . . and it was starting in a little over an hour.

Chapter 14

Made From Holy Water

G arry knocked on Lundstrom's door a short while later, looking sinfully sexy in a white shirt, tie, and navy suit. (Did I mention I wished we didn't have a wedding to go to?)

"Am I presentable?" He held out his arms and spun around, then lifted up his pant legs. "Look, I even wore socks."

"You look like a saint," I said.

"Baby, I may look like a saint, but I'm just a sinner gone astray.—Now *you*, my darlin', look like a choir girl about to commit a little mortal sin."

"That sounds about right."

This seems like an appropriate moment for me to add a quick note on the wonders of Catholicism (Catholicism as *I* see it anyway). Being "Catholic" is a relatively ambiguous label, at least for a "Cradle Catholic" like me. It requires limited participation, little to no evangelization, and nary an effort on one's part. If you're like me, or Garry for that matter, you've been Baptized, First Communioned, First Reconciled, and Confirmed all by the age of 13. As adults, we may not faithfully attend Sunday mass, nor go to confession, nor get married in the Catholic church. We may not agree with the fact that priests take a vow of celibacy, or maybe we're "pro-choice" or we believe in gay rights, but *darned* if we don't still call ourselves Catholic. That's the thing about us Catholics, we're under the impression we get to pick and choose which of the Vatican's rules apply to us.

"What about guilt," you say? "Don't Catholics carry within them, interminable amounts of guilt?" Exactly. Because of the "sinful" choices we sometimes make, we Catholics are masters at the art of living with guilt . . . not to be confused with *dealing with guilt*, which, in itself, is fodder for years of psychotherapy.

We arrived at the church just as the ceremony began and slipped into a back pew, a great vantage point from which to check out the guests. Ellie's side represented strongly with all of my girlfriends and her family, with whom I was close. (My very first job was working with Ellie at their family bakery during high school. More often than not, she and I were hung over from the previous night, and I'm ashamed to say that *sometimes*—only sometimes—the floor was still spinning as I served up those apple fritters.) On John's side stood several guys from the class ahead of me and what I assumed to be a number of his friends from college. That's when I spied a very familiar backside. *Oh shit*, I thought to myself, *it's Patrick Kelly* (my high school boyfriend). *How could I have forgotten he and John were fraternity brothers?* It'd been a couple years since I'd seen him, and I must admit, before Garry came into view, a thought or two of him had crossed my mind. —Now, not that I was looking or anything, but he did seem to be dateless. There's a certain satisfaction, isn't there, in seeing your ex-boyfriend dateless? Overweight, balding, and hating his job would be even better.

After mass, I tried to stick close to Garry, but there were seldom-seen friends to hug, new babies to coo over, and recent bits of gossip to discuss. Garry, right in his element, didn't seem uncomfortable, nervous, or out of place at all. He was, as always, the epitome of calm, confident, and laid-back; something I, myself, longed to be. We shuffled through the receiving line and Ellie and John about fell off their rockers. (In fact, allow me to pass on this simple observation: when a groom yells out "holy shit!" in the back church vestibule, he will not be looked upon favorably by his new in-laws.) Garry told me several times he didn't want to upstage the bride and groom, and I can assure you, he was a picture of humility.

Funny as it sounds, though, I could hear the buzz. I could feel the eyes on us.

Speaking of eyes on us, I noticed Patrick look in my direction more than once, and as Garry talked with Luke and Mia he sidled over.

"Hi Nikki. It's good to see you." He gave me one of those hugs that ex-boyfriends give in public; you know the kind . . . not too much body contact, a fake smile, a few pats on the back . . . so no one thinks there are any hard feelings involved.

"Hi Patrick. I forgot you and John were fraternity brothers. It's been a while since we've seen each other, hasn't it? How long has it been? A couple years?" (Actually, it was a New Year's Eve party two years earlier. He was drunk and professed his never-ending love for me—with absolutely no recollection of it the next day.)

We exchanged small talk as Garry walked over. "Um, Patrick, this is my friend, Garry." (I hesitated about whether or not to say LaForge but decided to be the nice, unpretentious girl I'd been raised to be. I was, after all, in the church of my Baptism). "Garry, this is Patrick Kelly."

They shook hands, and although I could bet Patrick knew who Garry was, I assumed Garry was clueless as to whom Patrick was. That is, until he walked away and Garry said, "So that's Mister First Love, huh?"

"You have a good memory," I said.

"Well, he was only lookin' your general direction about a thousand times today."

I kissed Garry on the cheek, "He may have been Mister First, but he wasn't Mister Right."

* * *

The reception followed at nearby Lakeland Country Club. Get this, when we walked in, the band, still setting up, had put on Garry LaForge songs for background music. How funny was that! Garry went with it, though. As I said before, he was in a jovial mood "from all the go-juice I drank while flyin'." (Go juice is extra-strong coffee, by the way. I wouldn't want you to think Garry is one of those out of control rock stars, fated for an episode on *Rock Stars That Hit Rock Bottom: The True Story Behind The Music.*) He struck up conversations with anyone willing to talk and spent a great deal of time with Ellie and John, who badgered him to play a song or two. He humbly declined at first, but as the night wore on and the tequila flowed freely, they managed to squeeze the humility right out of him.

The band happened to be decent, which was a big help. They also graciously let Garry borrow a guitar and take center stage. Garry played, "Conditional Love," a slow song that Ellie specifically requested, and received a rousing applause. Then, spurred on by the crowd, and another shot of tequila, he struck up one of my favorite tunes, "Between the Devil and the Deep,"

It was then, perched there on my bow-tied chair at the edge of the dance floor, that a revelation swept over me. I had one of those "light bulb moments" that Oprah talks about. I suddenly understood. I got it . . . Garry's voice, pure as liquid gold, Garry's lyrical genius, his effortless banter with the audience. People were drawn to him. He had charisma. He had a flocking. He had me wrapped around his finger. Hell, he had me before I even knew his name.

Afterward, although everyone cheered for more, Garry thanked the band profusely and turned the stage back over to the band. I thought he handled it, well, like a professional.

At one point in the evening, as I came out of the Ladies Room, Patrick cornered me in the hallway. When I say "cornered," I mean truly, he cornered me. And like Garry, he had plenty of tequila running through his veins.

"Nikki, Nikki, Nikki," he mumbled. "It must be tough on the ego to date someone who gets more attention than you do."

(According to my scorecard, Patrick was in no position to make such a statement.)

"You would certainly know about egos, now, wouldn't you?" (Honestly, I harbored no ill feelings toward Patrick. I'd come to terms with his behavior long ago.)

"Touché," he laughed. "I always did admire your sarcasm.

"Word has it he's renting a house on the lake. Writing some sort of book or something. I also heard he flies his own plane in and out of the Oakwood Shores airport. In fact, someone said he flew in today, just for the wedding." (*Okay, what's the deal with not using Garry's name?*)

"You're well informed about *him*," I mocked.

"Let's face it, Nik, your date's the talk of the party," Patrick said.

"Well, *Patrick*, as usual, it looks to me like you're the only one around here who's busy flappin' his jaws." And I slipped away before the conversation got any more memorable.

And so, we all danced ourselves silly and drank just enough to call it a great time. Ellie and John talked nonstop about what a wonderful wedding gift it was to have Garry there.

As far as I was concerned, the wonderful part of the evening didn't really begin until we arrived back at Garry's house. The ten day absence, along with the alcohol, made Garry particularly amorous, and I can tell you it's a good thing Lakeland Country Club was only four stop signs from home. As soon as we stepped inside Garry looked at me with his big brown eyes and said in his best Southern drawl, "Ah have been a patient boy all night long, Miss Nichole." Then he pulled off my coat and we made love right there against the door. It was passionate and exciting and left us breathless.

"If I was 20 years younger I'd make love to you for a month of Sundays."

* * *

We did make love again . . . in the morning; that time it was slow and sweet, and I swear we would have lingered in bed all day, but family calls, and missing Sunday afternoon at the Bocelli house is considered a sacrilege.

But first, listen to what happened next; it took me by complete surprise.

Garry was in the shower when he leaned his head out and said, ever so charmingly, "So when can I help you bring all your things over?"

I wasn't sure I'd heard him correctly. "Excuse me, *what* did you say?"

He stuck his head out from the curtain. All I could see were his dimples and water running down his face.

"You heard me just fine."

"No, I don't think I did. Could you clarify that please?"

"Why don't you come on in and I'll make it perfectly clear," he said.

Garry pulled me into the water, robe and all, and whispered in my ear, "Move in with me."

Before I had a chance to speak, he kissed me again and again. "Say yes."

My head got all light and the room started spinning. Was he really asking me to move in with him? Was this crazy, or what? Was I just setting myself up to get hurt? Oh God. I wanted to so badly, but I wasn't sure.

He lifted my chin up with his finger. "Nichole, I love you."

That's all he had to say. I was putty in his hands.

"Are you *sure* you want me to?" I asked.

"As sure as I've ever been."

* * *

Don't think I don't hear what y'all are sayin' right about now, "How on earth could Garry ask Nichole to move in with him in such a short amount of time?" Or better yet, "How could Garry LaForge be interested in some small town Midwestern girl who he saw simply joggin' by his house?" My reply to you is, "And why not?" And I ask you, "Why is it people have to date for three or five or ten years before figurin' out if they're meant for one another? I have a friend, Rick, who was on vacation in California, met a woman at a Bed & Breakfast in Santa Monica and three days later asked her to marry him. They've been together for 18 years now.) Hell, I was pushin' 40. That dating bullshit gets old quick. I knew what I was lookin' for in a woman, and Nichole Bocelli fit the bill.

Now, bein' separated from Nikki so soon after we'd gotten to know one another was tough on this ol' boy. I did a lot of thinkin' while I was home in Camellia Bay. Between Mom havin' a stroke and dealin' with ex-girlfriend problems, I was more than anxious to get back to a little Midwestern comfort, if you know what I mean. To put it simply, my mind was made up and there was no room for doubt. I was goin' to ask Nikki to move in with me. But to be honest with you, I had absolutely no idea what her reaction would be. I also wasn't too sure if or when I was goin' to tell her exactly why I'd gone down to Key West.

Chapter 15

A Good Love is So Hard to Find

My parents were thrilled to see Garry again, now that they'd been let in on the "secret." My dad was all smiles and talking a mile a minute. "We had no idea there was a star in our midst when we met you."

Modesty is one of Garry's most amiable qualities. "Naw, I'm just a regular ol' guy, Gino. I never had intentions of becomin' a star. Besides, I've got plenty of folks in my life who are more than happy to remind me what a sad and sorry hayseed I am."

Mom, Dad, Luke, and Mia shot a barrage of questions at Garry regarding his business, his life, etc. They held him captive the better part of the afternoon, which suited me just fine because I hadn't figured out the answer to *this* nagging question: *How the heck am I going to explain moving in with a man I'd practically just met?*

After Luke and Mia left for the Land of 10,000 Lakes, Garry brought up Thanksgiving with my parents.

"Now I don't know what you have planned for Thanksgivin', but I would love to have y'all over to my house to celebrate."

That was news to me.

"That is, if you're brave enough," Garry said. "You don't have plans to go anywhere, do you?"

"As a matter of fact," said my dad, "Jane and Steve have decided to come here for Christmas, so we won't go down to Dallas after all."

"Are you sure you're up for it, Garry?" my mom asked.

"Don't let him fool you," I said. "Garry comes from a family of great Southern cooks. In fact, his sister, Samantha, has her own four-star restaurant, *Sammi's*, in the French Quarter of New Orleans."

"Well, that sounds great to us," my mom said. "Thank you for the invitation."

"One other thing," Garry said, looking at my parents. (He was on a roll and I was stumped as to what he might say next. He looked unusually serious, though, and a twinge of nervousness shot through me.) "I realize that y'all don't know me from Adam's cat and that Nichole and I haven't known one another a minute more than Sunday. And let's face it, I *am* a bit older than 24 (they laughed). But I just want y'all to know how much I love your daughter and care about her."

Talk about Southern charm. Garry had my parents smiling from ear to ear and hanging on his every word. Me too, for that matter!

No one said a thing. I held my breath. I suppose my parents were taking in the word "love" and counting the number of days we'd known each other.

"I don't mean to render y'all speechless," Garry said to my mom with a wink. "I just wanted you to know that I've asked Nichole to move her things out of Lundstrom's house and into my house before she gets the boot next month. I thought y'all should know before word gets around. If Oakwood Shores is anything like Key West, the gossip's already spread over hell's half acre. In any event, I didn't want you to think we were keepin' a secret from you."

They didn't react. I knew Garry'd caught them off guard. In fact, they looked so unphased I wondered if they would say anything at all. I looked Garry in the eye and shrugged my shoulders.

Finally my mom said, "No, we haven't known you very long, Garry, but in the short time we *have* been around you, we like the person that you are. It's nice for us to see that you're a genuine, caring, and humble person, not some bigheaded rock star. And it's clear to us that you and Nichole have something special."

Then my dad added, "We happen to be very protective of Nichole, and like you, we happen to think she's a special person. If she's happy, then we're happy. That's all that matters to us. All we ask is that you take good care of our girl."

"I wouldn't think of doin' otherwise, Gino," Garry said, giving my dad one of those square in the eye looks that fathers like to receive from questionable boyfriends.

I didn't know what to say. I had the sinking feeling I was ten years old again!

"Why do I feel like everyone's talking about me as if I weren't here?" I demanded.

Garry put his arm around me. "I need to stop talkin', don't I?"

I shook my head yes.

Together we claimed a shallow victory. I was glad everything was out in the open and I can tell you, Garry had won over my parents big-time. They didn't say one word about my moving in with him.

Chapter 16

Plowin' Straight Ahead

"**Y**ou're doing what?" Sarah's voice raised an octave.

"I know, I know. It's fast, isn't it?" I added that obvious fact more for her benefit than for mine. *I* knew I was making a quick decision. I was looking for reassurance, that's all. You may think it silly of me, calling Sarah Lorenzo, the greatest skeptic on earth, for reassurance, but what can I say; I guess the Catholic in me needed a little extra guilt.

"I honestly don't know what to say, Nik," Sarah said. "I hope you're making the right decision. God knows *I* wouldn't move in with a guy I'd known for, what? two weeks? three weeks?"

Guilt duly received.

* * *

"How did he ask you? I heard it was a complete surprise! When are you moving in? Have you told your parents yet?"

It was Christi calling.

"I can't really talk now," I said. "But I promise I'll fill you in on all the details, later." I paced up and down my parent's driveway as Garry and my dad loaded boxes into the back of the Jeep. "Just tell me one thing, though; and be absolutely honest with me." I turned toward the street and whispered, "Do you think I'm making the right decision?"

"Are you crazy, Nikki? You are *so* making the right decision."

God bless friends like Christi.

* * *

And so, I moved. I had no idea where it was leading or if I was just crazy enough to be insane, but it felt right . . . and for once, I was proud of myself for flying so far from the nest.

Now, if you've never lived with someone before, then trust me when I say there's some mutual adjusting to be done those first few weeks . . . or months . . . or maybe even years (I'll let you know). Little things, like the fact that Garry's more of a night owl than I am or that he's more verbal throughout the day. Or (and this is a biggie) that he leads a "grander life" than I do, which results in countless hours on the phone, arranging, dealing, and negotiating. Now, in all fairness to Garry, I must say I'm not always the easiest person to live with. I happen to be a neat freak (okay, call me anal) and I'm also, to Garry's dismay, a morning person—up and whistlin' Dixie by 7. (At midnight Garry's just getting ready to roll.) There were moments, at first, when I thought, *How could Garry be interested in me? I'm just an average girl from the hicks. Maybe I haven't known him long enough. Maybe he hasn't known me long enough! Maybe I should have listened to Sarah, after all.* But every night, as Garry would slip into bed beside me, press his body up against mine, and whisper, "G'night billfish," then I knew—no, I was *absolutely sure*—I'd made the right decision.

* * *

The moment my last box hit the living room floor, Garry dove into his writing. (As you can imagine, he'd been neglecting it that past month). He said having me in the house was "good inspiration for his creative soul" (whatever that meant). As for me, I became more and more disillusioned with my work at Roger's. Computer aided boredom had me practically in tears every day, to the point where Garry, who'd usually gone to sleep only hours before, took to mumbling encouraging words just to get me moving in the morning.

"You know what you need, Nik?" Garry said one day after I'd gotten home from work.

"A stiff drink?" I joked.

"Yeah, that, and a well deserved overdue binge. I mean it. You've been workin' harder than a one-legged man in a butt kickin' contest."

"I swear, Garry, where you come up with those expressions, I'll never know. Do you *always* speak in idiom, or is that just for my Midwestern benefit?"

Garry laughed. "I'm afraid we LaForges are flagrant collectors of useless expressions. What started as a family joke has since become a family habit. It's a harmless addiction, I assure you. Be forewarned though, it's already rubbed off on Marty, and you very well may be its next victim.

"But like I was sayin', you deserve some time off for good behavior. I need to get out to LA before Christmas and meet with my management company. Why don't we spend a few days out there? You could do your Christmas shoppin' and soak up some rays. What d'ya say? I could have Jake and Leroy bring *Global Escort* up for the trip."

"What's *Global Escort*? And who are Jake and Leroy?"

"*Global Escort* is the most beautiful jet you'll ever set eyes on, and Jake and Leroy are my pilots. You'll love it, Nik; leather reclinin' seats, a full galley and bar, DVD, TV," He put his arms around me, "and most importantly, a private bedroom and bath in the back."

"When do we leave?" I asked, my head buried in his chest.

"As soon as the turkey's eaten."

* * *

My mom and dad were wonderful Thanksgiving guests, and Garry, a superb host. His easy-going nature and positive attitude put us all in unusually festive moods. While Garry cooked up a feast in the kitchen, I decided my parents were in need of a little "Garry LaForge the Entertainer 101." You see, the Garry my parents were familiar with, (and me too, for that matter) was the down-home, Southern-talkin', in-the-kitchen right now wearin' an apron kind of guy. So I sat them down in the living room . . .

"Most all of Garry's things are down in Key West, but I came across one of his DVDs of a live concert at Riverbend, in Ohio. Now before you watch this, it's important to understand a little bit about Garry's fans. They are, without a doubt, some of the most devoted followers in the music business. They're doctors and lawyers and office workers, just regular people who love to escape their every-day lives at least one weekend a summer when Garry comes to town. They're also some of the most organized and generous fans out there, donating their time and money to a variety of charities. In fact, Garry recently made a donation to Habitat for Humanity, and next month we'll be joining a group of his fans down in Gulf Shores to build homes for the hurricane victims. But, and this is a big "but," from what you're about to see, you'd never guess these people are philanthropists."

We had a hoot watching Garry's bigger than life stage persona, not to mention grown men dancing in hula skirts and countless women professing their undying love for Garry. But the guy in the kitchen, the one stuffing the turkey, thought otherwise.

Garry walked into the living room with a bottle of wine in his hand and noticed the TV. "What are y'all watchin'? Now that's no Thanksgivin' entertainment. In fact, that's downright sacrilegious. You're supposed to be watchin' football on TV. Not some joker makin' a fool of himself."

"Football?" I said. (Garry was intently watching the Alabama/Mississippi game in the kitchen). "We're from Illinois, Garry. This is home of the disappointing Illini and the bad news Bears. Watching you is much more entertaining."

"Well, if y'all insist on watchin' it, at least have yourselves a glass of wine. Nobody is allowed to watch that crazy concert without a drink in hand."

Mom and Dad idled with us in front of the fireplace after dinner. We talked and got to know each other better, and somehow, in my mind, I struggled to relate the two Garrys I was coming to know.

Chapter 17

That Sacred Cell

H ow on earth did we manage before cell phones? I don't know about you, but I have a love/hate relationship with mine. Let me start by saying that I was probably one of the last of my friends to submit to cell phone technology. Like you, I couldn't stand people who drove while talking on their phones, disregarding every single rule of the road. I also couldn't stand the audacity of people who thought I wanted to hear their phone conversations while waiting in line at the Stop 'N Shop. I like peace and quiet. As simple as that. I didn't want to become some sort of Pavlovian slave to a bell in my pocket.... Just call me, leave a message. I'll get back to you if I feel like talking. You know that saying, "if the phone doesn't ring, it's me?" Well, that was pretty much me.

Until I met Garry.

As I said before, Garry's phone is his business lifeline. He has one of those fancy 90 jillion dollar solid gold numbers that can simultaneously reach anyone on earth *and* launch the space shuttle *and* remind you that you forgot to take your heartburn medicine.

He never leaves home without it. He's always upgrading and downloading (or is it uploading???) things onto it—either that or he's talking about it. It drives me absolutely crazy! (Wait. This is supposed to be a happy part of the story. You don't want to hear about my pet peeves just yet, do you?) Anyway, I finally called a truce with the whole cell phone thing *only* because I love getting calls and texts from Garry. And if you call me, I may even answer it on occasion.

* * *

The day after Thanksgiving, Black Friday, I was up early, packed, and ready to head to L.A. when Garry's phone rang.

"Nikki, could you get that?" he called.

Answering Garry's phone is a game of Russian roulette . . . I never know who I'm going to get. And it didn't take me long to realize, every now and then the dragons come to call. Case in point: a week before, a woman named Brooke was extremely taken aback that I answered *Garry's* phone. "Just have Garry call me, okay? He has my number," she abruptly said.

I asked Garry who Brooke was.

"Brooke Walker is—I mean *was*—a lady I met in Miami. We were dating for a while . . . and then . . . we weren't."

I looked at Garry with a smirk. "As simple as that, huh?"

"Well, it's *definitely* not that simple. That's the short version."

"I've got time," I said. (I'd yet to hear details about the women in Garry's past and as much as we girlfriends whine and complain that we'd rather not hear the particulars, you *know* we don't mean it. As painful as the truth may be, let's face it, we want to know every stinkin' detail.)

Garry laughed, "I met Brooke Walker at a summer concert a couple of years ago. She had a backstage pass. She invited the boys and I for a jaunt on her daddy's yacht. We started dating. We saw one another when we could. She moved down to Key West."

"With you?" (*Please say no. Please say no.*)

"No, not with me. She and a girlfriend got an apartment. It was a doomed relationship from the word go. I couldn't handle her lies. She couldn't handle my absence."

"So how did it end?" I was very curious about this Brooke Walker. I knew I didn't like her already.

"I left."

"Left?"

"To come here."

(I didn't realize she was such a current ex-girlfriend.) "And?" I asked.

"And—that's all. As far as I'm concerned, it was never meant to be. It was over, done, finished."

I knew Garry's past was a well-worn epic novel, with me making a cameo somewhere around page 400. I also realized there were *several* Brooke Walkers out there . . . I just hoped they were all faded memories from the past. Still, it annoyed me when she called.

Another time I answered Garry' phone and it was Matt Lauer of all people! It's funny, the voice on the other end sounded so familiar, but I just couldn't place it. He even spelled out his last name for me. That's when it hit me . . . I was on the phone with the voice of the *Today* show!

I got to the point where I actually sighed with relief when his mother or one of his sisters called.

Well, that morning it wasn't Garry's mother, or his sister. It was none other than Harrison Ford! My voice had such an odd dreamlike quality to it when I called upstairs, "Garry, Harrison Ford is on the phone for you."

"Harrison called to say he's going to be in LA over the weekend and why don't we all get together," Garry said.

"Just the three of us?" I asked, nervous already at the thought.

"Three, four, five. With Harrison one never knows. He and his wife recently got a divorce. He's been spendin' lots of time in L.A. lately, so I'm guessin' there's a woman to blame."

And I thought meeting Garry LaForge was a nerve-wracking experience!

Chapter 18

Out in Hollywood

T he flight to LA was so out of the ordinary for me. I had never even flown first class, let alone in a private jet. There I was but a month earlier, resigning myself to a life of suburban psychosis, and now I was flying at 34,000 feet in a Gulfstream V with my rock star boyfriend on our way to the Four Seasons, Beverly Hills to hang out with Harrison Ford! —I never planned, in my imaginations, a situation so heavenly.

That two-hour time change has Midwesterners up bright and early on the west coast. That morning, Garry's fate was to sit in a sterile office on La Cienega Blvd. while I strolled down Rodeo Drive, bathed in glorious sunshine, taking in all the excess and pomposity that we call life in America. Now if you've never been to California, Rodeo Drive in particular, it's all that you think it is, the epitome of *see and be seen—* hair, nails, the hippest fashions, valet parking on every corner, not to mention oodles and oodles of money. In other words, I felt completely out of place (you know by now I'm not a "look at me" kind of girl). So, even though I had carte blanche with Garry's American Express, I spent most of the morning window-shopping and people watching.

Eventually I ventured back to the hotel where a message from Garry awaited. *Having lunch with Harrison and his girlfriend???* at 1:30.

There were those nerves again. My trip down Rodeo Drive had caused severe regression. The average girl inside my head reappeared, unsure about what to wear and even more unsure about what she was going to say.

Harrison chose Japanese. No, not the girlfriend, the restaurant, which was a treat, considering good sushi is hard to come by in Oakwood Shores. Harrison's mystery guest turned out to be a fellow actress, Calista Flockhart. I wasn't familiar with her work, which ruled out any shoptalk, but as luck would have it, she comes from a small town in Illinois *and* just happened to graduate high school the same year I did! As a matter of fact, Harrison also grew up in the Chicago area, only a few short train stops from Oakwood Shores. (Now, bear with me while I wax philosophical here) Thanks to Harrison and Calista, I began to realize that no matter how well known or how unknown we are, we're all just regular small town people at heart. Funny, isn't it? Sometimes it takes lunching with the big shots to realize we're not such little guys after all.

(By the way, if you think Garry and I have a big age difference, then the 22 years between Harrison and Calista would really shock you. Apparently Harrison's ex-wife isn't too happy about it either.)

All in all, lunch was a success and Harrison left us with an open invitation to visit his ranch in Wyoming. Two of his children live nearby with his ex and are always begging him to have "Uncle Garry" visit.

There's not much more to tell you about the rest of that weekend, other than we consumed obscene amounts of California sunshine, drove our rented convertible up into the Hollywood Hills, down to PCH and through Malibu, lunched at a quaint roadside café and wondered, more than once, why we ever had to go home.

But go home we did.

Come Monday we were back in Oakwood Shores. Cold, cloudy, gray November in Oakwood Shores.

Need I say more?

Chapter 19

I Do Believe I've Had Enough

I was faced with a particularly tough Monday. I remember coming home from work that evening and flopping down on the sofa, coat and all, so absolutely frustrated I wanted to cry.

Garry came in from the kitchen and saw me, prostrate, in the dark. "We need to have a discussion about your job."

"What's to talk about?" I mumbled.

"What's to talk about? Come on, Nik . . . the fact that you hate it? The fact that you're not happy Monday mornin' through Friday afternoon. The fact that it's tearin' you apart inside. I'm not stupid; I can see it. A blind man on a gallopin' horse can see it."

"A what?" (Sometimes it takes me a minute to figure out what the heck Garry's saying, especially when I'm exhausted.)

"I can't just quit, Garry. I need to figure out what to do next. I wish I had a passion like singing or writing like you do. I can't just live here and mooch off of you."

"And why not?" Garry asked so matter-of-factly that I took a moment to consider his comment.

I couldn't come up with an answer, but as much as I would have liked to quit everything and live the good life with Garry, I felt I'd be taking advantage of him and our situation. I mean, isn't that what everyone expected me to do? Live off Garry's money?

"I don't know, Garry. The quitting part is easy. Believe me. I'd have no problem going in tomorrow and telling Roger I'm through."

"Then do it, Nichole! Do it! I want you to be happy. I hate to see you agonizin' over your work every fuckin' day. You are such a positive, energetic, creative person, and I see your job imprisoning you."

"I'd feel guilty. Don't you get it?"

"Guilty about what?"

"Guilty about quitting a good job without having a plan. I can't take it easy. I mean, I have car payments. I have student loans."

"Do we always have to have plans, Nichole? You're bein' too rational again. You've got to let go of some of that control you like to have and just trust that it'll all work out. I'll help you, I promise. I'm good at flyin' by the seat of my pants."

He pulled me onto his lap. "Promise me you'll give it some serious consideration."

"I will."

"And by the way," he said, "regardin' those car payments and student loans . . ."

"Yeah?"

"They no longer exist."

* * *

It wasn't too difficult to quit my job. As I said, I knew that would be the easy part. Roger's disappointment was expected, although he confessed to having had his suspicions. He and Edie wished me well and were a bit perplexed as to what I'd do with my time, but they were also excited for me. (I have a hard time understanding people who claim they wouldn't know what to do with themselves if they didn't work. Or better yet, the guy working at Kmart who just won the Mega Millions and says, "There's no way I'm ever going to quit my job." I just don't get it.) Of course, the real difficulty came in telling my parents. They were less than pleased, to say the least. "You're too far ahead of yourself, Nichole," they said. "You've worked so hard at Roger's," they said. "We hate to see you quit," they said. Now don't be fooled. What they were actually saying was, "We're afraid Garry's going to dump you and leave you homeless, penniless, and jobless." I thought it best not to inform Garry of their thoughtful and loving concerns. Anyway, those two matters out of the way, I hurried home to share the good news.

You know that TGIF feeling you have at 5 o'clock on Friday afternoon? Well, take that joyous feeling and multiply it by infinity because that's how f-ing giddy I felt that evening. And you know I *must* have been loopy because I drove through the raging flurries of a predicted snowstorm with a big old grin stuck on my face. I even took a moment to catch one or two giant snowflakes on my tongue before going inside.

The house was dark. "Anybody home?" I called, stomping the snow from my boots. "Garry?" I followed the glow of the computer coming from the study. Garry sat, headphones on, laptop open, feet on the desk, starring out the window. He jumped when I walked in.

"Sorry to scare you," I said.

"Hey there good lookin'. I was just enjoyin' the show outside. Been a while since I've seen any snow. Supposed to dump 10 to 12 inches."

"I quit," I said.

It took him only a moment to get it. "You did?"

I could no longer hold back my smile. "I feel better already."

"Hot damn! You don't know how happy I am to hear that, baby. I am so goddamn happy for you! This calls for a celebration. I've been a regular Hemingway today, so we both deserve it. But first, come on over here."

I happened to have on a skirt that day, so I bounced over and straddled Garry on his lap. "Is this the kind of celebration you have in mind?" I asked.

Garry flashed a mischievous, one-dimpled smile. "This kind of celebration is always on my mind."

I unbuttoned Garry's jeans and repositioned myself right . . . down . . . on top. It was erotic, sensual, steamy sex. It was as if an enormous load had been lifted from my shoulders that day. I felt carefree. I felt wild.

"You should have quit your job long ago, my dear," Garry said afterward.

Chapter 20

Troubadours and Clowns

O kay, let's get this out of the way . . . Yes, I *was* living off
Garry, and no, it didn't take me long to rearrange all the
guilt in my mind. Still, every once in a while, Garry had to push me from
my safe harbor out into those trade winds, especially when it came to
my financial conscience. Keep in mind that although I was raised in an
upper middle-class environment, both my parents were products of a
self-sacrificing generation. At my house, we were taught to value hard
work and take pride in earning an honest dollar. I learned at an early
age that if I wanted a pair of Tommy Hilfiger jeans or a Louis Vuitton
bag or any item *at all* from Neiman Marcus or Lord & Taylor, I was
going to have to work for it. At my house, we ate Saltines, drank
powdered milk, and wrapped our sandwiches in waxed paper.

As a result, I was hard-pressed to give up my thrifty ways. For
example, I decided to throw a Christmas party at the house last year.
Actually, since Garry's birthday falls during the holiday season (he's a
"two turtle dove" guy), it was going to be a Christmas/birthday party. I
spent the better part of an afternoon trying to decide if it would be a
potluck party and who was going to bring what, or if I should try to
undertake all the cooking on my own. I borrowed dozens of my mom's
cookbooks, downloaded potential recipes, and was in the process of

assessing our cookware situation when I asked Garry for his opinion. He just laughed and threw an old phone book at me. "Nichole. Hire a caterer." As simple as that. See, I would have spent countless hours slaving in the kitchen!

* * *

With that good advice in hand, I promptly shooed Garry away from any further participation in the party planning itself. This was going to be *my* party, *my* personal tribute to the birth of Garry Jackson LaForge (and Jesus Christ too, for that matter). —And then, I wished I hadn't. Who is, after all, the king of party planning? Who is it that can guarantee, without a doubt, a good time had by all? Who is it that embodies the everlasting party spirit? Unfortunately, it was the man I was hoping to impress.

First things first, I thought. *Best friends.* Garry has two of them: Marty Anderson and Joshua Porter, and although I was last minute, I hoped they could both make it to the party. Marty told me he would definitely make it (his pregnant wife, Allison, wouldn't) and so did Josh. Of course, almost all of *my* friends could make it. (You know as well as I do, they were dying to stick their noses behind our closed doors; a truly pathetic bunch, the lot of them.)

I flew Marty and Josh into O'Hare with a limo waiting to bring them out to the house. I knew the evening was off to a good start when Garry opened the door and hollered out, "Well dip me in shit and call me ugly! Look what the cat drug in!" Apparently I scored one point in the initiative department for arranging that behind his back.

Speaking of scoring points . . . I didn't get an opportunity to talk much with the guys; the party kept me hopping, but I did notice that Josh and Jessica were getting along extremely well. And as much as I didn't *want* to notice (on my way to the bathroom through the dark study), Marty and Melanie were getting along even better. (I promise to discuss this later.)

Admiral of the Ocean. That's what Garry was that night . . . smoking cheap cheroots with the good ol' boys, keeping the drinks flowing and the music rolling. As for me, the proud party planner, I knew I'd made the impression I was hoping for as Garry stood before the glowing candles of his birthday cake, winked at me, and mouthed the words, "I love you."

Chapter 21

I Can't Help It . . .
I Just Tell the Truth

L est you think this fine tale is nothing but happiness and cheer, allow me to relate the following exchange:

The next morning, Marty won the early riser award. I joined him in the kitchen for some coffee and get-to-know-you conversation.

"Quite a party you threw last night, Nichole. You sure do have a mess of girlfriends. I can see why Garry likes it here."

"Well I'm hoping he likes it here because of me, not all my girlfriends."

"Oh, you don't have to worry your little head about that one bit. All I've heard from Bubba these days is 'Nichole this and Nichole that.'" (Don't you *hate* when men, especially men you don't know, say condescending things like that? Sorry to say, but you contractors out there are the worst. Working as a female architect, men often said things to me like ,"okay sweetie" and "thanks a bunch, hon" and "bless your little heart" and "aren't you a dear." Ugh!)

"Really?" I replied.

"Ooh yeah, Garry is in knee-deep; believe me. I haven't seen him this love-struck since . . ." He stopped short.

"Since what?" I asked, extremely curious and annoyed all at once.

We both looked up, startled. Garry arrived with a "Morning y'all" and a big kiss for me.

"Okay, am I missin' somethin'?" he asked.

"No," I said with a smile. "Marty was just going to tell me about the last time you were love-struck." I wanted Marty to know he couldn't play those games with me. I also wanted to make Garry talk.

Garry looked at Marty with wondering eyes. "So when *was* the last time I was 'love-struck,' Mr. Anderson?"

"Well, what I was referrin' to was one of your previous lengthy relationships. One that wasn't right for you, of course."

Marty was sidestepping the question.

I noticed Garry's eyes burn a hole right through Marty. This was getting ever more interesting for me.

"You're not talkin' about Brooke Walker, are you?" Garry asked rather defensively.

"That's the one," Marty said.

"For all y'all's information, I was never *love-struck* with Brooke Walker. If anything, she's the one *I* couldn't get rid of."

"Didn't she move down to Key West?" Josh asked as he entered the kitchen.

"I've heard about this Brooke Walker before; although I think Garry's holding out on me," I said jokingly. (Well, sort of jokingly.)

"I'm holdin' out on nothin'," Garry said.

I detected an edge to his voice. I also noticed that vein on his neck start to protrude.

"Listen, y'all, Brooke Walker is no more than a trust-fund brat. She thinks just because her daddy is rich and powerful she can do whatever she damn-well pleases."

"Like claimin' you're the father of her unborn child?" Marty asked, nonchalantly.

The sound of percolating coffee echoed from wall to wall.

Josh was genuinely surprised, but I could tell Marty was happy with himself. He looked right at me with a shitty grin on his face.

"Oh, I get it," I said to Marty, "baptism by fire." And I walked right out of that kitchen. I was peeved at him for being such an ass and even more peeved with Garry for not telling me about it personally.

I heard Garry snarl, "Can we please not mention Brooke Walker's name anymore around here! She's caused me enough headaches already."

"Jesus Christ, LaForge," Marty said. "Don't have a conniption fit. Nichole was gonna find out about it sooner or later."

"Enough Marty. End of Story!"

To say that I was not happy is putting it lightly. Allow me to make this perfectly clear. I was *pissed!* And humiliated at the same time. I mean, what did Marty think . . . that he was dealing with some naïve little girlfriend? Did he think I'd leave the room crying at the mention of another woman? And why the hell was Garry keeping it a secret from me anyway? Maybe he *was* the father of the baby. What then?

Upstairs, I threw on a pair of jeans and a sweatshirt, grabbed my purse, and bounded down the stairs, only to be met by Garry at the bottom.

"Listen," he started.

But I knew I had to get out of that house before I said or did something irrational, so I jumped right in, "You know what, Garry," (I made sure my voice wasn't more than an angry whisper . . . All I needed was for the guys to tease Garry about his "whiny" girlfriend.) "right now, I'm pretty pissed off."

He started getting defensive. "I'm willin' to talk about it, Nik, it's just that . . ."

"I will *not* discuss this when your friends are in the house," I said, walking to the front door.

Garry followed behind me, saying (in a more submissive tone), "We'll talk about it tomorrow, then. After they leave."

"Right." And I slammed the door behind me. (Okay. I shut it. I admit, I'm not a very good fighter. But I *wish* I had slammed it!)

Josh, Marty and Garry were off to Chicago that day and I gladly let them go. It was late when they returned, and although I was already snug in bed, Garry slid under the covers to face a wind chill colder than the one whirling outside.

Marty did his best to apologize to me the next morning. (I did, after all, possess some adulterous information that his wife would be rather interested to know about). As soon as the limo pulled away I put Lynyrd Skynyrd on the stereo, got on the treadmill, and worked out all my frustrations. I was thankful Garry gave me that time for myself. (Actually, he had no choice, held at bay by a sulking Italian girl.) Afterward, stretching outside on the balcony, breathing in the sharp, cold air, Garry joined me with a blanket in hand as a peace offering.

"I wasn't tryin' to keep a secret from you," he began. "I want you to know all there is to know about me and what's goin' on in my life."

"You realize you put me in an awkward situation yesterday morning, don't you?"

Garry shook his head.

I continued, "You should have told me everything that day I answered the phone and it was her."

"I should have. You're right. I'm sorry. Marty has a tendency to be over protective of me, but he can also be an ass. I assure you we had quite a discussion about it last night. Believe me, he will never play those games with you again."

Inside, I sat wrapped like a cocoon on the chair while Garry paced back and forth.

"Brooke Walker comes from a rich powerful family in Miami . . . the island-hoppin' crowd. She's good-lookin', knows how to have a good time, and could seduce the most God-fearin' Baptist preacher. I guess you could say I was easily enticed. Well, things between us were goin' along fairly well until I was on the road quite a bit and it became more and more difficult to have a long-distance relationship. So, like I told you, she moved down to Key West with a girlfriend. Remember, money wasn't her issue. What she didn't realize is that Key West is a small island and everybody eventually ends up knowin' everybody else's business. I kept hearin' rumors about Brooke sleepin' around while I was gone, but of course I didn't want to believe it, and when I confronted her, she'd adamantly deny it. On the other hand, she was endlessly jealous of *my* lifestyle and all the women that . . . um . . . are around the band, which is rather ironic, because she was one of the women I'd met at one of my shows."

I rolled my eyes. (Why do men feel the need to remind us what chic magnets they are?)

"Anyway, we commenced to argue more than we were gettin' along, so I decided to call it quits. I was sick and tired of playin' the fool, especially when my friend Ronny said he'd walked in on her screwin' a guy from Chino's Bar. It was a respectable break-up on my part. I didn't want it to end in a drama, so I made sure I spelled everything out clearly. *What I didn't realize* was that when Brooke Walker doesn't get her way, she gets vindictive. She called me about a month after we broke up to tell me she was pregnant and what was I going to do now?"

I interrupted, "So, you're telling me that someone else is the father of her baby?"

"You better believe it," Garry said.

"How do you know the baby's not yours?" I asked.

"Simple math. I was on the road and then when I *was* in town the last time—let's just say that it's not possible."

I was taking it all in. I didn't know what to say. I hoped to God Garry's math was right; it's human nature to miscalculate. I also hoped Miss Miami didn't turn it into a legal matter. Not that I didn't think Garry could handle it; it's just that he mentioned more than once that her father was a powerful man, and you know as well as I do that power is a dangerous drug.

"So what did she say when you told her it was impossible that the baby is yours?"

"Well, the first time, she was all weepy and played the victim. Said I was just scared and runnin' away from my responsibility; commitment-phobic, etc. Then, when I saw her a couple weeks ago, she was no longer the victim but a woman on a mission."

"So *that* was your "business" down in Key West?" I said plainly.

Garry didn't say anything. He walked over to the window and looked outside. He turned to me with furrowed eyebrows. "Nichole, let's get one thing straight. I have a "past" with women. Not because I'm tourin' all over the world and meetin' em left and right, but because I am a 38 year old male. Now, I'm not some sailor with a woman in every port, but you have to realize I've been involved in *several* relationships."

"I do realize that, Garry. And I'm sure I'll keep coming face to face with that the longer we're together. I just need you to be open and honest with me about your past. That's all."

Garry came over and knelt on one knee in front of my chair. "I love you, Nichole. *This* is the *only* relationship that matters to me."

"I love you too, Garry."

Believe it or not, that was a first for me. For weeks I'd been suppressing the urge to say those words, waiting for just the right moment. Well, that moment seemed as good as any to let my guard down. And Garry's dimples confirmed it.

Chapter 22

'Tis the Season

C hristmas: a time of love, a time of peace, a time for family (a time of wondering endlessly about Brooke Walker) . . .

"What kind of name is Brooke anyway?" Christi asked. "Sounds like some bubbly bimbo to me."

She was making me feel better already.

"And you *know* what she's telling Garry is one big fat lie."

"What if it's not?" I dared to venture.

"Nichole, how much do you trust Garry?" she asked.

"I trust him completely," I said.

"Do you trust him enough to . . . to not read your journal?"

"Yeah."

"How about to not look through your purse when you're gone?"

"Of course," I answered. I had a sudden flashback to my afternoon of snooping around Garry's house.

"Okay," Christi said. "Here's the real test. Do you trust him when he says he won't come, inside?"

"Huh? What do y. . . ?" It took a moment to figure out what she meant. *Ooh, that's a good one*, I thought. "I trust him.

"But now you've got me not trusting myself!"

* * *

I didn't bother to call Sarah. I was in no mood for I told you so's.

* * *

My sister, Jane, her husband, Steve, and their 11 month old, Rebecca, arrived at my parent's house several days before Christmas. Not only did boughs of holly deck my parent's halls, but helium-filled balloons and flowing streamers were hung in honor of Garry's birthday. We devoured my mother's German chocolate cake, chased Rebecca from room to room, and laughed endlessly at the gifts Garry received from my family: a sweater, a hat, gloves, a snow shovel, a window scraper, and an *80* pound bag of rock salt (appropriate gifts, considering a month earlier he hadn't even owned a winter coat). Garry, in turn, gave my parents a Christmas gift unlike any other they'd ever received: the use of either *Celestial Explorer* (his twin engine) or *Global Escort* (the jet) and his services as pilot, to fly anywhere they'd like for a winter vacation. Talk about thrilled! That gift had my mother dipping into the New Year's Eve champagne and my father holding a living room fashion show of his bathing suits. They told Garry he was being far too generous, but I knew Garry was just doing what he does best . . . making people happy.

As for Garry and me, we decided not to exchange presents until we were together after the holiday, which was just fine with me because my gift for Garry was running a little behind schedule.

The next morning, standing behind the windows of the Oakwood Shores airport, I was less than enthusiastic as *Celestial Explorer* went streaking southward toward Camellia Bay. I wanted so badly to go. I knew Garry'd be back to get me in a few days, but still, a part of me longed to ditch my family and spend every moment with him. I guess that's what they call being in love, isn't it?

For Garry it was a low-key Christmas/birthday with Aunt Betty taking over the holiday festivities due to Charlene's continuing recuperation from her stroke. According to Garry, her recovery was progressing better than expected and she and his dad, Charles (C.J.), looked forward to my visit.

Two days after Christmas, my mom and dad, along with Jane, Steve, and Rebecca gathered at the airport for my departure (or was it to get a tour of Garry's plane?). That time I wasn't nervous at all as he made his final approach. As Garry likes to say, I had a fun ticket in my pocket and my name was written all over that thing. I knew an awesome trip awaited me with the opportunity to dig deeper into the life of Garry—his family, his hometown, Key West, his friends, Brooke Walker (Okay, maybe not Brooke Walker.).

To my surprise, it was *Global Escort* that came barreling out of the sky. (Good thing Oakwood Shores Airport has a cornfield at the end of the runway!) Again, we waited for Garry to taxi in and for the staircase to descend before scurrying, backs bent, heads bowed, into blowing wind and bitter cold. Garry opened the door, wearing cargo shorts and a t-shirt! "Dang, it's cold enough out here to freeze the balls off a pool table! Hey, y'all! Come on up."

The last one on the plane, I received the most welcoming kiss and squeeze on the behind. Garry was full of energy and also full of surprises, a bouquet of camellias (the Alabama state flower) for me and some company for himself, his father! It pleased me that my parents got to meet C.J. I've always found the "meeting of the families" to be a validating point in a relationship; although I had a therapist once who found it odd that my parents hung out with my boyfriend's parents. (What's so odd about that?) Anyway, what a gentleman C.J. was, that long lost type of man who'd give up his seat for a lady.

Garry played tour guide but said we needed to make headway because a storm was moving in.

Unbeknownst to me, C.J., a retired naval officer and pilot, joined Garry in the cockpit. C.J. was exceedingly polite and very good-looking for a 69 year-old man. Garry told me that his parents were regular hard-working people . . . "down-to-earth, easy going and likeable." After spending time with C.J., I had to agree.

Prior to meeting Garry, my personal compass rarely wavered from north. It's not surprising, then, that once the plane hit the ground in Alabama I lost all sense of bearing. We'd crossed over into Garry's territory, and I subconsciously let him take the lead. (Which means I let him *think* he was in charge.) Garry opened the cockpit door and yelled back to me, "Welcome to Alabama, baby! Dump your winter gear and let me take you on a trip through
my life."

* * *

As far as I was concerned, I wished the whole Brooke Walker pregnancy situation never came to Nichole's ears. Better for me to deal with the consequences of my past by myself than to drag everybody else into the fires of hell with me. And as much as Nikki would hate for me to say this, in my eyes, she was still young and innocent. But in a good way. Lets' face it, it's a jungle out there, and Nikki had yet to be jaded by the daily unadulterated crap. In fact, I discovered early on that Nichole was raised in an all-American middle-class family that's a little less dysfunctional than most . . . I was just hopin' like hell she could say the same thing after meetin' mine.

Chapter 23

The Old Bayou

Anxiety swept over me as I gathered my things from the cabin. I was anxious about meeting Garry's mother and sister. Past experience has taught me that approval by your boyfriend's father is pretty much a given, but it's the women of the house who are the most discriminating. And I happen to think it's crucial to be liked and approved of by the women who raised your man.

We drove straight to the LaForge home in C.J.'s old blue Suburban; a 20 minute ride from the airport. The LaForges live in a picturesque middle-class neighborhood—formal Southern homes, white picket fences, fragrant magnolia trees. Garry told me he'd offered hundreds of times to buy his parents a new home—anywhere they wanted—but they refused, saying, "for 60 years, the LaForge Family has called this house home and no tax collector, developer or high falutin' son of ours is goin' ta make us leave." Garry assured me they were only joking about the "high falutin" part, but after seeing that charming cottage-style home for myself, I can't say that I blamed them.

Charlene slowly eased herself from the porch swing as we pulled in the drive. She greeted me with a warm welcome hug and a kiss on the cheek.

"Good to see ya. My, aren't you as pretty as red shoes! It's so nice to finally meet the woman that has our Garry all in a dither. How *was* your trip? How was the weather? Are y'all hungry? Sammi's got chicken salad and sweet tea waitin' for y'all on the back porch. Please, come on in."

And so it goes, right . . . talkative woman, quiet man. (Can't get a word in edgewise) C.J., soft-spoken and somewhat shy. Charlene, all Southern charm and hospitality. She linked arms and led me inside. "Make yourself useful, Garry dear, and put Nichole's things upstairs."

"Yes ma'am," Garry replied.

"Here's our Yankee girl," Sammi called out as we walked into the kitchen. "It's a pleasure to finally meet you, Nichole," she said with a hug. "Garry talks about you so often, I feel like I already know you. I'm Samantha, but Sammi's just fine. And this is my husband, Colton." *Wow, I thought, a hug from the brother-in-law too. Okay, I can relax a bit.*

"I hear things are goin' well for you and my baby brother up there in Illinois," Sammi said with a wink.

"That's right, Sammi," Garry exclaimed, bounding down the stairs. "The cotton's high and the fish are jumpin'!"

I discovered that afternoon that lunch at the LaForge household consists not only of a good home-cooked meal but an earful of Southern musings as well. Regarding the weather: "It was rainin' to beat sixty yesterday," On Aunt Betty's Christmas Turkey: "She tried her very best, bless her heart," Garry's high school girlfriend: "You'd think she hung the moon," On Marty: "Lord, that boy could sell a drownin' man a glass of water," and finally, on Garry: "You go at everything like you're killin' snakes with a stick." You get the idea. You also understand why I was "as quiet as a mouse." (See, we Yankees just can't do it.)

Peeking into the childhood of Garry added yet another piece to the puzzle in progress. I only wished I could turn back the hands of time and see what he was *really* like as a child. Speaking of turning back the hands of time, Charlene has kept Garry's room pretty much intact from the time he left home at 18. On display are baseball trophies, school certificates, Prom pictures. Oh, and in case you're wondering, that college diploma is *still* stuffed in the top drawer of his dresser. And despite the fact that there were twin beds in the room, Garry told me, with a wink, that I'd be sleeping across the hall in Susan's room.

Sammi and Colton left town the following day with a warning that we *must* go visit them in New Orleans "or else we'll tell Grandma Mary that you two have been eatin' supper before sayin' grace."

"Well that one went right over my head," I protested.

Garry grabbed me around the waist. "Eatin' supper before sayin' grace means livin' in sin, Nichole Marie. And our Grandma Mary happens to be more devout than the Pope himself."

That night, once Garry's parents had gone off to bed, we stayed up watching old home movies, although Garry had other thoughts on his mind. There's something so very mischievous about making love in your boyfriend's living room while his parents are asleep. It brought back a high school memory or two!

* * *

And so, one minute we were grubbin' on the living room floor and the next minute we were actually *creating* a living room floor . . .

Now I know I've already ridden this horse, but I'll go at it again: Garry's fans are some of the most charitable and fun-loving people I've ever met. Close to a hundred of them, completely unphased by the drizzle, helped build two Habitat for Humanity houses in Gulf Shores that next afternoon. Garry and I arrived, unannounced and unexpected, and spent a good six hours hammering and hoisting, laughing and joking. By the end of the day, we were rain-soaked and covered in grime, but the appreciation we received from the soon-to-be homeowners was worth each and every sore muscle that was to come. Also, Garry has this "thing" about being accessible to his fans. He's always willing to stop for an autograph or shake a hand or have a picture taken. Never once have I seen him lose his patience or his cool in such a situation. And believe me, there exist some mighty zealous fans out there. In any event, not to go on and on about Garry (but this *is* my story, you know), I have to say I was proud he'd not only sponsored the two homes, financially, but that he went into it truly expecting to pull up his sleeves and pitch right in.

* * *

Other than the Bocelli family's annual Spring Break trip to Florida, I'd never once set foot south of the Mason-Dixon Line. In those few short days in Camillia Bay, I discovered there's something so different about the South . . . the pace is much slower, the women are charming; the men, chivalrous. Everything is about family and tradition. There's a certain formality and order about the South. Or maybe it was simply the pleasure I took in hearing that ever-so-delightful gulf-coastal accent. (In case you're not aware, we Midwesterners are suckers for a Southern accent. Not a Southern *woman's* accent—no not at all . . . a Midwestern woman's hair stands on end the moment a Southern woman opens her mouth, all sweet and syrupy. Blech! But a Southern *man's* accent is a different story altogether. A Southern man's drawl gets us dizzier than a ride on Space Mountain.)

We stayed one more night and on the 30th bid farewell to C.J. and Charlene. I admit I had to fight back the tears as we departed; the genuine hospitality and outpouring of love from the LaForge family had touched the depths of my heart. (And here's the secret on this one: I really, really, *really* wanted to be a part of that family!)

C.J. kissed me on the cheek, saying, "Now you make sure that boy of ours takes good care of you, alright?"

And Charlene whispered in my ear, "We hope to see you often at our house, Nichole. We feel like you're just one of the family."

(Dangerous words to a girl who gets too far ahead of herself).

Chapter 24

Down Island

I t was a fairly short trip to the Sunshine State and a breathtaking flight at that. The weather served up just as we'd ordered and the views from the plane were phenomenal. As we approached, I realized that I was now entering the world of "Garry LaForge The Entertainer," and I didn't know what to expect.

The crew at the airport treated Garry as if he was their best friend. Slaps on the back were followed by lots of "yes sirs," not to mention three over-eager college girls waiting out front, completely oblivious to my existence.

"As you can see," Garry said, after he'd been drooled over for 15 minutes, "I'm a regular fixture here at Key West Airport. If this music gig doesn't work out, I'm sure I could get a job out on the tarmac."

"Or at least a couple of good lays back in baggage claim," I jabbed.

A taxi took us the quick 10-minute drive to Garry's house. From what I saw out the car window, Key West lived up to all the rumors I'd heard and all the pictures Garry'd painted in my mind . . . beautiful tropical vegetation, an array of Colonial and Victorian architecture, a blend of ocean air and flowers drifting on the breeze with, of course, a variety of colorful conchs thrown in. But as far as Garry's house went, I had no preconceived notions as to what it would look like. To tell you the truth, I just hoped it wouldn't be some black leather bachelor pad. Like most of the houses on his quiet street, it didn't seem like much from the outside—a three-car garage and a big stucco wall with a gate. But beyond that gate spoke a different story altogether—a tropical entry garden, a wooden footbridge crossing a meandering creek, and two spectacular hand-carved Indonesian doors, or as Garry calls them, "cause to pause." Inside, I was welcomed by a sprawling, one-level, open floor plan with floor to ceiling sliding doors which overlooked a deck, a pool, and the ocean beyond. I loved the light airiness of it and was duly impressed with the decorating; sort of 1800 Nautical meets the Beach Boys.

"Well, here it is, billfish. Home sweet home."

"It's beautiful, Garry. I love it."

He hooked my hand in his and gave me a tour of the house . . . dining area, study, two guest bedrooms, master bedroom and bath, sunk-in living room, kitchen, eating area, sun porch, laundry room, and finally, another guest suite off the garage. As I said, there was an expansive deck outside with a hot tub and pool. And that's not all . . . down by the water a sizeable boathouse hid under the palms, and beside it, a long pier where several of Garry's boats and his seaplane nodded their greetings. (Sorry to bore you with the plumber's tour, but I am, after all, an architect . . . or is it *was*?) I was speechless as I took it all in. The lush landscaping, along with the privacy of the house sweetly iced the cake.

"It's a palace, Garry. A tropical palace," I said.

"Seemingly," he said, laughing. "Just wait 'til the gypsies arrive in the palace and you'll be singin' a different tune."

Garry's refrigerator echoed when I opened it, so we called for pizza, enjoyed a swim, and eventually made our way to the master bedroom. Now, the most wonderful thing about Garry's bedroom (except for Garry of course), is the huge retractable glass ceiling over the bed. Believe me, to a Midwesterner, there's nothing better than warm sunshine on your naked body in the middle of winter.

And then, the doorbell rang.

"You've got to be kiddin'," Garry said as he grabbed the phone.

"Yeah, can I help you?" he asked, via the entry gate speaker system.

"Garry, Garry, Garry, we heard you were in town." It was a female voice, then another in the background, "Wake up you bum!"

I'm not sure I'm liking this, I thought. *Looks like I'm running into Garry's past sooner than I imagined.*

"I'll be right back," Garry said, jumping into his shorts.

I waited several minutes, then several more. Annoying flirtatious laughter at the door put me in motion. I threw on Garry's shirt and walked to the kitchen for a drink. I heard one of the women say, "Garry LaForge! You didn't tell us you weren't here alone!" Then another said, "Am I to assume you won't be my date for Smittie's party tomorrow night?" I couldn't believe she was flirting with Garry, knowing I stood right there in the kitchen! I'm not one for a catfight, but I decided to be bold and walked over to the door, wearing nothing more than Garry's t-shirt and a pleasant smile.

"Hi," I said, innocently.

"Your assumption is correct, Leoni," Garry said, trying to hold back his smile. "Hey y'all, this is Nichole. Nikki, this is Layla and Leoni." Before me stood two Hawaiian looking women . . . pretty . . . sisters . . . twins?

I shook their hands. The women chimed a pleasant hello and the pep rally came to an end.

"Well, ladies, it's quite possible we'll be seein' y'all tomorrow night. This pretty woman right here's pullin' the strings, so it'll be up to her."

He closed the door and unleashed an irresistible smile. "Gol dang. You are a woman to be reckoned with, Miss Nichole Marie."

I gave Garry a peck on the cheek. "So who are *Layla* and *Leoni?*"

"Layla and Leoni are sisters who I met through Smittie. Layla is Smittie's girlfriend and Leoni and I; well, let's just say we used to ride the winds of fortune together now and again."

"I don't want to know what 'riding the winds of fortune' means, but I'm so glad you said 'used to.'"

Garry put his hands under my t-shirt, "Now, where were we?"

Chapter 25

Sparkle of Treasure

T uesday on the island found us up and out early; first, to get some groceries before the stores closed for the holiday and, more importantly, for a quick tour of Key West. We drove Garry's red '68 Corvette, top down, soaking up the warm December breezes . . . through Old Town, Mallory Square, Southernmost Point, Hemingway's house . . . let's see . . . Truman's Little White House and . . . oh yeah, the ever popular Duval Street. Amazing, the number of attractions packed into that 2 by 4 space!

Actually, the newest attraction, and by far the hippest hangout on Duval, had to be Garry's latest venture, a café/club called, what else, Tropicana Jam. Garry's basically the financial backer and ultimate head honcho, but the café is, for the most part, run by an extremely qualified COO and several managers.

"What prompted me," Garry said, showing me around, "was the need here in Key West for a laid-back tropical oasis where you could stop in for a cheeseburger and cold beer during the day and come back at night to catch an up-and-coming band perform on an intimate stage."

And *Tropicana Jam* certainly was tropical, from the tiki bar right down to the grass-skirted waitresses, it was Bali Ha'i reincarnated.

We sat down for lunch—me and The Big Enchilada.

Afterward, we set our sights on Mallory Square, scene of Key West's infamous nightly sunset celebration and the inevitable fruitcake convention. Little did I know, though, we'd soon become one of the attractions ourselves. Pictures, autographs; everyone wanted a piece of Garry and I have to tell you, I've never been good at sharing—toys, candy, my bike, clothes, my car, and most certainly, not my boyfriend. The longer Garry chitchatted, the longer he posed for the cameras and lounged in the limelight, the more irritated I became. *A consummate performer* I told myself. *Giving back to his fans.* The only trouble is, Garry has a tendency to give too much. And you fans out there know it. Believe me. I've been witness to the personal relationship you all hold with Garry and my only complaint is that sometimes you just suck him dry and there's nothing left for me. Maybe Patrick Kelly hit it on the nail when he said, "It must be tough on the ego to have a date who gets more attention than you do." And since we're on the subject—I *know* you've been saying to yourself all along, *This guy is too perfect. Come on, Nichole, he's got to have some faults 'cause we know the ideal man doesn't really exist.* Well, of course he doesn't exist (take one look at the man who walks in *your* door tonight). Garry may be wonderful, but he sure can push my f-ing buttons when he wants to. In fact, a conversation arose between us just the other day in which I found myself on the end of the pier, yelling (competing with the departing plane's engine), "Life is *not* a performance, Garry Jackson LaForge!"

I carried my ill temper all the way back to the house, rearranging in my head the logistics of getting ready for New Year's Eve in under an hour. (Okay, we all know you men can shower, shave, and get ready for any occasion in 10 minutes flat. We get it. You remind us of it all the time. But *we* can't. Get over it. Stop bugging us about it. We're *not* going to change. Case closed.)

A FedEx truck parked outside Garry's house broke the silence between us.

"Hey," I said, cheering up a bit. "Your Christmas gift is here."

And so, you're wondering, what does one get a multi-millionaire musician/boyfriend for his birthday and Christmas? Well, thanks to my dad, I finagled a great deal on a Martin acoustic guitar that Garry had been incessantly pondering over. And thanks to Josh, I knew exactly what he wanted.

Garry carried the long box inside, saying, "I have to tell you, I have absolutely no clue as to what's inside this box, but seein' these "fragile" stickers all over it makes me as curious as a virgin on her weddin' night."

He set the carton down in the living room. "Now give me a few minutes to come up with a gift for you." And he disappeared into the bedroom.

I slipped into the study to get Garry's Christmas card. When I came back, there he was, lounging on the sofa, arms out, foot propped up on his knee. Perched beside him was a small beautifully wrapped box. (A suspiciously small square box, I might add.)

"Show me yours and I'll show you mine," he teased.

I presented Garry with a card, hoping he'd appreciate the thirty minutes I'd spent in Hallmark, finding just the right card—one where the words on the inside and the picture on the outside worked together in perfect harmony to convey exactly what I wanted to say—not to mention the time I'd put into composing my own thoughts and feelings, which I'd lovingly transcribed with my new $12 calligraphy pen.—He didn't. (I mean, he wasn't gushing and teary-eyed like I'd envisioned.)

With a kiss duly delivered, he quickly made his way through the packing tape . . . piles of foam on the floor . . . an inner box to pry open . . . more packaging . . . and finally, those huge dimples upon recognition of the embossed hard shell case: *C.F. Martin & Co.* From the look on Garry's face, I knew I'd found his sweet spot. (Instantly pardoned for bad behavior.) Speechless, he rubbed his hand over the case then gingerly unhinged the latches. The wider he opened the lid, the wider his eyes became.

"Holy shit, Nichole." He caressed the mahogany before carefully lifting the guitar from its plush bed.

"How'd you know?" he asked.

"Josh."

"Ah. I should have known. I love it. Absolutely love it. And look at this, *Southern Cross* on the headstock! I can't wait to play it! Thank you billfish. From the bottom of my heart I thank you. You sure do know how to please a man." He kissed me then held that guitar like a new father getting to know each and every square inch of his newborn. "Needs tuning, of course, but it feels wonderful."

"Now don't have a heart attack," I said, grabbing a black sharpie from the drawer. "There's one thing I need to do to complete your gift." I uncapped the marker and looked at Garry for approval before altering the soundboard of his guitar forever. Fortunately, he smiled and nodded his head, so I proceeded: *To Garry, Just you and me. Alone. Nichole Marie. XXX.* He read it, laughed, and gave me a bear hug and a big old sloppy kiss.

"Okay," he said, "now it's your turn. I hope my gift doesn't pale in comparison."

For a split second I'd forgotten about the small square box on the sofa . . . but only for a split second. I looked over at the box, then looked at Garry, then looked at the box again. My mind was in a state of confusion. It couldn't be what it looked like. I mean, we'd never even discussed marriage. (Sure, we'd talked about the future but always with severe caution on my part not to mention the "M" word.) It had to be something other than a ring, some other bauble or jewel. I thought, *What, in Garry's mind, could likely pale in comparison to an acoustic guitar?* (I knew the answer before I even opened it—EVERYTHING!)

Garry waved me over to the sofa to sit down next to him. I could actually feel my heart pounding in my chest. —I didn't know what to expect.

"I don't have a card for you," Garry said. (*Of course*) "But I do have some thoughts locked up inside my brain just waitin' to make a jail break."

I laughed. "Should I call the police?"

"Well, you better wait and hear what I have to say first. Then maybe you'll be callin' the police . . . Seriously now . . . in these past two months I've known you, you have changed my world, Nichole Marie. It's taken me many more years than it probably should have, but I can honestly say that now I get it. I get what life is all about. It's about bein' with the one you love. Sharin' *all* the moments of life, not just the big things—fame and celebrity—but the everyday little mundane things; especially the mundane things. Not only are you beautiful, Nik, but you are extremely intelligent, energetic, positive, fun, sensitive, sexy . . ." Garry hesitated.

"Feel free to continue," I said with a smile.

"You know I've never been one for tradition, but for some reason, you make me want to straighten up and fly right."

To my astonishment (and delight) Garry got down on his knee in front of me. He had the most serious look about him that caused my throat to tighten.

"What I'm tryin' to say, if you haven't already guessed, is that you have become my reason for livin', Nichole Marie, and I'd be a damn fool if I didn't ask you to spend the rest of your life with me." Holding the silver bow, he pulled off the lid of the box and flipped it over into the palm of his other hand. There, rested a classic black velvet case. There was no mistaking what was inside. I struggled for air as he slowly pulled back the lid to reveal the most stunning diamond ring I had ever seen.

My heart skipped a beat.

"I love you, Nichole. Will you marry me?"

I was speechless. Literally. I mean, there I was, standing at the crossroads of my future and all I could think was, *Is Garry LaForge really asking me, Nichole Marie Bocelli of Oakwood Shores, Illinois, to marry him?* My mind flashed back to all the men in my life—the good ones, the bad ones. The ones I thought I'd wanted to marry. The countless times I'd circled pictures of engagement rings in the Sunday paper. I always assumed I'd get married, but I never thought the asking would come as a complete surprise. And then, when it actually sunk in that I had just been proposed to, I thought, *Wait! I wasn't paying attention. You should have prefaced your speech with, "And now, listen up Nichole, I'm going to ask you to marry me" because I can't remember all those wonderful things you just said!* —That's when I realized Garry was waiting for my answer.

"Yes!" I replied with tears in my eyes. I put my hands on Garry's cheeks and kissed him. "Yes. My answer is yes. I love you."

"You had me shakin' in my boots for a minute, there," he said.

Garry slipped the ring on my finger, a band of sparkling diamond with a beautiful marquis set high in the center.

"It's gorgeous, Garry." I couldn't take my eyes off the ring, and I couldn't take my mind off the fact that Garry had just asked me to marry him!

"You really took me by surprise, Mr. LaForge."

"That was the plan, baby."

I continued to marvel at those brilliant rocks wrapped around my finger. And knowing, as every woman does, that the commonly accepted guideline for purchasing a diamond engagement ring is two months' salary, I knew I'd definitely made out on that deal. At first, I felt the ring was so conspicuous—a diamond as big as the Ritz. But then again, maybe I just wasn't used to wearing a ring. And believe me, I wasn't complaining one bit. Let's face it, have you *ever* met a woman who thought her engagement ring was simply too big?

"Did you pick this out on your own?" I asked.

"What? You don't think I could have done it on my own?"

"No, I didn't say that; I was just . . ."

Garry laughed. "Mom and Sammi helped me."

(I knew there had to be a woman behind that ring.)

"This calls for a celebration," he said.

"It certainly does," I said. "And remember what happened the last time you said that?"

Garry laughed. "Why don't you refresh my memory?"

And so I did.

* * *

Did I expect a yes from Nichole when I proposed to her? You bet I did, that is, until she took her sweet ol' time answerin' me. She said I took her by complete surprise, but I know what she was really thinkin'. She was thinkin', This guy's no day at the beach. Do I really want to spend the rest of my life with this Southern fool? *But I thank my lucky stars she did say yes. At least somethin' was goin' right with one woman in my life.*

Chapter 26

Different Islands, Different Worlds, Though We Really Are the Same

What is it about Garry that attracts me to him? (Other than his obvious sexy good looks.) I knew you were going to ask me that, so I'll let you in on a little secret: I hate when people ask me that question. Not that I can't come up with reasons why, it's just that some of the reasons have no concrete explanation and I know people can't stand to hear answers like "he makes me happy" or "he completes me." So, for your benefit, I'll take a moment to come up with some more specifics . . . First and foremost, Garry is down-to-earth . . . unpretentious . . . a HUGE requirement in a man of mine. I also like the fact that Garry has a lot of friends, yet doesn't *need* his friends. I appreciate the loner side of Garry. I wouldn't want to marry a guy who hangs out with "the guys" all the time.—Let's see, what else? I admire Garry's confidence in any and all situations. (I'm hoping that'll rub off on me). His creativity as a musician and a writer is inspiring (but that's a given), he loves nature and is a sporty guy; that's a big one (not to be confused with a man who "watches" sports). There are lots of other things, like the fact that he's generous and helpful, easy-going and funny. We have a lot in common, from the books we read, to how we butcher the French language, to our Catholic upbringing. You know, no matter what anyone says, I don't buy that saying that opposites attract. Okay, maybe they attract, but are they really happy? I *have* heard the saying, though, that the things you love and admire most about someone are the same things that will eventually drive you nuts about that person. It's true. For example, I love the fact that Garry is a traveler and world-explorer, but I hate that he has a hard time staying put. Also, I'm impressed by Garry's work ethic, but damned if he doesn't work too much. (And you already know how I feel about his devotion to his fans.) So there you have it. Those are the biggies. Except, of course, the money and the celebrity. You didn't think I was going to mention those two loveable attributes, did you? Although you'll notice I mentioned them last.

* * *

Looks like it's my turn . . .

> *What is it about Nikki that I love so much?*
> *Well, let me start by sayin' that all my life I've been taught to treat women with utmost solemn respect; as if women were God's divine creations—incarnates of the Virgin Mary herself. (I found that to be a penitential challenge as Sister Mary Mojo saw to it that my knuckles grew more and more calloused with each passin' year.) Anyway, I pretty much swore off women 'til the age of 18 when I was released from Catholic confinement, and it was then that I set about makin' up for lost time.*
> *As you are well aware, the life of a troubadour is full of hedonistic opportunities, of which I seldom abstained. Trouble is, as my music grew more and more popular, I began to notice a direct correlation between my expandin' assets and the number of women wantin' to make my acquaintance. Now that was all good and fine for a decade or so, but too much sugar for a dime gets old awfully quick, and with the big 4-0 lookin' me in the eye, the need to settle down swept over me like a tsunami.*

So I guess you could say Nichole came along in my life at just the right moment. Tired of all the remoras circlin' my tent, I found it ultimately refreshin' to meet a woman who didn't give a damn who the hell I was.

Now, I love Southern women. I truly do (Charlene Perkins LaForge happens to be one of the finest), but there's somethin' about a Northern woman that has always made my head spin. I don't want any of you Southern Belles out there gettin' your knickers in a bind over this. Keep in mind, I grew up in a world of wonderful Southern women. I have two sisters, no brothers, three Aunts, two nieces and seven cousins—a world of women.

Okay, I know what y'all are thinkin', But she's so much younger than you. *True. In fact, the 14 year age difference between us had me worryin' more than a whore in Sunday service. But truthfully, that was my only real concern. Within, I'd say, the first half-hour of our meetin' I could see that Nikki was a straight-forward, what-you-see is what-you-get kind of woman . . . And I liked what I saw.*

And let's face it, anybody who's ever seen her knows that Nichole's a beauty. A natural beauty, not a "don't kiss me 'cause you'll smudge my lip gloss" kind of girl but a woman who can catch a centerfield fly ball, whip up a mean chocolate cheesecake, calculate the moment of a steel beam, and still strut the red carpet with the best of 'em.

But most importantly, Nichole Marie Bocelli can put up with all my bullshit and still love me enough to give me refuge between voyages.

So there you have it. Any questions?

Chapter 27

Where's the Party?

W ith spirits high, we ventured into the wild festivities of New Year's Eve in Key West. Warm, breezy Key West. What a change of pace for me, leisurely rambling through town on a balmy New Year's Eve. Prior to that experience, ringing in the New Year for me meant snow and ice and driving (or should I say "sliding"), half-drunk, from party to party. In fact, I have vivid memories of the year Christi's car implanted itself at the bottom of an icy hill with no hope of getting out. Oh, the desperation we felt at missing the "New Year's party of the century."

Our evening plans included one of Garry's favorite hangouts, The Sandlot. We ate well, enjoyed the band, and even danced a number or two. Now you know I'm not much of a partier, but that night belonged to me, and Duval Street was glad to oblige. We wormed our way through the crowds . . . past Southard . . . then Fleming . . . and finally, Tropicana Jam. Now, no one at The Sandlot noticed "the ring." Probably because, as Garry noted, we were packed in "tighter than a cow's ass in fly season" . . . or perhaps, self-consciously, I kept my left hand down by my side. (I must confess, though, to a deep desire to gaze endlessly at my ring, but I knew that wouldn't be a cool thing to do in public.) Anyway, it was a different story at the café where our every move was analyzed. Molly, the COO, whom I'd met earlier in the day, was talking with Garry and me when she noticed "it." She stopped mid-sentence, looked directly at Garry then back down at my hand again. "Do I see an engagement ring on this lady's hand, Garry? I don't remember seeing one there this afternoon."

Garry shook his head. "That's why you get paid the big bucks to run this place, Molly. You're so damn thorough."

Suddenly, Molly jumped on stage. "Ladies and Gentlemen, Mr. Garry LaForge is in the house this evening."

Everyone looked around and spotted Garry, and a round of cheers went up.

"Oh no," Garry whispered to me under his breath as he smiled and saluted the crowd.

"He and his lovely fiancée, Nichole, are celebrating their engagement tonight. How about a round of champagne for everyone?"

The entire bar lifted their glasses to us and created quite an uproar. That's about the time I noticed over 500 eyes all looking at me. The eyes traveled directly from my face right down to my hand. Normally, I would have been overcome by worry, but after all, I didn't know a single person there (and the champagne was kicking in).

I noticed Garry keeping pretty close tabs on me throughout the evening. At one point, when I got up to use the bathroom, Garry realized I was heading toward the public restrooms and said, "Use the private bathroom back by the kitchen, Nikki. Just a forewarnin', you are no longer an anonymous person around here. That means privacy is hard to come by." As he kissed me, I realized I was going to have to rethink my way of doing things from then on.

Etiquette required we hang out for a while and lend an ear to a couple of the bands. Garry even got up and played along, much to everyone's delight. Come about 10:00 though, we made a gracious exit and swaggered over to Smittie's house for his annual New Year's Eve party. It's a good thing I'd already had countless glasses of champagne because I knew full well what I was about to encounter . . . all of Garry's friends and perhaps some women from his "past."

Before entering, Garry asked me, "Out in the open, or discreet?"

"I prefer discreet, butisthat really possible?" (Have you ever heard yourself talk when you're drunk? It's like you have no control over what you're saying; you're just a bystander overhearing yourself speak. I remember listening to my response and thinking, in horror, *Did I just slur my words? Oh my God, I hope I'm not slurring my words. Articulate, Nichole. Articulate.*

"Let's see how it goes. They're probably all snockered by now anyway. Just follow in my wake and you'll be fine."

We let ourselves in via a security guard disguised as a butler. Smittie, having clearly partaken in holiday libations, stumbled over to say hello. "Hey, Miss Oakwood Shores! I heard you were in town. Everybody was just talkin' 'bout you. —Oops, I wasn't supposed to say that, was I? Ah hell." He gave me a kiss on the cheek. "It's great to see you again, Nichole. Come on in. The gang's all here. Make yourselves at home. Layla's around some place. Garry, the set up's the same as last year; although if I recall correctly, you don't remember much from last year's party."

Garry gave Smittie a playful swat upside the head.

Smittie continued, "The drinks are poolside, the food's everywhere, and the heavier vices can be found by those who wish to partake."

Garry hooked my hand in his and led me out back where the waterfront people had converged. I instinctively scanned the area for recognizable faces . . . Marty, beside his very pregnant wife . . . Josh, surrounded by three lanky women, and finally, Ryden and Tyler. I felt more comfortable with familiarity within reach. Oh yes, and Layla and Leoni lingered about, of course, along with a throng of other well-heeled women. (I'm not paranoid, really I'm not, but I couldn't help notice that Leoni kept a close eye on Garry. For that matter, several of the women couldn't keep their eyes off him! Okay, I needed to get over that.)

I was well aware, that evening, that Marty endeavored to keep in my good graces. He eagerly introduced me to his wife, Allison, a cute blonde woman so very friendly (and pregnant) that I wondered why Marty had a wandering eye. She took an immediate liking to me, chitchatting as if she were president of the Junior League and I, a prospective member.

As I said, from the moment we arrived, Marty, in a great effort to suck-up, assumed the role of my personal attendant. While Allison and I yakked away, women continued to eye Garry. And the more they eyed Garry, the more conceited I became. As a result, what happened next must be blamed not only on outdoor lighting, but on a fair dose of shameful self-importance . . . Marty brought me a second glass of champagne which I "inadvertently" accepted with my left hand. The outdoor lighting hit my ring and that was the end of that. Marty took a hold of my wrist and pulled it right

out in front, into the circle of people we were talking with.

"Well good God Almighty!" he said.

"Nichole!" Allison cried. "When did this happen? I can hardly believe it. Congratulations!" She gave me a big sorority hug.

Garry stood nearby, his back to us, talking to some people, when Marty bellowed out, "LaForge, get your Southern ass over here!" (Warning: the more a Southern man and his friends drink, the more their inner redneck comes out).

Garry didn't hear him, (or was just ignoring him), so Marty, in obnoxious good ol' boy style, called out even louder, "I'm a talkin' to you, Bubba!—Can't help but notice your girlfriend here has a mighty big rock on her finger! Would you mind comin' over yonder and makin' some sense outta this?"

Garry may be used to being the center of attention but Marty's annoying public announcement wasn't exactly what I'd had in mind. I didn't appreciate every single person at the party starring at me. I reprimanded myself, *That's what you get for being arrogant, Nichole!*

Garry came over and took my hand in his. "Well I'll be damned, Miss Nichole, you might coulda told me you was afixin' to get hitched. Ida never taken advantage of your sweet hospitality had I known that."

The spotlight was on me and I had no choice but to play along. (It was a test of sorts. I knew it . . . *Let's see if she holds her own. Let's see if she fits in.*) I gave it my best shot. "I declare, Garry LaForge," (picture a Midwesterner doing a bad imitation of Scarlet O'Hara) "I don't recollect you mindin' much about this here ring on my finger last night."

Laughter echoed around the pool.

Marty put his arm around me, "Who said anything about a damnyankee? This one's a keeper, Bubba."

"And by the way," Marty looked over at Garry, "you have now officially entered the portal of monogamy. No more foolin' around for you, pretty boy." (I almost choked on my champagne at that remark!)

"What's this I hear about a huge rock?" Smittie said, coming over with Josh, Ryden, and Tyler.

Instead of looking at my ring, they grabbed a hold of Garry and, like a gang of coked-up cowboys, threw him into the pool . . . their own personal way of saying "congratulations." (Thankfully it was only a guy thing.)

All in all, the evening lived up to my expectations. I met everyone in the band, including their significant others, and apparently I passed the test because I was welcomed like a family member. I couldn't have been happier that night as I fell, drunk as Cooter Browne, into bed. (See, Southernese is contagious!)

Chapter 28

Legal Problems Gettin' Thick and Hazy

I t was a New Year's Day of sleeping late and hanging low. Garry snored his way through the morning and into the afternoon. I finally drug myself out of bed at one, went for a swim, and called Christi.

"... suddenly everyone was looking at my ring, asking questions and congratulating us. And then, instead of all the women staring at Garry, they were whispering—and eyeing me!"

"They're just jealous, that's all," Christi reassured.

"I'm sure they were saying to each other, *Who the hell is she? How old do you think she is? And by the way, why is she here in our territory?*"

"Well, screw 'em," Christi added.

"Oh, hang on," I said. "I hear the doorbell. —I'll let Garry get it."

"Have you told your parents yet?" Christi asked.

"No, not yet. You're the first! But do me a favor, don't tell any of the other girls just yet, okay? I need a little while to digest this myself before I get bombarded by everyone. —Oh, there's the doorbell again. I'm gonna try to revive Garry. I'll talk with you later."

"Garry?" I called. Looking through the sliding doors, I could see that sobriety was a long time coming. I opened the door and called in, "Garry? Someone's at the gate. Do you want me to answer it?"

He was dead to the world. The doorbell rang again. Whoever it was, was persistent. I closed the door and picked up the pool phone. "Hello?"

"I'm looking for Garry." The voice was familiar. It was a woman, and she sounded like she was someone.

"Garry's sleeping. Is it something I could help with, or is it possible you could come back later?" (I know, I know. Sometimes I'm just too damn polite for my own good.)

She snapped at me, "I'm sure you can't help, considering I don't know who you are and NO, I can't come back later. Just tell Garry that Brooke needs to talk to him."

Bingo. Thus, the familiar voice—and a rather bitchy one at that! I didn't care to get in the middle of that one, although I had to bite my tongue from giving her a piece of my mind. I decided to let Garry handle it.

I tromped back to the bedroom and woke Garry up. "Garry." I shook him once, then again harder. "Garry, you need to wake up. — Brooke Walker is at the gate and won't go away."

"Huh?. . . What?. . . Did you say Brooke?"

"Yes, I did say Brooke. And she's very bitchy," I said, walking into the bathroom.

"Ah, fuck," he muttered under his breath.

Okay, do I go back out to the pool or do I hang out inside, maybe catching a bit of the drama? I decided to just do my own thing and trust that Garry would fill me in later. I needed to keep busy. I went back out to the pool. I swam. I paced around the yard. I poked around in the boathouse. I kicked around in the surf. I dangled my feet at the end of the pier . . . all the while suppressing my every gut-wrenching urge to go take a peek. Was she good-looking in an "oh, she's cute" sort of way? Or was she a beauty as in "damn, she's hot!" Hell, I didn't even know if she was blonde or brunette. What was I supposed to do? Ask Garry? Show him that I cared? —Not in a long shot.

I couldn't take it anymore. I decided to take matters into my own hands. Just as I stood up to go inside, Garry came strolling down the pier. (What's that saying? *He who hesitates . . .*) We sat together in silence, watching seabirds doing touch and goes.

"Good mornin'," he finally said.

I smiled but waited for him to say more.

"You're right, she *is* awfully bitchy. I've been questionin' my sanity for ever gettin' involved with her."

I let him talk.

"She wants me to take a blood test."

"What did *you* say?"

"Well, first of all, the blood test deal wouldn't be until after the baby is born, which is the end of March.

"What did I say? I said HELL NO!"

"And so?"

"And so I think I better get in touch with my lawyer and talk to Ronny about that guy from Chino's she was sleepin' with.

"And by the way, I didn't mention a word about you. I don't want to drag you into this or have her confront you in any way. Alright?"

"You know I'm already drug into this, Garry."

"What can I say, Nichole? I'm tryin' my best here."

I patted him on the knee. "I still love you, though."

"Wanna go for a ride?" Garry said, nodding toward his sailboat, *Perpetual Motion.*

It's amazing how an afternoon of floating around the world's backyard can blow all your worries away.

Chapter 29

Tryin' to Learn About Bassinettes

K ey West held us captive a few more days. Ten below zero was nothing to rush home to. Besides, Garry needed to speak with his attorney and also take care of some band business. Oh yeah, and go fly-fishing. Have I never mentioned his second love before? (...and don't get me started on the subject of surfing.)

While Garry was off chasing the proverbial "big one," I took the opportunity to do some exploring on my own. He'd left me the Corvette to drive, and once I'd mastered the ever-so-small clutch, I gladly became Monroe County's burden for the day. I spent one entire morning driving north on US1, just getting lost in the little towns along the way. I guess that's one thing Garry and I have in common, we both like to explore; albeit his explorations prove a little more "grand" than mine. Like I told you earlier, I spent my junior year of college studying architecture in Versailles, but that only made me long for more adventure and made my Midwestern existence that much more intolerable.

Then another day, while Garry and Marty fished the flats, I accepted a lunch date with Allison. How particularly kind of her to have me over, considering she was due to give birth at any moment. She said getting together would take her mind off the delivery. So we ate a little cool conch salad on her best china and swapped stories from our childhoods.

She continued to marvel at the fact that Garry and I were getting married. "He's quite the catch, Nichole. I know many a woman who would kill to be in your shoes."

"I know," I said. "I saw them all giving me the evil eye at Smittie's party the other night."

Allison laughed. "Those women you saw whisperin' at Smittie's party are nothin' but gold-diggers. Believe me, I know. They're glamorized groupies; that's all they are. But those of us who truly know and love Garry—his closest friends—are ecstatic to see that he has finally found an amazin' woman. I mean it, Nichole. He is one lovesick boy." (I don't know about you, but in my book, flattery gets you everywhere. I decided right then and there that I liked Allison.)

That moment of camaraderie opened the door to a nagging question I'd been having . . . "It's probably difficult, when you're with someone in the entertainment industry, to know if people like you because of who you are, or just because you're the girlfriend or wife of the celebrity. How do you deal with that?" (I made it sound like I assumed she was having the same problem.—I'm anything, if not diplomatic.)

Allison laughed. "Although Marty likes to think he's a celebrity, I'm afraid that question doesn't apply to me. All I know is that we have never once liked any woman Garry has brought to the table. That is, until *you* came along. Just between you, me, and the hitchin' post, I heard all the guys in the band talkin' the other night about how great they think you are."

I also realized right then that Allison was going to be an invaluable source of inside information. Actually, prior to that lunch, I considered Allison Marty's pretty little trophy wife—a woman whom I thought was either completely blind or overly patient. What I discovered, though, was a savvy woman who knew all the vices of her man, yet loved him just the same. Heck, they'd been going together since the eighth grade. I don't think she knew the extent to which Marty indulged in those vices, but nonetheless, she was smarter than I thought. (I only hoped that Melanie, "Miss Girls Just Wanna Have Fun," realized what she was getting herself into.)

It didn't dawn on me at the time, but I now understand Marty's eagerness for Allison and I to get to know one another. He assumed I would find her engaging (which I did), likeable (which was true), and too kind-hearted to disclose to Allison Marty's bad behavior (which was right). So tell me then, why was *I* the one feeling so guilty?

Speaking of Marty, I couldn't help but question his judgment in leaving Allison to go out on the water that day, but, like Garry, Marty has wandering toes.

We were told they would try to stay within cell phone range. And it was a good thing too, because come about dessert, Allison went into sudden and serious labor. It took both of us by complete surprise. She wasn't sure at first, but quickly thereafter, the contractions were 5 minutes apart.

Up until that very moment, I knew pretty much nothing about the whole labor and delivery process. I am a youngest child, which excludes the idea that I had to deal with baby issues in childhood. And I guess I must have been absent in Health Class when that subject was being taught. Anyway, I'm always up for whatever comes my way, and at that moment, I was surely in the hot seat.

I called Marty . . . got his voice mail. I called Garry . . . same thing. *Shit!* We called Allison's doctor who told us to head to the hospital right away. Allison's best friend, Audrey, promised to meet us there. As Allison settled in, I did my best to encourage her while still calling Marty's cell. Finally, I got through to Garry. In the background Allison begged for an epidural.

"Garry! Did you guys get my messages?"

"No, but I see I have some missed calls."

"Well, tell Marty he better get to the hospital immediately. Allison is in serious labor and it won't be much longer. How far away are you guys?"

Garry relayed the message to Marty. Marty got on the phone.

"Nichole, let me talk with Allison."

I looked in on Allison, who was having a major contraction while a nurse checked her dilation. (Within moments, I'd become master of all terminology labor and delivery: dilation, effacement, Lamaze breathing, transition labor, episiotomies; believe me, I could talk the lingo with the best of them.)

"She can't talk right now, Marty. How far out are you?"

"Bout a half hour, as the crow flies. We've already left. Tell her I'm on my way. Is Audrey there?"

"Audrey's here and the doctor's due any moment."

After I hung up, I went in and told Allison that Marty was on his way. I didn't dare say he was a half hour away, though. She did not look pleased. The nurse announced a dilation of 8½ . . . too late for an epidural. Poor Allison; between that news and Marty's absence, all her Southern Belle composure was lost. I had no idea she was capable of such profanity. Marty was going to have some serious hell to pay!

Audrey and I did all we could to ease Allison's pain and give her the courage to hang in there. I remember wondering just how painful the contractions could be. Were they as painful as the broken arm I'd experienced when I was ten? Or the car door that got slammed on my hand when I was seventeen? Or the van that crashed into me on my bike when I was nineteen? —And by the way, Sister Clement, are we really supposed to believe that labor pain is God's way of punishing Eve for eating the apple? As Allison let out the most heart-wrenching cry, I decided maybe I *would* look into the possibility of a C-section one day.

With each contraction, my contempt for Marty grew. I'm sure he had no clue as to what Allison was going through without him. I wasn't too happy with Garry either, for agreeing to go fishing with Marty in the first place. (Charlene had already warned me, "Garry Jackson LaForge has had a problem sittin' still since he was knee-high to a gator in the bayou." I was beginning to understand.)

The doctor arrived soon after and checked Allison again. He declared her ready to go. From there, things just steamrolled. With Audrey on one side and me on the other, Allison pushed to our steady count of ten. The nurses were impressed with her aggressive efforts, considering it was her first delivery. I think, no, I'm *sure*, she had Marty's absence to thank for that.

Then, just as the baby's head was crowning, we heard someone running down the hall. Marty arrived, out of breath, with enough time to hold Allison's hand and watch Caroline Grace enter the world. We were all awash in tears of joy as they laid that little miracle on Allison's chest.

We lingered until she was deemed a perfectly fit baby girl, then Audrey and I left the room. Teary-eyed, I bumped right into Garry who stood outside the door.

"Oh my gosh, Garry! You should have seen that! It was the most amazing thing I've ever witnessed."

Garry hugged me. "Well?"

"Well what?"

"A boy? A girl?"

"Oh! A girl. Caroline Grace. She's beautiful. You should go in and see her. I'm sure they wouldn't mind.—And by the way, if you ever do to me what Marty did today, you can kiss your ass goodbye."

"I wouldn't *dream* of doin' such a thing," he said, crossing his heart.

Once the doctor came out and a nurse or two, we decided to go in. Garry, like me, couldn't get over how tiny Caroline Grace was and how pure and innocent. Each of us took turns holding her, but when Garry, in particular, cradled her in his arms, a strong maternal instinct pulled at my heartstrings. Garry saw the look in my eyes. "Patience, my dear . . . patience," he said.

Marty and Allison laughed.

That night, while lying in bed under an open roof of stars, Garry and I discussed our future family life. Garry made it quite clear to me that he wasn't yet ready to start a family, but that "one day, by and by" we'd have a whole "heap" of LaForges.

"There are days, like today," I said wistfully, "in witnessing the miracle of birth and seeing that precious little baby, that I want to be pregnant so badly."

"I can certainly accommodate, my dear," Garry said, rolling on top of me.

"Are you joking? Have you already forgotten your recent pregnancy troubles?"

"NO," Garry answered. "I haven't forgotten. Not one little bit. And my attorney's goin' to remind me of it again tomorrow mornin'. —I thank you sincerely for that moment of gravity."

And we went to sleep.

Chapter 30

Sharks That Swim on the Land

G arry was as excited as a little boy in a pile of mud the next day, our last in Key West. He wanted me to go along with him to his attorney's, but that's not what he looked forward to. We'd been invited to lunch with his friend, and former college roommate, Ronny Collins, who happens to be a flight instructor at the Key West Naval Air Station, and afterward we'd been promised an "exclusive" tour of the base.

As for me, I was no foreigner to military bases. That year I studied in France, I shared one too many beers with a US Army Officer at Oktoberfest and subsequently spent many a weekend on and off base in Germany. (Remember, I mentioned dating some jerks?) All in all, the experience hardened me, so I'd have to say I wasn't as thrilled about the tour as Garry was.

First, we stopped at the hospital, laden with gifts for Caroline Grace and Allison. We said our goodbyes and promised to keep in touch. Allison and I had become quite close, as you can imagine, due to the circumstances the day before.

Then it was off to see Garry's attorney, Chavis Worthington. I thought I'd feel awkward, attending a meeting about Garry's ex-girlfriend's pregnancy, but I didn't. I found Chavis a bit of a strange bird (think hockey's Don Cherry), which is par for the course in Key West, but Garry told me he's an ace in court. "Nothing to worry about, Garry boy," he said with confidence. He assured us he could easily handle the case, and I could tell a weight was lifted off Garry's shoulders.

The naval base awaited . . . We pulled up to the main gate in the Corvette. "Garry LaForge and Nichole Bocelli here to see Commander Ron Collins."

It took the shore patrolman at the gate a moment to register the name LaForge in his brain. He scanned his list and found our names as a child-like smile spread across his face. "Mr. LaForge and Ms. Bocelli, welcome to Key West Naval Air Facility. Commander Collins will be meetin' y'all at the Officer's Club.—And on a personal note, sir, it's a pleasure to meet you. I'm a big fan. I have every single CD of yours and faithfully attend your summer concerts."

"Why thank you, sir," Garry said. "I sure do appreciate that."

Officer Barnes continued, "If there's ever anything I can do for you, you just let me know. I mean it. If y'all run into any delinquents here on base, just tell 'em Lieutenant Barnes will be hot on their tail. That'll scare 'em for sure. Everybody south of the Seven Mile Bridge knows who I am, although I s'pose you're used to such a thing, aren't you? I guess you could say I'm a regular celebrity, myself, 'round here. Workin' at the gate like this, I know practically each and every name of everybody who comes and goes on this base." His was visibly proud, puffing up his chest, adjusting his belt buckle. I had to stifle a laugh, considering 1.) a line of 5 or 6 cars waited behind us while he jibber-jabbered on and on and 2.) he looked to be no more than 5 pounds heavier than me!

"Thank you, Lieutenant Barnes. It's a pleasure to be here, and I *promise*, if there's ever anything I need, you'll be the first man I call." Garry and the soldier exchanged salutes and we were on our way.

Talk about conspicuous . . . a classy little white and red Corvette cruising through a sea of standard issue. To my surprise, not only was the Officer's Club chic, but it sported a magnificent view of the Gulf. We ordered drinks and waited at the bar while a slew of male officers milled about. Women were definitely in short supply. Garry left to use the bathroom just as a group of young officers saddled up next to me at the bar. My watch read half past twelve, but according to them it was 5 o'clock somewhere, and I was the nearest catch at hand. Within moments, three of them scooted over closer to me, trying to play it cool with their smoothest pick-up lines. They provided ample amusement until Commander Collins arrived.

"Nichole Bocelli, I presume?" Ronny said.

I looked up, smiled, and nodded.

The three guys seemed annoyed that an outranking officer was honing in on their catch. But as I said, he was a Commander and they, apparently, were mere Lieutenants.

"With all due respect, sir," one of the bolder ones said, "we were just getting to know this beautiful lady here."

"Save your respect for the lady, gentlemen. I'm afraid she's already spoken for."

They looked disappointed. "They always go for the Commanders, don't they?" one of them said.

"Not this Commander, y'all. This lady is Garry LaForge's girlfriend," he said, nodding toward Garry as he approached.

Their eyes lit up in surprise.

"Fiancée," Garry added as he arrived by my side.

The three lieutenants apologized for disturbing me and withered away. Garry introduced me to Ronny, an extremely personable, well-mannered fly-boy.

"Thanks for saving me," I said.

"You have to watch yourself around here," Ronny replied. "This place is full of landsharks, especially with a beautiful lady like yourself around."

"Speaking of landsharks," Garry muttered under his breath . . . Just then, Mr. Tall, Dark, and Handsome breezed by our table, looking stunning in his dress whites. He was impressive. So impressive, in fact, that I had a difficult time keeping my eyes to myself. Don't tell Garry, but Mr. Tall, Dark, and Handsome caught me glancing at him more than once. After the second time, he smiled at me, stood up, and started walking toward our table. *What have I done?* I thought, my face turning every shade of a Florida sunset.

"Hey Ronny," he said.

"Hey Hunter. How's it going? Hunter, you know Garry, don't you?"

He does? I thought.

"Garry LaForge," Hunter said matter-of-factly.

Garry stood up and extended his hand. "I think we met at Shayla Zimmerman's party a while back, didn't we?"

"That's possible," was his reply.

That's possible? That's possible? I wasn't sure how Garry would react to that one. I'd never seen someone act so indifferently toward him. Was it arrogance or innate confidence?

They shook hands then Garry introduced me. "Nichole, this is Hunter . . ."

"Rayburn," he said, taking my hand and holding it just a little longer than necessary. I'm not sure Garry noticed that, or the wink Hunter gave me when he went on his way. I was flattered. Military bases sure are good for the female ego.

As we ate lunch, Garry and Ronny discussed, among other things, the Brooke Walker situation—well, sort of. Garry never mentioned the pregnancy, just that he wanted to know the name of the guy from Chino's she was screwing.

"Actually, it's ironic you mention that because the guy used to hang around with Hunter. His name is Avery, Blake Avery. He's a bartender at Chino's; at least he used to be. I haven't been there in ages. I'll ask Hunter if he knows anything more."

After lunch Ronny took us on an awesome tour of the base, including an up-close-and-personal with several fighter jets. (See Garry salivate.) (Actually, see Garry remind me for the millionth time of his dream to tag along with the Blue Angels.) But the truly spectacular moment of our tour occurred as we walked out of the hangar. Directly in front of us, an F/18 Hornet came roaring through the sky, so low it sent Garry's baseball cap flying. If you've never seen a fighter jet flying upside down tilting its wings back and forth at 200 feet off the ground, take it from me, it's breathtaking and horrifying at the same time! Garry and I looked at Ronny in amazement, that is, after we recovered from our heart attacks.

"What in God's name is that all about?" Garry asked.

"It's a new procedure we've been teaching the pilots called "distress flying." Fortunately, they're only practicing. What it is, is a way of signaling distress to personnel on the ground. In other words, it tells everyone to clear the area and get help immediately because a problem aircraft is heading their way. Not to wave my own flag, but I'm proud to say that another instructor and I are the innovators of this new maneuver. In fact, there's an award ceremony later today; that's why so many of us are wearing our dress uniforms."

We were winding things up with Ronny when we noticed Hunter in the parking lot getting into a hot little roadster.

"Hunter!" Ronny called out. "Hey, Hunter, Garry here was asking me about your friend over at Chino's Bar. Blake Avery. Does he still work there?"

Hunter sauntered over. "You know, Garry," he said, leaning against the Corvette (Yes, I said *leaning* against the Corvette.), "I haven't seen Blake in quite a while. But I do know he's not working at Chino's anymore. I can contact some people who may know where he is, though. Do you want me to look into it? How can I reach you?"

"I'll give you my number. Call me when you have some information," Garry grumbled, eyeing invisible smudges on his fender.

"Sure. Are you going to be in town a while?" Hunter asked.

"No, we're headin' back to Illinois tomorrow."

Hunter looked at me with raised eyebrows. "Illinois?"

"That's where Nichole's from," Garry said, then turned to say goodbye to Ronny.

Hunter smiled at me, "Ah ha. A lovely Midwestern woman."

I didn't know what to say, so I just smiled.

". . . with a mesmerizing smile. Too bad you're going back to Illinois tomorrow." (I'm afraid he had me pegged. I'm a sucker for a flirt.)

"Why's that?" I asked.

He couldn't answer, though. Ronny came over to say goodbye.

As we drove home Garry stated, out of the blue, "Hunter's got an eye on you."

"What makes you say that?" I acted as innocent as I possibly could.

"Please, Nichole. I wasn't born yesterday. I saw the way he was lookin' at you. I know the guy; he's a cocky Annapol"ass" pilot. He thinks he can have any woman he wants. —He better think again."

* * *

I never met a naval aviator I didn't admire . . . that is, until I met Hunter Rayburn. Some time ago, Shala Zimmerman was throwin' a little party at her Daddy's golf club up Miami way, and for some unknown reason Hunter Rayburn happened to be on her guest list. All night long, he was eyein' Brooke like a starved dog at a 4th of July picnic. And there he was again, in my face, droolin' all over Nichole. I tell ya, if I didn't think he held the key to some important information regardin' Brooke's pregnancy, I'd of knocked his pretty boy face into the middle of next week.

Now, I know you're also wonderin' about my friend Marty. I won't drag you through the sordid details of why Martin Anderson and I are and always will remain great friends. I realize he can be a dickhead. And everybody knows he's windier than a bag of assholes, but God love him, his heart is in the right place. He and I have been through the gates of hell and back, and I know despite all his faults, he's always got my back.

Chapter 31

What Do the Ladies Say?

B ack to Illinois. It was cold—lung-stinging cold—and snowy, but I didn't mind one bit that time. I felt cozy and warm in the lap of happiness. I was living a completely different life than a mere 3 months earlier. Garry dove into his book with a vengeance while I spent my time playing Kristi Yamaguchi out back. I had Garry borrow my dad's snow blower to make a rink on the ice, and there were already lights out there, so we just readjusted them to shine onto the rink. That way I could skate at night. Garry said he loved looking up from his laptop to see me skating. He said I looked footloose and fancy free. I even went so far as to buy him a pair of CCMs and a stick for Valentine's Day. (How romantic of me, huh?) Admittedly, Garry never could adjust to land and had only been skating once in his life, but he was out there practicing a little bit every day. He said it took his mind off work. As for me, I took great pleasure in finally having a talent that outshined Garry's!

The following week I invited my friends over for a skating/slumber party—just the girls. At that point I had only told Christi about our engagement (and my family, of course, who were thrilled beyond belief). I figured it'd be a good occasion.

Sarah, Christi, Amanda, Melanie, and Jessica piled through the door on a cold Saturday evening. Garry was in the kitchen when they arrived. I swear, they had barely dropped their bags when Amanda looked at me, shocked. "Nichole!" She grabbed my hand. "What is that massive rock on your finger?"

Then Melanie added, in her boisterous voice, "How the hell did you find this guy, Bocelli?"

I could hear Garry laugh from the kitchen.

"Oh my God, is Garry here?" she whispered. "I didn't know he'd be home. What a gorgeous ring, Mr. LaForge," she called into the kitchen.

"Thanks," Garry called back. "And for all y'all's information, she didn't find *me* . . . I found *her*."

Amanda held my hand prisoner as everyone gazed at my ring.

"Did you get engaged over Christmas?" Sarah asked.

"New Year's Eve actually."

"Well, we want details you know," Melanie pressed.

I smiled. "I guess it was supposed to be at his parent's house right after Christmas, but *my* Christmas present for Garry was running behind schedule." I knew the next question out of their mouths . . . "A guitar. So, we didn't exchange gifts until New Year's Eve." They were silent, waiting for more. "In Key West. At Garry's house."

Silence still. (My girlfriends are so predictable.)

I whispered, "Yes, he got down on his knee." (I knew that's what they wanted to know.)

"How exciting!" Christi said with a wink, as if she'd just heard the news.

"Have you set a date yet?" Jessica asked.

"Not an exact date. We're thinking this fall sometime—after the summer tour."

"You'll get married in Oakwood Shores, won't you?" Sarah asked.

"Of course," I said.

Garry came out to say hello to the girls. They congratulated us and complimented him on the beautiful ring. My goal that evening was to loosen them up a bit around Garry, liquefy those formal postures, wipe those polite schoolgirl smiles right off their faces.

"Nikki's got pizza in the oven for y'all and Bon Jovi playin' out at the rink," Garry said. "And the drinks are on the way. What more could you want?"

"Five of your sexiest single friends," Melanie said, never one to need
loosening up.

"I very well could arrange that, ladies. We'll have to have y'all down to our place in Key West. Maybe in March or April. I usually stay out of town during Spring Break season, but I bet y'all could use a breather from this ice-box."

Their eyes lit up at the thought of it. They all agreed it was a great idea. (Of course they did!)

Just a side note: I had yet to think of Garry's house in Key West as "our place." It was odd, yet exciting, to hear him say that.

We fastened our skates and enjoyed a merry old time on the ice. Garry served up hot chocolate and hot buttered rum ("Somethin' to keep y'all warm."), and the girls talked him into lacing up and joining us outside.

At one point in the evening, while inside using the bathroom, I heard Garry's cell phone ring in the study.

"Hello," I answered.

There was a pause, then, "Hey. —Is this Nichole?"

I recognized the voice immediately. It was Hunter Rayburn.

"Yes it is."

"This is Hunter Rayburn, Nichole. I didn't expect to hear *your* voice on the end of the line."

He obviously didn't know that Garry and I were living together, let alone engaged.

"Well here I am," I said, the hot rum running through my system.

"And where is Garry?"

"He's out back ice-skating."

"Ice-skating? Let me guess . . . you're not in Florida, are you?"

"No, we're in Oakwood Shores. Illinois, that is."

"Oakwood Shores. Now that sounds like a charming place. And what does one do for excitement in *Oakwood Shores*?"

"Well, at this moment I'm having my friends over for a party."

"A party girl, huh? I didn't think you were a party girl."

I didn't know whether to be offended or not. "What *did* you think I was, then?"

"Thoughts about you are between me and my daydreams, darlin'."

Once again, he'd stolen my voice. And I know I said it before, but I'll say it again, I'm a sucker for a flirt.

"Do you want me to go get Garry for you?"

"No, not really. I'm thoroughly enjoying speaking with you . . . I'm not making you uncomfortable, am I?"

"No, you're not making *me* uncomfortable, but I'm sure Garry wouldn't find much comfort in it."

At that moment, Amanda and Sarah walked into the study, and I experienced what I can only describe as "cookie-jar guilt." I quickly said to Hunter, "Hey, I've gotta go. Is there something I can tell Garry?"

"Tell Garry I found Blake Avery for him. He can call me about it. And tell him a very pregnant Brooke Walker is spreading all sorts of rumors around town."

"I'll tell him," I said.

"When do I get to see you again, Nichole?"

"Hunter."

"What?"

"You're going to get yourself in trouble," I said.

"Just maybe you're worth the trouble."

"Goodbye," I said, laughing.

Back outside, I skated over to Garry and told him that Hunter had called.

"Why didn't you come get me?" he asked.

"He said you could call him back."

Garry thought for a moment. "He wanted to talk with you, didn't he?"

I didn't know how to answer that one. Technically, knowing Garry's dislike of him, I shouldn't have been engaging in flirtatious banter with Hunter. But, after all, it *was* rather harmless, and I have to admit, rather fun.

"I told him you were out skating, but that I could go get you." *Quick, change the subject*, I thought. "He said to tell you he knows where

Blake Avery is and to also tell you that a very pregnant Brooke Walker is spreading rumors about you around town."

"Asshole," Garry muttered under his breath.

"Who? Hunter Rayburn or Blake Avery?"

"Both," he said, skating off.

* * *

Garry joined us inside for pizza but eventually wandered off upstairs. My friends took the opportunity to ask me all sorts of prying questions about Garry—his life, our future, etc. Lest you think my head was growing big from all the attention, I'd like to point out that it was *not* my objective to turn that evening into "the life and times of Nichole Bocelli." I made sure we gave fair play to everyone else's current dramas: Sarah's roommate's obsession with tanning, Amanda's unattractive boss who continually asks her out, Christi's battles with her on-again off-again boyfriend. However, we never *did* get around to discussing a certain someone's fling with a married man; although, over stiff drinks and steady laughter we were well on our way to solving a majority of the world's problems.

Garry snuck downstairs around midnight, wearing his boxer shorts and looking, well, *good*.

"Hey, y'all, I was dozin' off upstairs and thought I'd better come down and say g'night."

He came over and kissed me. "See ya in the mornin'. G'night ladies."

A hush fell over the room as he climbed the stairs to bed.

"Allow me to say what is on everyone's mind right now," Melanie stated in her drunkenness. "You are so fucking lucky Miss Bocelli. Do you realize that?"

Everybody concurred.

"Stop it you guys," I said, embarrassed.

"How's the sex?" Melanie whispered. "I bet it's *steamy*. Am I right?"

"Melanie!" Sarah said.

But she went on, "No, really. I'm sure everyone here has been wondering that. Wondering what it must be like to be with Garry LaForge . . . to hear that dreamy Southern accent in bed every night, to live the life he's leading. Come on you guys, admit it."

Christi nodded her head.

Jessica laughed, "Well, now that you mention it."

"Yes, yes, we've all been wondering," Amanda said.

"Good thing I'm extremely buzzed, you guys." They fell silent again, hanging on my every word, waiting for my response. "First of all, Melanie, I'm sure you know a little something about dreamy Southern accents in bed." (Roaring laughter—even Melanie) "And yes, I realize how lucky I am. Every single morning I have to look over at Garry when I wake up just to make sure it's not some whacked-out dream I'm having. And as far as the sex goes . . . let's just say that your choice of adjectives was accurate."

* * *

The next morning my parents arrived at Garry's house bright and early. Garry was making good on his Christmas gift by flying them down to San Diego for a winter get-away. My friends, although suffering from lack of sleep and horrendous hangovers, managed to throw on their jeans for a trip to the airport and a tour of the plane. (I simply had to mention the word "private jet" and they were all over it.)

"So ladies, how about joinin' Nichole down in Key West for Spring Break? I've got a fishin' trip planned for the end of March and I'd be more than happy to give all y'all a lift down in the plane."

Everyone agreed it would be a wonderful idea. (Surprise, surprise.)

Chapter 32

Pale Invaders

A nd so, come end of March, we, and all the other tan crusaders took over Key West for some Spring Break fun: Sarah, Christi, Amanda, Melanie, Jessica, and me. Garry flew the six of us down—six overly-excited twenty-four year olds with a license to chill.

Garry announced over the PA system, "Shall I call ahead and warn the men of Key West that six lovely, eligible ladies are comin' to town?"

I looked at my friends. "Did he just say *six* eligible ladies?"

"Scratch that," Garry said over the PA. "Make that *five* eligible ladies."

I called up front, "And remember Garry, you promised them five of your sexiest single friends."

"I can assure you ladies, I am not a man of empty promises," he answered.

Garry had arranged a limo for our arrival. "If there's one thing I learned growin' up in a house full of women, if you treat the ladies right, life ain't nothin' but a breeze." (Another reason to love a Southern man.)

The fact that it was sunny and 82 degrees in Florida and snowy and 5 degrees in Illinois helped heighten our spirits. I remember as a child, stepping off the plane in Florida every spring and realizing there was this whole other world where people wore shorts, t-shirts, and flip flops in the middle of February! I'm sure the locals could spot us Northerners coming a mile away with our corduroy pants, turtlenecks, and down jackets over our arms (sleeves stiff with hats, gloves, and scarves). I recall, most specifically, the smell of orange blossoms as we drove our rental car, windows down, toward the shore. It was a divine smell, having spent the previous five months breathing nothing but forced-air out of floor vents. I'll tell ya, you Floridians may not enjoy the tourist invasion you receive every spring, but have pity on us Northerners . . . I know for a fact that Cabin Fever is real, and it's ugly.

"I had Joshy stock the fridge for us," Garry said when we arrived, "so make yourselves at home. There's plenty of room for everybody; just let Nikki or me know if y'all need anything. Let me remind you that this is *your* vacation, ladies. I don't give a shit about the dishes or makin' the beds or what time y'all come in at night. I just wanna see bikinis by the pool and boat drinks in your hands."

While Garry unloaded the luggage, I gave the girls a tour of the house and the grounds. If I were to pinpoint an exact moment when I felt a sense of personal attachment to the house in Key West, that was it. (I mean, wasn't that *my* box of tampons under the sink in Garry LaForge's bathroom?)

A night out on the town was almost a given, but quite honestly, I'd have been happy curled up on the sofa next to Garry watching a good foreign movie. So, Tropicana Jam became our compromise. I drove the Corvette, Jessica took the Jeep, and Melanie hitched a ride with Garry on his Harley. We were quite the motorcade—Garry, with six ladies in tow! My friends were impressed with the café but mostly impressed with the rock star treatment we received. As expected, Tropicana Jam crawled with Spring Breakers, yet Molly was sure to give us a great table and excellent service. Poor Garry hardly got his meal down, though. Energized fans claimed his full attention—attention no longer paid to me. That familiar irritation began to boil in my bones, and I had to keep telling myself, *It's a mutual respect, Nikki. These fans keep Garry in business and he has an obligation to be accessible to them.* Thankfully, my girlfriends provided ample diversion to this disgruntled bride-to-be.

Soon after our arrival, Marty and Josh made an appearance. I couldn't blame Josh. I thought he and Jessica made a perfect couple. Josh is a fantastic friend to Garry, a relentless joker, a talented musician, and easy to talk to, not to mention a fine sight to look at. I already considered him one of *my* friends. Marty, on the other hand, I *could* blame. I know you're probably thinking that I can't stand Marty, and I know you also probably can't figure out how Garry could have such a best friend, but you have to understand that despite his constant screw-ups and misguided exploits, Marty has a way about him that calls for forgiveness, no matter what he does. I was beginning to understand what Garry meant when he said "everybody loves Marty." Overall, I know he means well and I also know he'd do absolutely anything for Garry. My only concern at that point was for Allison and Caroline Grace. I didn't want Allison to think I purposely harbored such a secret. Okay, that's not the only reason. Actually, it's not the real reason at all. You see, I found Marty's unfaithfulness disturbing. Not that I found Melanie's behavior any less troubling, but Marty was, after all, in a different position than Melanie. Anyway, the rationale rolling around in my brain went something like this: *If Marty, Garry's best friend, can so easily cheat on his adoring wife, then what's to say Garry would not do the same? In effect, what kind of influence does Mr. Anderson have over Mr. LaForge?* I was torn. Garry felt I should let Marty and Allison deal with their own consequences as they'd been doing since the age of thirteen.—As you'll see, that proved to be a mental struggle for me.

Upon Ryden and Tyler's arrival at Tropicana Jam, I commented to Garry, "Hey mister, you'll have to cough up two more friends if you intend to keep your promise."

"Don't worry, ladies. By next weekend I *will* come through for you. Although I have a hunch y'all'll round up five men of your own b'fore I even hook my first fish."

I know Garry wasn't in a mood to entertain that night, but like I said, he has real heart for his fans, so he played a little something between sets.

"Hey y'all. Normally I'm not in town this time of year, but love's been doin' crazy things to me lately. Speakin' of love, this song I'm gonna play is a new one in my repertoire, one that I've never played in public before."

He bummed a couple barstools from the bar, took center stage, and played "Been Tryin' To Catch Up With You," accompanied by Josh on harmonica. After a well-deserved standing ovation, a tired Garry kissed me and told me he was heading home. Before leaving he said, "I don't mind y'all bringin' people back to the house, just be vigilant about who it is you bring back. Remember, there's no rewind and no replay."

The only people through Garry's doors that night were Ryden, Tyler, Marty, and Josh. Somehow, between the two guest rooms, the study, the living room sofa, and the boathouse, everyone found a place to sleep... or in Marty's case, a place to stay until 2 a.m.

* * *

The following morning Garry, Ryden, and Tyler were set to drop in on the hungry and unsuspecting fish of the Dry Tortugas. The plan was to fly *Southern Cross*, Garry's seaplane, west to the Fort Jefferson area and spend several days getting their fishing fix before joining us the next weekend.—Did I mind the fact that Garry was going fishing? Not one bit. First of all, I had my own circus of fun planned for that week, but most importantly, fishing is a sacred rite for Garry, a religious experience of sorts, "an encounter with the divine," he'd once told me. (I tried not to laugh.) Simply put, if Garry couldn't fish, then Garry wasn't happy. And if Garry wasn't happy . . . well, that's an easy one.

And so, my joyful angler was up bright and early Monday morning, seeking some "special attention" before leaving. Not a bad way to start the day.

Several of us, coffee in hand, made it out to the end of the pier in time to see the fishermen off. I had never before seen Garry fly *Southern Cross* and I must say, it was spectacular watching those silver wings take from sea to air and slowly fade out of sight.

Chapter 33

The Dark Side of the Moon is on the Rise

H ere's where things started to get complicated.
Monday afternoon found us cruising the gift shops, taking a trolley tour, and soaking in all the craziness of the Conch Republic. Garry was right when he said that Key West is a small island; I'd only been in town once before, yet I ran into several people I recognized while we were out. Jessica, Melanie, and Christi made friends of their own while surfing around town. The three of them skipped into Tropicana Jam (our meeting point), having clearly gone one too many rounds on the Conch Train. "We've been invited to a party tonight, ladies."

"Where?" we all replied.

"Well," Christi said, "we're not sure exactly *where*, but it's on a private beach somewhere, and we're supposed to meet the two guys here at 7:00. And we promise, you won't be disappointed. They're hot!"

"Are you sure they aren't a couple of whackos? There are a lot of those here in Key West," I said. "And, more importantly, are you sure they're straight?"

"Oh, they're definitely straight," Melanie replied. "In fact, one of them is a Navy fighter pilot."

"Their names are Blake and . . ."

"Hunter?" I said.

"Oh my God, how did you know?" Christi asked. "Do you know them?"

"Something like that. I met Hunter last time I was in town, and I know *of* Blake."

"Do they know you're friends of mine?"

"No. I don't think we mentioned it. Did we?" Jessica asked.

"I didn't," Christi said.

"No. Not me," Melanie replied.

"So they're coming here at 7? All I can say is it's a good thing Garry's not in town."

"Why do you say that?" Sarah asked.

"Because Garry has issues with both of those guys—one that involves me and one that involves an ex-girlfriend."

All eyebrows were raised.

"Sorry guys. I've been sworn to secrecy," I said.

Seven o'clock was fast approaching, so we ordered dinner at the café. (I just have to tell you, I loved saying this, "Put it on Garry's tab, please.") We were finishing up when Hunter and some pretty boy with bleach in his hair walked in. I happened to be in back talking with Molly when I spotted them.

Yes, they were hot, no question about it, and I really have to admit, given different circumstances, I may have been interested in Hunter. He had a sexy flirtatious way about him that permeated through me. But, they say the life of a sailor steers a wandering course, and I'm afraid Hunter Rayburn is one sailor who would wander much too far for my taste. Anyway, I digress.

You should have seen the look on Hunter's face when he caught sight of me heading toward the table. I had the upper hand on that one.

"Hello there Mr. Rayburn."

His face lit up. "Nichole! I thought you were going to tell me when you were coming to town." His eyes quickly scanned the room for Garry before giving me an ever-so-tight hug.

"I see you've met some of my friends from Oakwood Shores," I said.

He looked surprised. "These beautiful women are friends of yours? I should have known. My God, are all the women in Illinois this good-looking?"

My friends were awestruck by this seemingly handsome and charming man. Introductions were made all around. When Hunter got to me he said to Blake, "This here is the lovely Nichole Bocelli, girlfriend of Garry LaForge; although soon to be swept off her feet by Hunter Rayburn."

Poor Blake. To borrow one of Garry's valuable expressions, "he didn't know whether to scratch his watch or wind his ass." And you should have seen the look on my friends' faces when Hunter said such a thing.

I laughed. "I told you, Hunter. You're looking for trouble. And I'm not Garry's *girlfriend*; I'm Garry's *fiancée*; soon to be Mrs. LaForge."

Hunter made as if someone had shot an arrow in his heart. He then leaned in, his rough cheek grazing mine, and whispered in my ear, "You're kidding me, right? You and Garry are engaged?" He seemed genuinely disturbed.

"Astonishing news, isn't it?" I whispered back.

He pressed his moist lips against my ear. "I guess I'll just have to work a little faster . . . and a lot harder."

Chapter 34

Brown Eyed Girl

T he party was, in fact, on a private beach, near the Navy base. Not that I'm blaming my girlfriends or anything, but they *were* rather enthusiastic about the whole party idea, and if it were not for them, I would certainly have passed on Hunter's invitation. (At least I like to think I would have.) But that's hindsight, and I have no one but myself to blame for my insufferable behavior . . .

The beer was flowing, shrimp were boiling, and the bonfires were lit. We met a bevy of friendly people and didn't get back to the house until 3 a.m.! As to be expected, Hunter's flirting was relentless. I'm absolutely sure Garry wouldn't have liked it one bit. And, to make matters worse, I was in no shape to drive, so for some dumb-ass reason, I let Hunter drive me home in the Corvette! Garry's words hung in the back of my brain, "Just be careful who y'all bring back to the house with you." If Garry knew Hunter was driving his Corvette and that Blake Avery sat drinking a beer in his kitchen, I guarantee you, I'd be takin' a one-way walk down Eternity Street.

My intentions to say goodbye and thank you at the gate drifted out to sea as Hunter and Blake insisted on walking us in. While we waited for their cab, the subject of Brooke Walker came up.

"I'm afraid that topic's been banned in this house," I warned. "Garry would jerk a knot in my tail if he knew you were here, Blake. — And you too, Hunter."

Hunter flashed a playful smile.

My friends listened intently, those who weren't already passed out from drunkenness or fatigue.

"You know she had the baby a couple of weeks ago," Blake said.

I wasn't expecting that one. She must have had the baby early. "Boy or girl?" I asked.

"A girl," Blake said.

"And how do *you* know?" I asked.

"How else, the Coconut Telegraph. Key West is a whole 'nother world," he said.

"I'm beginning to figure that out."

The cabbie rang at the gate. Relieved, I walked my two overdrawn guests out front.

Before leaving, Blake added, "The baby has brown eyes, Nichole."

"And what's that supposed to mean?" I asked.

"Both Brooke and I have blue eyes. You figure it out," he said, getting into the cab.

I stood there, wide-eyed and suddenly stone sober.

Hunter turned to me. "Thanks for a wonderful evening, Nik. Now I expect to see you again this week, alright."

His words didn't register in my brain. The only words circulating through my head were *brown* and *eyes*—Garry's brown eyes!

Before I had a chance to object, Hunter leaned in and kissed me (and it wasn't a peck on the cheek), then slid into the cab, winked, and was gone.

Thank God it was almost 4 in the morning or I wouldn't have slept at all that night.

Chapter 35

El Diablo

A nd so I slept. I slept and slept and slept some more. The girls were concerned about me. I blamed it on a bad hangover, but the truth was, I didn't want to wake up and face a possible reality that I so desperately didn't want to believe. I also knew, as a child who's disobeyed his parents knows, that my behavior the previous night had been less than model.

Have you ever heard the expression, "Doing the Duval Crawl?" Well, it's a Key West phrase which refers to the act of frequenting the many bars that line the sidewalks of Duval Street. That evening, preparations were underway for just such an event. As for myself, I hung around the house in one of Garry's big oxfords, assuring the girls I'd be fine at home without them. And, because my judgment was no longer obscured by alcohol, I remembered no one else was "allowed" to drive the Corvette; therefore, I offered to call a cab to escort my girlfriends into town.

"Actually, Blake offered to come get us," Melanie said. "He should be here any minute."

At least she didn't say Hunter.

"Nik," Amanda called out, "Blake is at the gate. Do you mind if I buzz him in?"

"Go ahead. Just push star 9," I said.

I was in the pantry, leaning over, looking for something to eat when I felt two hands under my shirt, very low on my hips.

"Staying in by yourself tonight, Nichole?"

I jumped and quickly turned around when I heard Hunter's voice. He wore his flight suit and had me practically pinned against the shelves with his wings.

"God, you scared me!" I said.

"You seem nervous. Is everything ok?" His placed his arm on the shelf behind my shoulder, blocking my exit. Not only was the situation making me uncomfortable, if someone were to walk in on us, I'd have some explaining to do.

"No, I mean yeah. I'm fine," I said, ducking under his arm. A sudden flash of Garry coming home early and finding me half-dressed and in the pantry with Hunter Rayburn had gotten me flustered. The sound of heals on the foyer tile made it worse.

I called out, "You guys aren't leaving yet, are you?"

Blake poked his head into the pantry. "Coming or not?"

"Go on ahead," Hunter said. "I'll catch up with you later."

What? Did I just hear Hunter say he's going to stay here with me . . . alone . . . dressed only in Garry's shirt and my bikini bottoms!

I looked Hunter square in the eyes. "That's *not* a good idea," I said.

But everyone was already gone.

Shit! I thought.

"What's not a good idea?" he said, tossing his hat onto the sofa and making himself right at home. "I'm not making you uncomfortable am I?"

"You seem to be very skilled at it."

"I'm skilled at a lot of things," he said, putting his boots up on the coffee table and settling in.

I remained firmly planted in the kitchen. "Hunter. What are you doing here?"

"You kept me up late last night, and I had a long, exhausting day at work, so I thought I'd hang out here with you, have a quiet evening, get to know you better. It's the least you could do," he said with a most angelic smile.

I just shook my head. "You're not going away, are you?"

"Not easily," he quipped. His boyish grin did wonders to melt my icy glare.

There was silence. Hunter casually leafed through one of Garry's fly-fishing magazines as if he was relaxing at home in his pajamas. I resigned myself to the fact that he wasn't going to leave. And he did seem harmless enough. And although you may have your doubts at this point (because you *do* realize, don't you, that I found him irresistibly charming and overwhelmingly handsome), I knew I wasn't going to do anything regrettable.

"Well, I guess I don't need to tell you to make yourself at home. I was just scrounging for something to eat. Have you eaten yet?" I walked into the bedroom to change (closing the door behind me, mind you).

"I haven't eaten a thing since this morning," Hunter called from the living room. "I'm *very* hungry!"

I emerged from the master bath wearing nothing but my bikini bottoms, and guess who I bumped into. "Holy Shit! – Hunter!" I quickly grabbed Garry's shirt from the bed and covered myself, although he'd already received full exposure.

"Sorry I scared you," he said. "I was just going to ask if you wanted me to order take-out."

I gave him a 'yeah, right' look and said, in my sternest, most serious voice, "Listen, mister, promise me you'll behave yourself and I'll let you stay. Got it?"

He put his hand over his heart. "On my honor, darlin'; although you don't have to change your clothes on my account. I'm kinda likin' the outfit you got goin' on right there."

My folded arms and tapping foot sent Hunter scurrying from the room.

I remember talking to myself as I got dressed, *Keep it light, keep it casual, Nik.*

We ordered Chinese and channel flipped most of the evening. I did my best to keep things light, but Hunter dove into the heaviest of subjects, his life as a Navy brat—about having lived in 7 different states and 5 different countries since he was three feet tall.

"My father was my hero," he reminisced, "but unfortunately, he was at sea most of my childhood."

"How did your family handle his constant absence?" I asked.

"It was just me and my mom. I handled it with drugs and alcohol.—*She* handled it by cheating on my father.—He handled it by committing suicide."

I was taken aback. Hunter said it so matter-of-factly that I began to reconsider my current state of bitchiness.

"It was years ago. I was 18, in my first week at the Naval Academy."

I didn't know what to say except for the standard, "I'm so sorry, Hunter." I felt rotten for having been so rough on him.

"So what about your life in Illinois?" he asked. "Wait," he put his fingers to his temples. "An aura of idyllic childhood encircles you. Am I right?"

Apparently my five sentence version didn't satisfy his curiosity. It's not that I hadn't planned to tell him more (especially after he'd been so forthcoming with me), the reality is I was having a tough time keeping my eyes open. My head kept bobbing up and down while the *Weather Channel* girl gave her South Florida Sunshine Report. I woke up as Hunter was carrying me into my bedroom.

Now, severe panic *should* have swept over me, right? But something strange was happening. I was so very, very drowsy, which was odd, considering I'd slept on and off all day long.

"What are you doing?" I casually asked.

"Carrying you to bed, sleepy head," he said.

For some reason, that sounded completely rational to me, and I put my head on his shoulder. I recall he smelled like Drakkar Noir—a weakness of mine. As he laid me down on the bed he caught sight of the glass ceiling above. A spectacular full moon covered the bed in a golden glow."

"Wow, would you look at that!" he said, lying down next to me to get a better look. "I could get used to this bedroom."

Despite extreme efforts to keep my eyes open, I continued to doze off, knowing full well a potential sticky situation was brewing.

"Hunter, you can't stay here," I said, but it came out of my mouth as a whisper.

That's when he leaned over and kissed me . . . hard.

"And . . . you can't . . . do that anymore." I barely got it out before I succumbed to an intense desire to sleep.

What happened next was like swimming through the murky waters of the lake with my eyes open. I wasn't sure if I was having a dream or not, and I was confused as to what was going on. I do remember hands. Hands between my legs. I thought it was Garry, of course, and became aroused, but it wasn't Garry's voice I heard whisper in my ear moments later, "I've been
waiting for this moment, Nichole."

That's when I realized several things: 1) It wasn't Garry straddling me; it was Hunter! 2) I no longer had my shorts on, and 3) I had not asked for this . . . or had I? I was disoriented and seemed to be slipping in and out of sleep. There were moments when I knew what was going on, but ultimately I had no power to stop it.

The rest of the story was told to me by Josh.

Apparently Josh had run into my friends in town and they told him I wasn't feeling up to going out. He and Jessica went back to the house to see if they could convince me otherwise. They rang at the gate a couple times, but no one answered, which Josh found odd considering Hunter's car was parked out front. So Josh used his spare key to let himself in. He said he called my name when he opened the door, but again, there was no answer. The second time he called out, Hunter slipped out of the bedroom, closing the door quietly behind him. I guess he told Josh and Jessica that I'd fallen asleep on the sofa and he had just carried me to bed. Of course, they believed him. (Why wouldn't they? There he was, after all, in his Navy uniform.) He grabbed his hat from the coffee table and bid them both good night. That would have been all good and fine for Lieutenant-Commander Rayburn, but in his haste to leave the house, he hadn't gotten a chance to clean up our drinks in the living room. It wasn't until the next morning that they discovered the truth.

Sarah knocked on my bedroom door and received no answer. She cracked the door open and peeked in. She told me she found it unusual that I was sleeping on top of the comforter with no underwear on. She said she called out my name again, but still, I didn't respond, so she rushed off to find Christi and Amanda. The three of them sat on the edge of the bed and shook me. I guess they freaked out when I wouldn't wake up. They put a blanket over me (thank you) and called everyone else into the room, including Josh. That's when two and two were put together. Josh checked my pulse, which was very weak, then called 911. He found the glasses which Hunter and I had been drinking out of and told no one to touch them. He said he then had a tough decision to make: try to get a hold of Garry right away or wait and hear what the paramedics said. He chose to wait. (*I* would have called Garry first, but obviously I had no say in the matter.)

Before long, the paramedics concluded that I had probably been given some sort of drug, like the date rape drug. They said my vitals were in an extreme repressed state. They then called the police (standard protocol) who took photos of the scene, interviewed everyone in the house, and got as much information on Hunter Rayburn as they could. The paramedics said they needed to transport me to the hospital for drug tests, rape tests, and general observation.

Off we went. ("Sirens?"—"No sirens, Nik.")

Josh tried to reach Garry via cell phone, to no avail. (Note to self: buy Garry a satellite phone!) Josh then called Marty who said he'd go to the airport and try to reach Garry via radio if he happened to be flying at the time. By the grace of God, it worked. Marty told Garry he couldn't explain exactly what was going on because he was in a public place making an announcement over the public airways.

Apparently, what he said was, "Garry, this is Marty. I don't know what you're doin' right now, Bubba, but give it a lick and a promise and get your ass here immediately."

"What is it? Is it my mom?—Is it Nichole?!"

"It's Nichole. She's at the hospital," Marty said.

"Damnit, Marty, just tell me, is she alright!?"

"We think so," Marty answered.

"I'm already gone. Tell her I'm on my way."

Chapter 36

He Came Unglued

T his time it was *Garry's* running feet echoing down the hospital corridor. My girlfriends, along with Josh, Marty, and Allison had been keeping vigil when he arrived.

FYI: at that point, the drug tests had come back positive for sedatives in my system, and the results of the rape test had yet to come back.

Garry was in a panic!

(Quickly, allow me to explain the kind of panic he was in. Today, as I left the pool over at the club, a barefoot man ran past me out the door at breakneck speed. The look of terror on his face was so disturbing that it made me stop dead in my tracks. It wasn't as if he was in a hurry to retrieve a forgotten towel or goggles from his car. He'd forgotten something much more important. He'd forgotten his baby! He opened that car door, grabbed that baby out of the 100 degree heat, and held him close to his cheek, thinking, I'm sure, of the horror that could have been. I know I'll never forget the look on that man's face today as he ran outside to save his baby's life because it was the *exact* same look on Garry's face last year when he sprinted through my hospital room door.)

I was slipping in and out of consciousness when Garry arrived but caught bits and pieces of the conversation and it went something like this . . .

"Would somebody please tell me what the *hell* is goin' on here?"

Good old Josh volunteered his head. "Apparently, Hunter Rayburn slipped some kind of drug into Nichole's drink last night, and she wouldn't wake up this morning."

"What do you mean, *Hunter Rayburn*?" The aggression in Garry's voice halted my breathing.

"He was over at the house. Last night," Josh said with hesitation.

"*My* house?" Garry growled. He was mad as hell. (*Breathe, Nichole, breathe.*)

I nervously watched my friends trickle from the room. No one wanted to be around when it hit the fan.

"Tell me, Josh, why would Hunter Rayburn have been at *my* house last night?" Now Garry was fuming.

"The girls had been partying with Hunter Rayburn and Blake Avery the past couple of nights."

"*Blake Avery* was at my house too?" Garry roared.

I didn't need to see clearly to know that I was in for a good tongue-lashing. And poor Josh. I wouldn't have wanted to be in his shoes, the bearer of such news.

Garry looked over at me. (I quickly shut my eyes. Are you kidding? I knew at that point, the sympathy card was my only hope.) "You and I need to talk about this out in the hall, Josh," he ordered.

But first, Garry walked over to my bed, put his hand on my forehead, and smoothed back my hair. I lifted my eyelids just a bit. He smelled like saltwater and fish and had a two-day beard going, but he was the most beautiful sight to my blurry eyes.

"Tell me this," he said to Josh, "where's the doctor? Is she goin' to be alright?"

"The doctor said he'd check in on her periodically. She just started coming to. He said she's going to be fine. The drugs will slowly wear off and then she'll have a hell of a hangover. They need to keep her overnight for observation, though."

The nurse came in. "I need to get some more tests, so if you gentlemen would please give us some privacy."

"What kind of tests?" Garry asked in a snippy voice.

The nurse looked at Garry; she knew who he was, and although she knew the answer, she still had to ask. "Are you a relative, Mr. LaForge?"

"She's my fiancée," Garry answered.

Josh left the room.

"Mr. LaForge, it seems the rape test we took earlier was inconclusive, so I need to take more samples."

I was conscious enough to know that Garry was about to explode. He looked up at the ceiling and let out a heavy sigh. "Do what you need to do, but I'm not goin' anywhere."

Garry stood, arms crossed, next to the IV pole while the nurse poked and prodded me like a Holstein. When she left, Garry said to me (in a not so pleasant tone, mind you), "Are you alright?"

I could only nod my head.

"Good," he muttered, then disappeared into the hall.

"Where the hell is Josh!" I heard him bellow.

I remember thinking that the nurse should have taken *Garry's* blood pressure at that moment because I guarantee you, it was off the charts!

Eventually, the doctor made an appearance. He shook Garry's hand. "Mister LaForge, I'm Doctor Benson; I was on call this morning when they brought Nichole in. She *was*, in fact, under heavy sedation— sleeping pills—far too high a dosage for her body weight. She's lucky she didn't slip beyond an unconscious state. As you can see, she's gaining more lucidity and will continue to all day long. However, she will probably have a severe headache or migraine later today, but we'll be able to manage the pain for her. We'll have to keep her overnight for observation, though."

"What about the other tests?" I sensed Garry's concern and anxiety. "The rape tests? The nurse said the results were inconclusive?"

"Yes, I was getting to that. Unfortunately, the *initial* test results were inconclusive due to a problem with the lab work, but the more recent tests *were*, in fact, positive for both sperm and semen."

I looked over at Garry who stood, rubbing his forehead, trying like hell not to explode. "What about Monday?" he suddenly asked.

The doctor looked confused.

"Monday mornin', before I left to go fishing, we had sex. Is two days ago too long ago for the lab to pick up sperm results?"

"No, not at all. That could, of course, account for the sperm, but we can't guarantee the identity unless you were willing to give us a sperm sample."

Garry looked over at me and scowled. "Of course," he said firmly.

Bless me Garry, for I have sinned. Given the chance I wouldn't do it again. I couldn't figure out why Garry had yet to go ballistic on me. Had he come to his senses and understood that Hunter Rayburn's actions were absolutely inexcusable, no matter what I did or didn't do? Or was he just waiting for the perfect moment to pull the plug?

"There's also the matter of the police, Mr. LaForge. They were contacted by the paramedics and were out at the sight, which I believe was at your house?" Garry nodded. "They have some evidence that may concern you. Your friends Marty and Josh have been in contact with them and I'm sure they can fill you in on everything else. There's a bit of paperwork involved, but we won't worry about that until the morning. In the meantime, Doctor Craven will be the Attending and will look in on Nichole. If you need anything else, she can certainly help you or she can give me a call." He patted Garry on the back. "She's a lucky girl. She's going to be alright."

Poor Garry; the doctor sent the nurse back in with a container for him "to use" and said she'd take it to the lab whenever he was finished. She left the room, and as Garry headed over to the bathroom I said, "I'm so sorry, Garry."

"Sorry? Are you kiddin' me?"

He was talking to himself as he closed the door of the bathroom. "Hunter Rayburn. Now there's somebody who's gonna be *fuckin'* sorry."

Chapter 37

They're Checkin' the Evidence

O n the upside, I was about 90% conscious by late afternoon. On the downside, a massive headache had set in, along with severe nausea and vomiting. I confess, I'm a big baby when it comes to throwing up. Normally when I'm sick, which isn't often, I'll do anything *not* to throw up. I'll drink sparkling water. I'll suck air for hours. I'll even call on the mercy of God to spare me that terrible fate. That afternoon was no exception.

My girlfriends, along with Josh, Ryden, Tyler, Marty, and Allison hung out at the hospital all day, which was a blessing considering I wasn't looking forward to time alone with Garry. No one really asked me about the previous evening other than to sincerely apologize for leaving me alone with Hunter. Garry and I assured them that no one was to blame. But it was Josh and Jessica who were beating themselves up over it. "I knew we should have gone in and checked on you, Nik. How stupid of us," Jessica said with tears in her eyes.

"He looked like a fucking Boy Scout in his Navy uniform," Josh added.

By dinnertime, Garry and I urged everyone to go back to the house and thanked them for keeping me company. But first, a general discussion ensued about keeping the matter private. Garry warned,

"This is the kind of thing people like to read about, so be careful where and with whom y'all discuss this situation. I don't want to read it in a magazine."

Two officers from the Key West Police Department stopped by the room after dinner. (Not my dinner. I couldn't eat a thing. Garry, fortunately, took his unpleasant attitude elsewhere to eat.) The police said they were waiting for the final sperm test results before any charges could be filed, although they *had* run tests on the two glasses Josh had given them. One tested positive for sedatives. Unfortunately, that glass contained only *my* set of fingerprints, so that wasn't much help. They said they were trying to find the whereabouts of Lieutenant-Commander Hunter Rayburn, but it seems he left "on assignment" that morning to a "classified location."

No sooner had those officers left the room than Garry grabbed a metal bedpan and threw it against the wall. "Classified location my fuckin' ass!" he yelled at no one in particular. (That nerve-wracking sound still reverberates in my ears.)

I started to cry. I didn't mean to, but I was an emotional basketcase. Alligator tears swam down my cheeks. I'm surprised it took me that long. You see, I'm a self-professed cry-baby. That is, self-professed only to myself. To everyone else I'm a rock—calm, collect—a leader. I didn't want Garry to see me crying, so I closed my eyes when he came over.

"I'm sorry, Nik, but I am so *fuckin'* upset! Do you *know* how upset I am?"

I nodded.

"What the hell were you thinkin', hangin' out with Hunter Rayburn!? I go away for one night and . . ." He stopped short.

I knew what he wanted to say. He wanted to say that I'd broken the trust between us.

"I made a mistake," I said sheepishly.

Garry ignored my feeble attempt at penance.

"Do you remember anything?"

"I remember some things," I said and started in on the story. Garry listened intently, making no comments or judgments, which I sincerely appreciated. Afterward, he mercifully kissed both of my eyelids and wiped a tear from his own.

When I finished, the attending doctor, Dr. Clara Craven, arrived with the results of the sperm test. "I need to let you know that the sample you gave us this afternoon, Mr. LaForge, matches positively with a specimen found in Nichole. Sperm is viable for up to 72 hours, so that explains that."

Garry breathed a sigh of relief.

"What it doesn't explain is the other set of sperm and semen found in Nichole."

My heart sank to the pit of my stomach. I looked over at Garry whose face was as white as a mainsail.

She put her hand on my shoulder. "Therefore, it's the conclusion of this hospital that, barring any other consensual sexual partners in the past two days, rape is, in fact, an issue. From this point forward, it's imperative we follow hospital rape protocol. I'll send someone in with that information for you.—I'm so sorry."

That was it. The worst moment of my life.

And I must tell you, it was a terrible sight to see Garry crash and burn before my eyes.

* * *

What followed was a rough night for both of us, Garry, for pacing the cage, plotting and planning his next move, and me for being wide-awake, fighting a migraine and the dry-heaves. Now I'm no stranger to hospitals (I kept my parents hopping back and forth to Oakwood Shores General all their live long days. Let's see: stitches in my nose, stitches in my knee, a broken arm at Girl Scout camp, glass in my hand from Chemistry class, a concussion from being hit by a van, a broken ankle from ice-skating, another broken ankle from slipping on wet grass.—I'm sure you're thinking, *geez, she's a real klutz*, but actually I like to think that I just play hard.) But, as I was saying . . . although I'd spent a lot of time in hospitals, it's never been easy to sleep in one. You can hear people walking in the halls all night long and random announcements being made over the PA system. You have nurses gossiping at the desk, not to mention one of them checking your vitals every 30 minutes. And that night, as the clock over the door ticked endlessly, I was haunted by the reality of what had happened to me. Sad but true, it was a blessing to have been rendered unconscious. I imagine my mental state would have crumbled beyond recognition had I been forced against my conscious will. Better to have no recollection of the whole damn thing!

* * *

Just for starters, Ryden, Tyler, and I were flyin' high over the Dry Tortugas, a haul of grouper, snapper, and wahoo chillin' in the back, when Marty's voice rang out over the airways. I was goin' out of my mind, not knowin' what the hell was happenin' with Nichole . . . and I have absolutely no recollection of flyin' back to Key West because my thoughts at that moment weren't too clear. All I know is that I ran down that hospital corridor, scared shitless as to what I'd find behind door number three.

Seein' Nikki lyin' there half-conscious nearly broke my heart, but at the same time it set me into a rage. And when I heard the word "Hunter Rayburn" within the first five seconds of my arrival, I became as angry as . . . as angry as . . . well, as angry as a man who's fiancée just got drugged, raped, and dumped at the Lower Keys Medical Center! I tried my very best not to lose it in front of Nichole. I had to step outside in the hall just to get some fresh air. ("I'll find Blake Avery for you, Garry. You can count on me." Can you believe that son-of-a-bitch!) Anyway, "The Girls of Oakwood Shores" were out there shakin' in their shoes, avoidin' me like shit on a sidewalk. I can't say that I blamed them. I was a loose cannon. In fact, I regret havin' thrown that bedpan against the wall. I looked over at Nikki and slowly down her cheek there came a tear. Okay, I admit, I'd been actin' like a ragin' idiot (hindsight is 20/20) and it was Nikki who'd been doin' her best to be stoic about the whole damn thing. That's why I resolved right then and there I wouldn't burden her with the details of my inevitable bounty hunt.

As you can imagine, I was beaten down even before the rape test results came back. But I have to say, there are few things in this lifetime

*that have made this grown man cry, and those test results about topped
the charts.*

Chapter 38

May Be Some Charges Pressed

I n the morning, after Garry and I had made our peace with one another (which was around 2 am), police reports and criminal charges were the order of the day, and as much as it pained me, I had to recount the event yet again for the official record. We were assured that "justice will prevail" and that the naval authorities, although evasive as to the whereabouts of Lieutenant-Commander Rayburn, would ultimately comply, etc. etc. But at the end of the day, I knew the retribution against Hunter Rayburn lay solely in Garry's hands. And there was no way he was going to let it rest.

As for me, I looked like a wreck and felt even worse. Thankfully, my migraine had vanished, but I was sore . . . and I'm sure I don't have to tell you where. All I wanted to do was go back to the house and get on with life as it was supposed to be.

However, one major concern played a continuous loop in my brain . . . the fact that I could have been pregnant. Now sometimes life throws us curveballs and that happened to be one of them. I had been on the pill for several months, resulting in terrible headaches, so my gynecologist recommended a break from one prescription before changing to another. I was between prescriptions and as a result, Garry and I had been using extreme caution. That is, except for Monday morning when we'd come up short in the condom department and decided to throw caution to the wind.

Chapter 39

Just Tryin' to Make Some Sense of it All

U pon my release, we told everyone the results of the tests, and I personally thanked Jessica and Josh for coming home when they did. God knows what else could have happened to me.

That day, my every wish was Garry's command. He showed concern not only for my physical health but for my mental state as well. I assured him frequently of my sanity; although I can tell you, that sucker was pretty elusive.

"I feel so bad, Garry," I said as we left the hospital.

"Is your headache back? I'll get you settled at home then run out for your prescription."

"No, no, it's not that. I feel bad about the girls. I'm afraid I've spoiled their Spring Break. They're supposed to be having fun. This is *definitely* not fun."

Garry sighed. "Nichole Bocelli, I'm gonna pull over and send you home on the short bus if you don't stop worryin' for other people's happiness."

I turned my head away, having absolutely no power to stop the stray tears.

He stopped, reconsidering I'm sure, his fragile fiancée. He gave me one of those parental pats on the knee. "Don't worry, billfish, I can arrange fun. I'm master of all things fun."

(I take it back, the part about being sane, that is. There I was, being driven home from the hospital after being drugged and raped, and all I worried about was whether or not my girlfriends were having fun. What kind of nutcase am I?)

And so, Garry made sure Josh, Ryden, and Tyler took the girls out on the boat that afternoon and, despite everyone's protests, out to the clubs that night. My dear sweet girlfriends had stripped our bedroom clean and bought us beautiful new bedding, along with silk pajamas for me. I appreciated that more than anyone could have known. In fact, I cried when I first walked in and saw the makeover. Unfortunately, sleep was not my ally that night, no matter how safe I felt in Garry's arms.

Somewhere around midnight, when I heard everyone arrive back at the house, I rolled over and said to Garry, ever so quietly, "Do you know that Brooke Walker had her baby?" (I don't know why I brought it up. I guess I was in a pissy mood and wanted to stir the pot.)

If Garry wasn't awake before, he sure was then. "I know," he mumbled.

"Blake Avery said the baby has brown eyes," I said.

Garry waited a moment before answering. "And?"

"Blake Avery has blue eyes and so does Brooke Walker. Doesn't she?" I didn't say a word more.

Garry sat up. "Nichole, you're not doubtin' me, are you?"

He didn't give me a chance to answer.

"Either Blake Avery is lyin' or somebody else is the father. In any event, we'll soon have a definitive answer when I take the DNA test."

I was surprised. "I thought it was against your principle?"

"You're right, it is, but the Walkers have a noose around my neck. And Chavis is recommendin' it."

"Sorry about that," I whispered.

Garry rolled over. "Just another shitty day in paradise."

Chapter 40

Blow All My Worries Away

By Saturday morning, "Holy Saturday," and the last day of Spring Break in Key West for my friends, I'd had enough of the tip-toeing going on in the house and told Garry I wanted, no, NEEDED, to have some fun. Garry immediately disappeared to the corner grocery, brought back everything but the kitchen sink and loaded it onto his 28 foot cruiser, *Sweet Home*. Within an hour, three speedboats idled at our pier, packed for a day on *No Man's Key*. *No Man's Key* is a wildlife refuge about a 25-minute boat ride from Garry's house. It's a favorite picnic/beachcombing spot of Garry and his friends and according to them is usually peaceful and deserted, even during Spring Break.

To the delight of my friends, Garry came through on his promise of five single men: Josh, Ryden, Tyler, Michael, and Aaron (percussion and horns). Marty and Smittie tagged along too, but they brought Allison and Layla, so they didn't count in the deal.

Oh, before I forget . . . that afternoon as I was "sleeping" on the boat, I overheard a conversation between Garry and Marty:

"Hey, Bubba, I just wanted to give you a heads-up regardin' the other mornin' at your house—when Josh and the girls found Nichole—I was there." (My eyes inadvertently opened when I heard that fascinating bit of news. Fortunately neither of them saw me.)

Marty continued, "I spent the night. In the boathouse."

"Really?" Garry replied.

"Yeah, and it looks like I'm in a real fix because of it. The police stopped by the house yesterday lookin' for me to verify some information on the police report—some information I'd given them the mornin' of the rape. Needless to say, Allison came down on me like bees in a honey tree."

"I'm surprised she came along today," Garry said. "Does she know it's Melanie?"

"No, she doesn't know it's Melanie. At least I don't think she does. She said the only reason she's comin' along today is to support Nichole, but I have a hunch she's here on a fact findin' mission."

"Looks to me like you're knee deep in shit, my friend," Garry said.

"Looks to me like I gotta find a way to shovel the shit back in the horse," Marty replied.

I waited for Garry to say more. I thought, *Go ahead Garry, give it to him good; serve him up a good dose of admonishment. That's exactly what Marty needs.* But all I got was, "Jesus Christ, Martin Anderson, Saint Ignatius you are not." (How it is men can keep things so simple, I'll never understand.)

A day of fun on *No Man's Key* proved to be a magic kind of medicine. We swam and barbequed, drank and sunbathed, played volleyball and Frisbee. Some of the guys surfed. Others did a little shore fishing. (Marty, I noticed, tried to avoid eye-contact with Melanie at all costs). And when the sun went down we ate and drank some more and were treated to an evening of fiddle tunes under the stars. The girls kept telling Garry and me what a great time they were having. I lost track along the way of who hooked up with whom, but all in all, everyone ended the evening back at the house on a happy note. It truly *was* a holy Saturday. As for myself, I slept like an angel that night.

* * *

Easter morning dawned early as I once again answered Garry's cell phone. (If you're calling early, it's my voice you'll hear on the end of the line.) It was Ronny Collins. I could tell he was surprised I answered the phone. He apologized on behalf of the honor of all U.S. Naval Officers. I told him it wasn't necessary. Beyond that, I didn't know what to say, and Ronny seemed hesitant in speaking with me, so I just figured he'd called to speak with Garry about Hunter Rayburn. I wondered exactly what information they were exchanging.

"Why don't I have Garry give you a call, Ronny?"

There was silence. Then, "I just wanted to let you know, again, Nichole, I'm so very sorry. I'll do everything I can from the naval aspect of things, but if there's anything more I can do for you, just let me know."

"There is one thing, Ronny."

"Of course," he answered.

"Will you make sure Garry doesn't get himself into trouble?"

"I'll consider it my duty."

* * *

The recess bell rang that afternoon, calling us back to our otherwise ordinary lives. Garry insisted I come along, not yet wanting to leave me alone in Key West. And I'm no chicken, but I have to tell you, knowing Hunter Rayburn was still out there somewhere made me more than a little uneasy.

Barring the Hunter situation, Spring Break in Key West was a hell of a time. (Don't think I'm making light of it; I'm the last person who'd make light of that week's events.) We even decided to make it an annual pilgrimage. My girlfriends felt they had come to know Garry so much better after that week—the good, the bad, *and* the ugly, and I know they now consider him a good friend. Or as Melanie put it, "I wouldn't kick him out of my bed for eatin' crackers." (To which I replied, "Melanie, who *would* you kick out of your bed for eatin' crackers?")

* * *

I gotta say, Nikki's girlfriends impressed me—the way they stuck by her throughout the entire ordeal, not to mention the fact that they had our house in ship shape condition when we arrived from the hospital, complete with a bedroom makeover, which, I happen to know, touched Nikki's heart more than words could say. I'm glad for Nik she's got such great friends.

Speakin' of friends, allow me a soap box moment regardin' the Marty/Melanie situation. Now I'll be the first to confess to the endless temptations out on the road. And no one knows better than yours truly that the lure of the wild is simply magnetic. It's just that some choose to partake in it a whole hell of a lot more than others. I can recall, on more than one occasion, Marty out runnin' around when he should have been home countin' sheep. But, I swear to you, Marty does not indulge in such foolhardy behavior on a regular basis. It is my opinion, and only my opinion, mind you, that about the time Caroline Grace was due to be born, Marty was goin' through a personal crisis of sorts—feelin' like his wild days were through. And most likely that's what sent him down that river of betrayal. And if I know Marty, he'll wind up lookin' for absolution, not accountability.

Don't get me wrong, I don't agree with Marty's behavior. Not one bit. But far be it from me to get involved in Marty and Allison's personal affairs. I've known those two for over 30 years now and I'm still tryin' to make a little sense of it all. And anyway, I had more important things on my mind.

Chapter 41

I Got Presents

T he Easter ham was just out of the oven when we arrived at
my parent's house. Our week in Florida had worn us quite
thin, and oddly enough, it was comforting to be landlocked in the Land
of Lincoln. (And *no*, we still hadn't told my parents about the rape. We
thought it best not to upset them. At least not yet.)

"Can you stay for a while, Garry?" my mom asked.

"Unfortunately, I can't," Garry said. "I'm afraid my days as a
gentleman of leisure are over. Or as we say in Alabama, 'the creek is
risin' and I'm up to my ass in alligators.' If I'm gonna get the show on
the road by Memorial Day weekend, I've got a mess of work to do."

What you don't know, but what I knew at the time is that I had a
bit of a dilemma. You see, I didn't want to hang out in Key West by
myself while Garry worked all the time; however, the lease on the
house in Oakwood Shores was due to expire.

"Garry, it's completely up to you," I said several days later. "If
you don't want to extend the lease, I don't mind staying at my parent's
house when I'm in town. I guess the real question is, do *you* mind
staying at my parent's house?"

Garry laughed and threw a fat accordion file on the table in
front of me.

"Okay. I give. What's this?"

"Happy Easter," he said.

It took me a moment to figure out what he meant. "You're kidding me?"

He shook his head and flashed those irresistible dimples.

"When did you . . .?" I started to ask.

"Closed on it this mornin'. The house is officially ours. I know how much you love this place, and you know I'd do anything in the whole wide world for you."

I stood up and hugged Garry. "You are just full of surprises, aren't you?"

"Now that's the good news. The bad news is that come Monday the previous owners are comin' to take all their furniture away."

"Yikes!" I said.

"Now for more good news. Once the house is emptied of *their* things, we'll need an architect such as yourself to fix this place up and fill it with *our* things. I have no doubt you'll do a fine job. I trust you entirely."

We smiled at each other in recognition of the deeper meaning of that comment.

"I've noticed my 'To Do List' keeps getting longer," I said. "If I didn't know better, Garry LaForge, I'd think you were trying to keep me busy—keep my mind occupied."

"Well, my dear, my schedule is about to become as wild as a ricochet, and I don't want you to feel neglected while I'm out singin' for our supper."

* * *

And so, Garry left for Key West, and I moved into my parent's house while our "new house" was emptied of everything not belonging to us. I really did have so many things to do. I had a wedding to plan within six months, a house to rip apart and redo, and, oh yeah, an absent period to worry about.

Chapter 42

Life's Hard Sometimes

I knew right away. All the telltale signs were there: sensitive breasts, bloated stomach, mood swings, lack of appetite. I didn't tell a soul. And although I knew it was on everyone's mind (that is, everyone who knew about the incident), no one asked me the inevitable question. In fact, no one talked about "it" anymore, even though it'd happened just weeks before.

By the end of April, I was going out of my mind. I couldn't eat, couldn't sleep, couldn't even bring myself to buy one of those damn home pregnancy tests! (Why bother at that point.) My parents were worried about me. I was dropping weight like a wrestler, but they chalked it up to home-renovation and wedding stress. Like I told you, I'm good at appearances—calm, cool, and collect on the outside, a basketcase on the inside. How does that saying go? *I'm FINE: Freaked-out, Insecure, Neurotic, & Emotional.*

I was plagued by doubts. And who better to call to confirm those doubts than Sarah, right?

"I can hardly believe all this is happening to you, Nik," she sympathized. "I feel so bad."

"Can you believe my biggest worry used to be whether to take my one week vacation in the summer or in the winter?"(I admit, I was wallowing in my sorrows.)

"What do you think you'll do?" Sarah asked.

"I'm not sure. All I know is I want things back the way they were."

"You mean the way things were before Spring Break or the way things were before Garry?"

"I mean, maybe my boring old life in Oakwood Shores wasn't so bad after all. —Everything was just hopscotching along, and then BAM. Now it's one big mess. Maybe I should have listened to my parents and joined that church group after all," I said.

"So does this mean I can call my cousin Anthony?" Sarah asked.

"Maybe not just yet."

* * *

One need not delve too deeply into the mind of a rape victim to figure out it's pretty screwed up in there. Looking back, I realize it was natural in such a situation for me to blame not only Hunter Rayburn (that was a given) but to blame myself as well. (*If I only hadn't been such a goddamn flirt!*) I even blamed myself for ever getting involved with Garry in the first place. (*If I'd have never met Garry . . .*) In fact, I spent every waking moment obsessively reviewing my actions and cursing the resulting consequences.

As a girl, when I needed time to reflect I'd either lock myself in the bathroom or sit out back behind the garage on the air conditioning unit. In later years I'd seek solace out in the woods or on farm roads with my bike. None of those seemed viable options, so I did the next best thing. I became a recluse. I resolved to distance myself from Garry—distance myself from all the folly and frivolity. I stopped mentioning Garry's name in conversation. I stopped listening to his music, and I stopped wearing my ring. I mean, who was I to think I could make such a leap?

Garry tried to come visit several times, but I insisted he stay and work. He even suggested a weekend trip to Sammi and Colton's in New Orleans.

"What do you mean you don't want to go to New Orleans? You've been beggin' me to take you there for the past three months."

I didn't answer.

"You're pregnant, aren't you?"

I couldn't answer. The tears were welling up in my eyes.

"Nichole? —Answer me."

I could hear Garry's distant voice as my trembling hand put down the receiver. "Nichole? God damn it!"

Chapter 43

You're Drivin' This Boy Insane

T he next thing I knew, the sun was streaming through my blinds. The bedroom clock read 10:30, a half hour earlier than the day before. My dad was already up and gone, and for all I knew, I was alone in the house when I heard a knock at the front door. Unfortunately, weakness and fatigue had a grip on me, not to mention a newfound nausea in the pit of my stomach. The knock came again, louder, more insistent. I guess my mom wasn't home after all. I threw on my robe and ran downstairs with just enough time to open the door before a massive wave of nausea sent me running to the bathroom. Garry, walking back to the taxi, must have turned when he heard the door.

"Nik?" he called.

No sooner had he stepped into the bathroom than it all came out.

"Oh baby," he said, kneeling beside me.

I slumped into his arms, completely spent. I was too exhausted even to cry.

"Can you stand up?"

I shook my head no.

"Have you been to the doctor, Nichole?"

I mouthed the word no.

Garry scooped me up in his arms. "Good God, girl, you're nothin' but skin and bones." He headed for the front door just as my mom arrived home.

"Garry! What's wrong?" she asked.

"I need to get Nichole to the hospital. She's weaker than a garden hose." I closed my eyes and buried my head into Garry's shoulder. "And if I'm not mistaken, she's pregnant."

* * *

The hospital confirmed that I was, indeed, still pregnant—six weeks. Add to that, a 12 pound weight loss, topped off by severe dehydration, and I was a mess.

"What the hell are you doin' to yourself, Nichole?" Garry was clearly pissed off; didn't even give me a chance to answer. "Are you purposely tryin' to lose this baby? Because if you are, you'd better open your mouth and start explainin' this fucked up plan of yours."

A shudder went down my spine. I hated being spoken to that way. He stood over my bed and looked me square in the eye, demanding an answer. We both knew it was a conversation we'd been avoiding since the rape.

I mustered every ounce of energy I had. "There's no *plan*, Garry. Do you think I like being in this position? Do you think I *planned* to be raped last month? I don't want to be pregnant! But I don't want to have an abortion either. I mean I'm *scared* to have an abortion. Is that so abnormal? The thing is, I know I have to do it; and time is running out."

"What do you mean, you *have* to do it? Nobody is forcin' you to do anything. Least of all me."

"Come on Garry, there's a 50/50 chance this baby isn't even yours. Do you want to raise Hunter Rayburn's baby? I don't think so. And by the way, I clearly recall you saying you're definitely not ready to have children. I think your exact words were, 'one day, by and by.'"

Evidently, I'd hit a nerve (don't forget, I'm a youngest child, therefore excel at playing victim), so I continued, ". . . and what if I *do* decide to have this baby. There's no way I'm getting married in September. What am I supposed to do, walk down the aisle 6½ months pregnant?"

Garry stood with his arms crossed, probably wondering if I was ever going to stop

"I just want my old life back," I said, with my last ounce of energy.

From the look on Garry's face, I knew he was about to spit fire.

"You want your old life back?" he raged. "I've been tryin' my damndest to make this work, Nichole, but you have been avoidin' me all month. I bust my ass flyin' here this mornin' and this is all I get from you? You want your old life back!" He stormed over to the door and spun on his heel. "You better watch your step at the wishin' well, darlin', 'cause you just might *get* what you're wishin' for."

And then—

He disappeared before my very eyes.

Chapter 44

Drinkin' Double

Seven weeks (pregnant): no word from Garry. Eight weeks: not even a phone call. My parents were on the phone, though. Against my wishes, they'd called the Key West Police Department and they'd also called the U.S. Navy (to no avail). I begged them with all my heart not to call Garry. I begged them to leave me alone in my misery.

I spent countless hours over at the house on the lake. I'd taken to sitting out back on the glider, trying to avoid all the noise and construction dust. The fact of the matter is, I fully realized I was living on borrowed days. The calendar and I waged a mental tug of war over that baby, one day filled with courage, the next, consumed in a purgatory of guilt. Although not opposed to abortion, I'd always thought of abortion as something "other people" did. When it came right down to it and I was faced with such a decision about my *own* circumstances, I realized I'd been paying lip service to the Pro-choice point of view all along. Deep in my heart of hearts, I knew giving up that baby was not an option for me, whether it was Garry's baby or not.

One afternoon, just after the work crew had gone home, I sat outside gliding with my headphones on, listening to . . . I'm not sure what, but definitely *not* Garry's music, when my phone rang. The screen showed a Key West number that I didn't recognize.

"Hello?"

"Nichole? This is Allison." Caroline Grace screeched in the background. "Hang on a sec."

"Hey, Nik. I know I haven't talked to you in an age, but I was just wonderin' . . . Have you talked with Garry lately?"

I wasn't sure exactly what Allison knew about Garry and me. "No, I haven't. Why do you ask?"

"Well, the reason is . . ." She sort of hemmed and hawed. "You see . . . I know things are a bit shaky between you and Garry these days, but I wasn't sure you were aware of the *unique* situation occurin' down here."

I knew enough of Southern Belle propriety to know that a "unique situation" was a major problem.

"What unique situation is that?" I asked.

"Now, Marty would be just furious with me if he knew I was talkin' to you about this, but sometimes it's up to us women to set things straight. You see, for the past several weeks, Garry has been a smokin' and drinkin' fool. Marty says Garry's high all the time and is constantly late to rehearsals. It seems he has no interest whatsoever in gettin' the tour together. Now, normally, I'd find that to be none of my little ol' business, but it just so happens that Garry hasn't been seen in days. He was supposed to have a photo shoot on Friday with Corona, but he never showed up. Marty went over and checked the house. *Southern Cross* is gone, so we were thinkin' maybe he'd headed up your way."

"No, he's not here. But now you've got me worried." (I had visions of Garry lying dead in some godforsaken place.) "Has anyone tried to call him?"

I knew better than anyone that Garry would never forget his cell phone. Hell, he'd been teasing me from the day we'd met about forgetting to carry mine with me. He must have been pretty messed up to leave home without it.

"But, hold on, that's not the end of this story." She continued, "Just about the time when Marty was decidin' whether or not to give you a call, our phone rang and it was none other than Garry, himself.

Seems he's caused a great ballyhoo down in *Cuba* of all places; some kind of bar fight. Well, as you can imagine, he landed himself right in jail."

"Cuba? Why in the world would he have gone to . . ." Then it hit me; Garry had gone to Cuba looking for Hunter Rayburn.

"He was looking for Hunter Rayburn, wasn't he?" I asked.

"Apparently so. Marty's down there this very minute, straightenin' things out."

"Who's detaining him?" I asked. "The Cubans or the U.S.?"

"He's on base in Guantanamo Bay."

"And when are they due back?"

"Sometime tomorrow evenin'."

They say the average person has about 60,000 thoughts per day. At that moment I had only two: first, what a schmuck I'd been and second, how quickly I could get down to Key West.

"I just thought you should know what's been goin' on," Allison said. "I know if I was in your position, I'd want a friend to tell me everything she knew. That's what friends are for, right?"

("*I'd want a friend to tell me everything she knew.*" *Well if that's not an open invitation, I don't know what is. She's practically begging me to tell her about Marty and Melanie. Should I? Shouldn't I?)*

"Allison . . . I . . ."

"Yes?"

"I . . . I appreciate your call, Allison. I've been sitting here on my stubborn butt waiting for Garry to come apologize to *me*, but it looks like *I'm* the one who needs to do some apologizing."

(Obviously, I chickened out.)

Chapter 45

Savin' the World on His Own

With a purse full of Saltines and one concerned father left at the curb, I flew to Key West the next morning. I took a cab over to Garry's and was shocked to find that he'd changed the entry gate security code. (Maybe things were worse off than I had feared.)

I nabbed the taxi just as it was pulling away and headed over to Marty and Allison's house.

"Come on in," Allison said. "Marty just called. He's over at the airport and says Garry should be arriving any time now."

"How did Garry manage to fly to Cuba?" I asked. "I thought Cuban MiGs shoot you out of the sky if you fly to Cuba."

"Well, accordin' to Marty, it's rather simple to arrange a landin' permit. You simply give the Cuban government your flight information, along with a good reason for goin', and a 24-hour notice, and that's that.—But he didn't fly into Havana, anyway. He flew into Guantanamo Bay."

"What did he tell them his reason for going was?" I asked.

"Seems the Navy has a Criminal Investigation Service located at Guantanamo Bay. He'd arranged to meet with them and discuss the Navy's 'lack of cooperation' in arrestin' Hunter Rayburn; although from what Marty tells me, Garry's got it in his head that Hunter is hidin' out

somewhere in Havana. You know Garry, once he gets an itch in his head, he'll scratch it 'til
it bleeds."

"So where does the bar fight and arrest come in?"

"Marty says Garry was gettin' the same ol' run-around regardin' Hunter, so he decided to do some investigatin' of his own out at the bars at night. Well, I s'pose if you combine one part anger with one part broken heart and mix in a whole mess of drinkin', you're bound to end up behind bars."

I had to sit down. Things were starting to weigh heavy on my mind . . . and my body as well.

"I declare, Nichole, where *are* my manners. Here you are pregnant and tired and I am ramblin' on without even offerin' you a drink. Would you like to join me in a cup of herbal tea? Have you eaten supper yet? —And by the way, did I ever mention I once put together a 300 guest weddin' in two weeks flat?"

Chapter 46

Causin' Lots of Trouble

M arty drove me over to Garry's house.
"I'm not too sure why you're here, Nichole, but I *am* sure my wife's got somethin' to do with this."

I nodded my head. I really didn't feel like having a conversation with Marty. First of all, I felt like shit, both mentally and physically. And second of all, I wasn't about to waste my energy discussing my relationship problems with the king of domestic deception.

"Let me tell you, Nichole, your fiancé has been one miserable cuss. He's been drunk now for over two weeks. Night and day he's been raisin' hell. I swear he has been nothin' but trouble lookin' for a place to happen.

"I s'pose you know he caused one hell of a ruckus down in Cuba and was thrown out of the country yesterday."

"I know, Marty," I said.

He continued, "I have witnessed Garry go through some hard times, but this one takes the cake. He has hit rock bottom, or to put it more clearly, he's been rode hard and put away wet."

(Marty's one of those guys who likes to hear his own voice.)

Chapter 47

*Down Here
on the Knees of My Heart*

T he wind was picking up as I stepped onto the back deck. I
could see Garry squatting down, grappling with *Southern
Cross's* tie-lines, so I took a deep breath and tread, ever so quietly,
across the yard and down onto the pier. I stood about ten feet from
Garry, a bit unsure of the depth of the water into which I was about to
jump.

"Looks like a big storm's comin' soon," Garry called out, without
looking up from his work.

"Well, it looks to me like it's coming in from the *south*, not the
north," I called back.

From under his armpit Garry delivered a half-smile, leading me
to believe things were going to be all right. I could also see that his face
had been used as target practice, complete with a swollen eye and half
a dozen stitches lined up like soldiers across his forehead.

He stood up and turned to me, "I must look a mess, I must
admit."

"That's an understatement," I said, cautiously stepping closer.

"It's an occupational hazard."

"And what occupation would that be?"

"Haven't you heard? I am currently your very own, personal, Defender of Justice and Honor." He did a bow with a flourish.

I couldn't help but laugh. "From the looks of your face, Captain America, I'd say you're a bit short on expertise."

"Don't you be fooled one bit," he said. "I've got the devil at the crossroads. I just need to refine my plan of action, that's all."

An awkward silence ensued as Garry began to unload his gear.

I knew it was my turn at bat.

"I was wrong, Garry," I said with conviction.

He pulled his last bag from the plane, sat down on the heap, and put his head in his hands. He looked spent.

I went on, "I've thought long and hard these past couple weeks about what I want to do with my life. I've been going half-mad trying to figure it all out. I've tried to let go, I really have . . . but you're still on my mind.—I don't want my old life back.—I don't want to raise this baby by myself. I need you in my life, Garry." I stepped just a bit closer. "I love you."

He looked me right in the eye. "I can't promise you a smooth passage, Nichole. I have a bank of bad habits bigger than a polygamist's grocery bill."

(I never thought I'd say it, but I sure had missed those corny expressions.)

"I'm not looking for perfection, Garry. I just want to live happily ever after every now and then."

He continued sitting on his bags, gazing at the lightening on the horizon. I walked over and knelt in front of him.

"I'm putting it all on the line, Garry. I'm resolved not to let this craziness tear us apart."

Then, just like that first night in Lakeland, Garry put his hand behind my head and pulled me toward him with a passionate kiss. "Looks to me like we've got a weddin' to talk about," he said.

"Funny you should mention that . . ."

Chapter 48

Don't Try to Explain It Just Nod Your Head

Y ou're probably wondering, like I was, why my code hadn't worked on Garry's front gate that afternoon. I may be a hot-headed Italian girl, but I've never been one to hold my anger for long. I have the amazing ability to blow my top one moment then go merrily on my way the next. Because Garry and I had never had an argument of such magnitude before, I wasn't sure just how long or how far he was capable of carrying his anger. I honestly thought he'd changed the security code as a way of changing channels on the "Nichole chapter" of his life. I thought, *Wow, I never knew Garry could be so cold-hearted.* I was impressed by his resolve. I felt duly punished.

I was wrong.

Marty explained that Garry had the entire security system reconfigured after the rape. ("Could you please stop referring to it as 'The Rape', Marty?") There was the addition of a camera at the front gate and one out back with a couple of strategically placed "panic" buttons linked directly to the Key West Police Department, topped off by some sort of system that shoots laser beams from here to kingdom come. In effect, Garry had spent countless hours and thousands of dollars working hard to protect me, not punish me. It was really rather impressive, but to tell you the truth, although it made my life safer, Garry's concern was holding me hostage.

After giving me the rundown on the new system, Garry said, "Hey, I've got some interesting news."

"Oh yeah?"

"The results came back from the DNA tests."

"And? Should I be scared?" I asked, half joking. I'd be lying if I said the thought of Garry being the father of Brooke Walker's baby hadn't crossed my mind more than once (try every waking minute).

"No. I'm not the father, of course. But get this, neither is Blake Avery. You'll never guess who the father is; well, it's all speculation at this point."

I thought long and hard for a moment. Then it hit me like a hurricane.

"Hunter Rayburn."

Garry was stunned. "How the hell did you know?"

"A lucky guess?" I said. "How do *you* know?"

"Ronny. He called me yesterday. It seems the Walkers are puttin' pressure on the Navy to disclose Rayburn's 'classified location.' Funny how it all coincided with my DNA results."

"So I guess both you *and* Brooke Walker are on a quest to find Hunter Rayburn," I said.

"Well, let's just say we both want blood from him, but for different reasons." Garry laughed at his own wit.

"Explain to me again why the Navy is protecting Rayburn?" I asked, having never really gotten an answer.

"Word has it Hunter Rayburn is not only an Aviation Officer for the Navy, but has some secret military information locked up in that masochistic mind of his. And of course, it doesn't hurt that his daddy was *Vice-Admiral* John-Henry Rayburn."

"I knew his father was in the Navy, but I didn't know he was a *Vice-Admiral*," I said.

Garry continued, "Ronny told me Rayburn's father committed suicide while on duty."

"I know. He told me. He said it happened at The Naval Academy. Do you think the Navy feels they owe him something because of what happened?"

"Not that they *owe* him something. It's that they're *afraid* of him. Ronny says that before he died, Rayburn's father passed on some classified information to his son that, if released, would put the Navy in a tail-spin."

"What kind of information? I mean, does Ronny know what it is?" I asked. "Did he tell you?"

"Nichole, giving out Top Secret information to former college roommates could get somebody in a heap of trouble," Garry said.

"Do you think anybody but top brass knows where Rayburn is?" I asked.

Garry raised his eyebrows suspiciously and walked out of the room.

"Garry? Garry!" I called out. "*Possessing* Top Secret information from former college roommates can also get somebody in a heap of trouble."

He didn't answer.

"Don't do anything irrational!" I knew he heard me but was refusing to answer.

* * *

Sometimes it's easy to forget that I have a job. (Easy for other people to forget, not for me.) I like to make it look effortless—like I just show up wearin' my flip-flops, shorts and t-shirt, strap on the ol' guitar and have a go at it. But the truth is, there's a whole lot more to it than that. The band and I spend numerous hours rehearsin' and arrangin', not to mention writin' the songs. There are photo shoots, radio interviews, TV appearances, and an entire corporate dance that goes on behind the scenes. Every year, come about March, I make the transition from man of leisure to concert commando. I can't tell you how many nights I've fallen asleep on that reclinin' chair at the studio. That's why I was more than happy to buy the house in Oakwood Shores for Nikki. In light of the

Hunter Rayburn situation, she needed to be near family and friends while I was busy workin'.

Now, I had my suspicions Nichole was pregnant. With every phone conversation we had, she was growin' more and more distant. But I knew for a fact she was keepin' somethin' locked up inside when she turned down a trip to New Orleans. To say that I was furious with Nikki is an understatement. Normally I'm a pretty even keel kind of guy—easy to get along with and quick to overlook others faults, but that woman of mine sure knows how to tear my sails and break my oars. See, I had been bustin' my ass at work and rackin' my brain figurin' out how the hell I was gonna track down Hunter Rayburn, and all I got from Nichole was a lack of gratitude and a nasty attitude. Suffice it to say, I jumped off the deep end. I reverted back to my old ways of drinkin' and smokin'. (Only trouble was, I'd forgotten how that monster chews you up and spits you out.)

It was in that spirit I followed my intuition down to Guantanamo Bay. I was God's own drunk and a fearless man. Admittedly, my plan wasn't foolproof, which basically meant I didn't know what the hell I was goin' to do once I got there. I do know I was feelin' kind of half-assed and would have picked a fight with anybody willin' to get in my way. And as you know, everybody did.

I was battered and torn, and I needed a new plan of action. And I swear, if Nikki hadn't shown up on the pier that day, I would have regrouped, refueled, and headed back at it again.

Chapter 49

Make the Best of a Bad Situation

Every year, for the past 12 years, Garry has kicked off his summer concert season on Memorial Day Weekend in Miami—no ifs, ands, or buts. The original plan was to turn it into a Bocelli/LaForge get-together, allowing our families to meet one another and feel connected before the wedding. But, as every sailor knows, sometimes you have to tack starboard in order to get to port.

* * *

So just how *does* one plan a wedding in two short weeks? Especially a certain someone who was still commode hugging sick each and every morning? With lots of help, that's how. Lots of help from dear, sweet Allison. (She said she owed me one. I wasn't so sure about that.) Somehow, in a mere 14 days, she and the Ritz Carlton wedding coordinator had worked their matrimonial magic, from my dress right down to the font on the thank you notes.

And what about invitations? Now that was a bit more difficult . . . or was it? Every person we truly loved and cherished would be at the concert on Saturday, so we figured why not just make it a surprise wedding. After all, it was practically a surprise for Garry and me. All we had to do was tell everyone we were having a special pre-concert lunch before the show. Sounds simple, right?

Chapter 50

Rubbin' Shoulders With the Stars

A s for Garry, his reckless binge left him with a mess of loose ends to tie up. Somehow, though, he managed to give the devil his due, and by the end of May, the show was on the road. Or as Garry so eloquently put it, "It's time to kick the tires and light the fires."

The whole gang met at the Key West Airport where *Global Escort* stood ready for a summer of active duty. The gathering reminded me of a combination pep-rally/military send off. I mingled with all the significant others and families, bidding our loved-ones goodbye and good luck. Most of us, of course, were going up to Miami a day or two later, but in all actuality, it was a farewell celebration in honor of the *entire* summer tour.

Garry pleaded with me to fly up to Miami with him, but with one final dress fitting on Thursday, there was no way I could go. Besides, after Miami, the band was due in Atlanta for more of the same, and I preferred to drive back to Key West than be a groupie in the wings. (Not exactly the honeymoon I'd always dreamed of.) Anyway . . .

Energized and feeling surprisingly good (for a weary pregnant woman), I loaded my bags into the car Friday morning and hit the cruise control. Garry called me somewhere in the middle of the Seven Mile Bridge.

"Hey there billfish, are you ready for 'The Crazy Parade' this weekend?"

"As long as you're Grand Marshall of 'The Crazy Parade'—whatever that is—I'm ready for it," I said.

"Well, here's the deal. As you know, both our families are due here at the hotel today by four o'clock, right? So that means I need to have a covert rendezvous with you in our room no later than one."

I got his point. "Are you serious?" I said, laughing.

"And why wouldn't I be?"

"If I meet you in our room at one o'clock today, then how can I be your *blushing* bride at one o'clock tomorrow?"

Garry laughed, "See ya at one."

* * *

Some girls dream of and plan their wedding from the age of five. I was never one of those girls. Yet, I always assumed I'd get married. In fact, I never questioned whether or not I would. (Is that strange?) In hindsight, I realize it was a good thing I didn't have a specific vision of what I wanted my wedding to be like, because no matter what that idea *would have* been, I can guarantee you, the actual wedding was nothing like it . . .

Garry and I talked for a good hour, which made the time fly by, and before I knew it, I was pulling under the portico of the Ritz Carlton, Biscayne Bay. The Corvette was whisked away, as were my bags. Summer, the concierge, took care of my check-in; although, I swear she thought I was joking when I laid claim to the LaForge suite. I tried not to let her see my puckered lips as she dialed Garry's number, but I will admit to oozing malice when Garry appeared moments later with a huge smile on his face.

Summer was suddenly dripping with honey. "Oh, hello Mister LaForge. I was just checking Ms. Bocelli in."

I gave her my 'Yeah, right' look, hugging and kissing Garry in front of her, being sure my engagement ring shined directly in her face.

A perky redhead in a crisp linen suit called out to us, "Welcome to the Ritz Carlton, Mr. LaForge and Ms. Bocelli." She looked both ways then whispered, "I'm Emily Edwards your wedding coordinator. What a pleasure it is to finally meet you." She flashed her Ritz Carlton smile and shook our hands. "I trust Summer is accommodating you in your check-in, aren't you, Summer? After all, it isn't every day we have such a prominent bride and groom in our midst." I admit, Emily was a bit over the top, but she knew her stuff and that's all that mattered to me. And I can tell you, from that moment forward, Summer was on her knees!

Garry turned to me and said, "I'd love to show you all the amenities this fine establishment has to offer, but I can hardly step outside my door without runnin' into somebody from the band who has a question about the show or somebody I haven't seen in ages and wants to chat. We'll have a look see later. Right now, I'm afraid we'll be takin' the unscenic route to our room."

He hooked my hand in his and led me in a very round-about way to The Crown Suite. However, Garry's "secret route" wasn't so secret after all. We bumped into James Taylor then Don Henley and finally, Ed Bradley who were also taking "unscenic routes" to their rooms.

"Looks like we avoided that problem," I remarked as we arrived 25 minutes later.

Garry quickly slipped the "Do Not Disturb" sign on the door (although he warned me his friends would ignore it), and treated me to my own royal welcome.

While ordering room service, a knock came at the door. It was Allison.

"Hey y'all. Sorry to disturb you. I take it you've met Emily. Isn't she just precious? Now I want you two to know that she and I have got everything under control. You don't have to worry your heads 'bout a thing. Just show up on time, and I'll take care of the rest. And by the way, Jackson Browne is invitin' everybody to a party in his room this evenin' after we sneak off and run through the ceremony, of course. Anywho, I'm off and runnin'. I've got my cell with me if y'all need anything. I'll see you two lovebirds in the gazebo at 7:30."

"Thanks Allison!" Garry called from the bathroom.

A party in Jackson Browne's room! I couldn't wait to meet Jackson Browne.

"I can't wait for you to meet Jackson, Nik. I already told him you love his music more than mine."

"You did not!"

"I did too," he said.

"You know that's not true."

"Remember that first night we met and I asked you to pick the music of the evenin'? Did you pick *my* music? No. You picked Jackson's."

Suddenly, another knock at the door.

"I told you my friends can't read," Garry said.

That time it was Harrison Ford. "Hey Nichole. Hope I'm not bothering you."

"Hi Harrison. Come on in. I'm so glad you could come. Is Calista here with you?"

"No, she couldn't make it. Hey, um, I don't mean to bug you guys, but I was just wondering if Gregory and Susan have arrived yet?"

It took me a moment to remember that he and Garry's brother-in-law, Gregory, were buddies and happened to live near each other in Wyoming.

"No, but they're due in soon," I said.

No sooner had Harrison selected his import, than there was another knock at the door—Josh and Marty. I rolled my eyes as Marty handed me the "Do Not Disturb" sign saying, "Hey y'all, did you know this was on your door?"

Garry gave me a clever little glance.

Shortly after room service arrived (and just before everyone dove into *my* lunch), there was yet another knock on our door. The LaForges made their entrance, along with the Rosenbergs and the Devereauxs. Garry had just closed the door when I heard the unmistakable laughter of "The Girls of Oakwood Shores" (as Garry and his friends had come to refer to them). The five of them, bikini-clad and in rare form, had clearly partaken in happy hour down by the pool.

"Did I just get introduced to Harrison Ford?" Melanie whispered in my ear. "And what is Jackson's party?"

You know that old routine, where the clowns just keep coming and coming out of that small Volkswagen? Well, our suite became exactly like that. I think Ryden and Tyler were the next to show up, although I lost track; so many people were packed into our room. Eventually, my family arrived, and after going through yet another round robin of introductions, Garry declared "The Crazy Parade" well under way.

* * *

I know for sure you're wondering how the heck my entire family and all my girlfriends could afford round trip airfare to Miami and a three-night stay at the Ritz Carlton, Biscayne Bay. (Let's face it, we weren't talking the Holiday Inn.) Well, that's exactly what I'd asked Garry a couple of weeks earlier. And this was the answer I got: "Don't get your knickers in a bunch, Nichole Marie. I've got everything tied down and locked up."

"Which means . . .?" I asked.

"Which means it's all taken care of—airfare, hotel, and concert tickets; signed, sealed, and already delivered." He flashed his million dollar smile.

"Your Mama done taught you right, Mr. LaForge," I said with a kiss.

Chapter 51

La Vie Dansant

When I woke up Saturday morning, I was tired as I could be.

"Good mornin' my bride-to-be," Garry said, all bright and cheery.

It's my wedding day, I thought . . . then rolled over and filled my mouth with oyster crackers.

After a phone interview with a Miami radio station, Garry's bodyguard, Reggie, (a huge Jamaican guy who scared even me) knocked on our door. "I be ready when you are, boss."

Garry turned to me, "Now, as you are well aware, I'm signed on for the nightshift this evenin', so I've got some final arrangin' to do over at the arena. But I promise, I'll be back faster than a hot knife through butter."

* * *

My family members are not known for their excitability— they're normally a semi-serious bunch. But that morning, while eating breakfast in our room, they were out of control. I mean it. I could *not* get a word in edgewise. On and on they chattered, "We're having such a great time," "Garry's family is wonderful," "What a time we had at Jackson's party," "What should we wear to lunch today," "We can't wait for the show tonight," "We insist on paying for *something*, Nichole." Quite honestly, I'd never seen them, collectively, in such good moods and having so much fun. And I didn't mind one bit. Their incessant chatter (or chin music as Garry calls it) had a way of calming my nerves. It was a relief to have them to myself and finally talk candidly.—Well, not *that* candidly. As much as I wanted to tell them about the wedding, I was a good girl and kept my mouth shut.

Moments after devouring our Eggs Benedict, Summer stopped by with a note. "Good morning Ms. Bocelli," she gushed. "I just received this message from Mr. LaForge and was told to pass it on to you. I hope y'all are enjoying your stay here at the Ritz Carlton. If there's anything else I can do for you . . ." blah, blah, blah.

"Thank you," I said . . . and shut the door, holding a beautifully monogrammed Ritz Carlton envelope.

"It's a note from Garry. It says:

'Good morning y'all. Sorry I had to rush off to work so early. We'll have time to catch up later. In the meantime, I've arranged a trip to the beauty salon for you ladies and massages for you men. I want to make sure y'all are well taken care of before Nichole and I wear you out with today's festivities. I hope you're enjoying yourselves. See y'all at lunch.
With love,
Garry'."

Off to the spa we trooped—hair, nails, make-up, massages, steam baths; you name it, we had it done. By the time they were through with us, we could have signed an endorsement deal to make Cesar Ritz himself proud.

I did make sure the salon took care of me first, though. After all, I had to go back upstairs and put on a big white dress . . .

"I'm suddenly not feeling so well," I said. "I need to go lie down for a while. I'll meet you guys at lunch, okay?—Where again did you say that lunch is going to be Allison?"

Chapter 52

I Ask Her to Marry Me and Be My Wife

Our guests were stunned. I saw it in their eyes as I spied from the balcony. Most people, arriving to see rows of white chairs lined up in front of a flower-laden gazebo, thought they'd stumbled upon the wrong party. More often than not, I'd catch them looking down at their luncheon invitations, making sure they were supposed to be on the south lawn. Then, once it dawned on them what was happening, smiles of delight lit up their faces.

While Emily and her assistant directed everyone to their seats, Allison hung by my side, assuring me of things like: I didn't look as bloated as I felt, or that my family and friends wouldn't be angry with me for having a surprise wedding, or most importantly, that Garry would show up on time.

And he did.

In fact, I got a lump in my throat when I saw him standing there in the gazebo, the sparkling ocean beyond. He looked like Bogie in his white dinner jacket, fidgeting a bit, shifting his weight from left to right, his eyes nervously scanning the horizon. Once he spotted me, though, a smile of relief set him straight on his feet.

With Pachelbel's "Canon" as a guiding force, I began my walk down the white carpet, locking eyes with Garry, daring not look any place but straight ahead because the one and only time my eyes did wander, I caught Brad Pitt grinning at me and practically stumbled at the altar!

I don't recall the exact details of the ceremony, although I do know that Garry didn't take his piercing brown eyes off me for one moment as we stood before that priest. And somehow, he managed to smile his magical dimpled smile through his vows while *I*, on the other hand, sputtered mine out through sniffles and tears of joy.

Yes, it was a gloriously beautiful day. What made it all happen is still a mystery to me, but one way or another, Allison had pulled it off. (I know, I know. Now *I* was the one owing a favor.)

And so, our joyously tearful wedding begot a celebratory champagne lunch, which in turn, gave birth to a festive reception—a reception minus the groom, of course.

Before leaving, Garry whispered in my ear, "Save the last dance for me."

Chapter 53

Tryin' to Find a Little Privacy

M uch to my dismay, I wasn't whisked away to a luxurious honeymoon cabana on a private island. Instead, a white stretch limo ushered me to the Bay Arena, a state-of-the-art concert venue—pavilion seating, plenty of lawn seats for the brave, two or three VIP rooms. According to Garry, because it sits right on Biscayne Bay, the setting sun provides a spectacular backdrop to the evening shows. The crowds had already set up camp as we pulled into the parking lot. My parents, neophytes in the world of Garry LaForge tailgating, were captivated by the pre-show shenanigans. Personally, I resolved to get a closer look before the Sunday afternoon show.

Garry was right in the middle of a sound check when we arrived. The dancers, Rhonda and Tea, were working out last minute changes, and the lighting crew hung from the scaffolding, fixing some sort of menacing problem. Garry was all business as we watched from the wings. When he saw me, his eyes lit up and he sang into the microphone, "Here comes the bride. All dressed in - hula gear!" He turned to the band. "That's it y'all. Go have yourselves a beer and relax. We'll meet back here at 6:30."

"Hey billfish. Hey y'all! You came just in time. Now the fun can begin." He picked me up and twirled me around.

I walked over to center stage and looked out at the sea of empty seats. It was hard to believe that within a matter of minutes each and every one would be occupied by a Garry LaForge fan. "So this is the view from the bridge," I said. "I can imagine the rush you must feel with thousands of fans screaming at you."

"That depends exactly *what* they're screamin'," Sammi teased.

Garry laughed. "That's true. With the ear monitors in, I can hardly hear a thing. Maybe I don't want to know what they're *really* sayin'."

Marty called to us, "Hey there honeymooners. Y'all better make a quick exit. They just opened the stadium doors."

Apparently the music business is full of assorted pre-concert rituals, from incense to prayers to heavy metal. Not so for Garry. One shot of tequila with the guys and he's good to go. I kissed him goodbye, slapped him on the behind for good luck, and ventured up to the VIP room where an endless spread of food and drinks awaited, along with the best seats in the house . . . which was a good thing because I was *exhausted!*

The carnival began with Rhonda and Tea dancing the samba while the "crowd pleasers," as Garry calls them, warmed up the crowd with Frisbees, beach balls, and t-shirts. The entire stadium drank and danced in the aisles. And you should have seen the lawn-dwellers— pure debauchery! All that before Garry even got on stage!

When Garry did arrive on stage, the crowd went crazy.

"Hello Miami!" A huge cheer went up. "Let the summer games begin!"

Now I don't know much about show business, but it seemed to me to be an enormous success. Everyone enjoyed it, but I'm sure, beyond a doubt, I enjoyed it the most; especially when Garry said, before singing "Been Tryin' To Catch Up With You," "This one is for the ever lovely and ever mine, *my bride* from this afternoon, Nichole Marie." What a thrill to see Garry in his true element. Sure, we'd been in the presence of several fans before but nothing like that. I was awestruck at seeing thousands upon thousands of people gathered for one purpose only: Garry.

Afterwards everyone gathered backstage to congratulate Garry and the band—family members, friends, and even a few fortunate fans with backstage passes. Limos escorted us back to the hotel where the party somehow ended up in our suite. It must have been 1 or 2 a.m. when Garry opened the door to our bedroom and called out, "Does anybody here recall that this is my weddin' night?"

Nobody seemed to care much; at least no one made a quick exit, but I knew Garry really didn't mind because he added, "Well, it looks like y'all are dug in here like Appalachian tics. Just make sure you lock the door on your way out, will ya?"

* * *

I'd like to say I was the helpful, sensitive type who took part in the weddin' plannin' every step of the way. But I wasn't . . . I was busy payin' for my sins on earth. Which was quite alright because I was marryin' the kind of woman who carries a sextant in her purse. Nichole Bocelli is the most organized, get-it-done woman I have ever been privileged to know. How she and Allison arranged that weddin' in two short weeks is beyond my comprehension. Although, to tell ya the truth, we could've gotten married at the VFW Hall, and still, I would've been as happy as a tornado in a trailer park.

Chapter 54

He's Crazy and Dangerous

Marriage: Day 1.

All the kinks having been worked out at the previous night's show, Garry and I took the opportunity that morning to work out some kinks of our own. (Are you kidding . . . I was asleep the moment my head hit the pillow the night before.)

That afternoon I did something I knew Garry wouldn't approve of, and I'm sure you'll understand why I chose not to tell him. My girlfriends and I planned to mingle amongst the tailgaters before the show. I knew for a fact Garry would think it was a bad idea, not because he didn't trust his fans, but because he was overly protective of me, not to mention the baby, and I didn't want to worry him. With our parents safe and secure backstage, the rest of us donned our tropical gear and headed to parking lot central. With drinks in hand (no, no, not me), we strolled up and down the aisles, watching, laughing, dancing, singing, and even partaking on occasion. No one seemed to be the wiser as to whom we actually were. We did run into Colton, though, who was videotaping footage for the show. We, of course, threatened him with severe torture if word were to get back to Garry.

According to Garry, there's a heavy line between Saturday night's show and Sunday afternoon's. Overnight, the crowd had grown younger, the party atmosphere much more distinct. We opted to watch the action from the fifth row. Front and center. It was actually, if possible, even more exciting for me to be a part of the audience that afternoon. Garry waltzed on stage, again, to an explosion of cheers. He cast his eyes to the left, then his eyes to the right, looking for us. Finally, with a hand to his forehead for shade, we were spotted and given a thumbs up. "Let's hit it," Garry called out. But just as the band started in on the first song, a trio of fighter jets roared overhead. Garry smiled and looked up. The crowd cheered for what they thought was a staged fly-by. Garry himself, thought it was an awesome sight, that is, until the jets continued to fly sorties right above the stadium! The sound was deafening, completely drowning him out. I'm sure I wasn't the only one who noticed the hidden irritation on Garry's face.

"Looks like those crazy Navy flyers have crashed our party this afternoon," he said in good humor.

He tried his best to play the second song of the set then said, "We're gonna take a little break right now, but I promise all y'all, we'll be right back as soon as we give ol' Uncle Sam a call."

Rhonda and Tea twirled across the stage while Colton's video footage rolled, bigger than life, on the jumbotrons above. The crowd got a real kick out of watching themselves. The film continued running as Garry returned on stage to attempt another song. Something happened, though, while he sang . . . He'd been gazing up at the screen to his right when a look of surprise came to his face. Suddenly, his words started coming out wrong. It took him a moment or two to regain consciousness, but something wasn't right. I knew it. He was rushing the tempo in order to finish the song and kept looking over in the wings. I decided to head back stage to see what was going on.—But first, I had to go to the bathroom soooo bad (You pregnant ladies know what I'm talking about.), and there it was, the Ladies Room, with *no* line—practically an impossibility at a Garry LaForge concert. Just my luck.

Or was it?

Three or four women hurried out as I hustled in. Then, while I washed my hands at the sink, I noticed, in the mirror, someone looking at me. I turned around and there was Hunter Rayburn, within three feet, leaning against the wall, arms folded across his chest! My heart skipped a beat and suddenly a couple of things became clear: first, the disturbance of the fighter jets was no accident, and second, Garry's sudden look of panic a few moments earlier had to do with the man in the mirror. Hunter Rayburn was wreaking havoc in our lives and quite honestly, I was scared.

"So we meet again, Nichole."

I tried not to look frightened, but all I kept thinking of was the fact that Hunter Rayburn stood between me and my only way out. I also cursed the fact that no one else was in the bathroom.

"What do you want?" I tried to sound firm.

A sinister smile came to his face. "You know very well what I want, Nichole. And I happen to know *you* want it too."

I was seething. "Are you crazy? You *raped* me! You drugged me and raped me!"

"That's not the way I see it. If I recall, you rather enjoyed our encounter. (*Encounter!*) It's just a shame you were so tired . . . and too bad your friends came home and disturbed us."

Now I was beyond angry. "So tired!—If I had wanted you so badly, like you say, then why would you have to drug me to get me into bed? Do you know you almost killed me? Do you realize I'm preg . . ." *Oh shit*, I thought. *I didn't mean to let that slip.* I was boiling with rage.

"He shook his head and stepped a little closer, a satisfied grin on his face. "Did you just say you're—*pregnant*?"

I didn't say a word. I'd forgotten to exhale.

"My mother was pregnant when my father killed himself," he said.

All I heard were the words "pregnant" and "kill" in the same sentence, and I knew I needed to get out of there.

"What does that have to do with anything?" I said, trying to buy some time.

"Maybe it just has everything to do with everything.—You see, my father had been invited to the Naval Academy as an opening ceremony speaker when my mother broke the news to him. She told him she'd been having an affair with a retired navy captain and that the baby was his. My father never showed up for the ceremony, so I went looking for him—and guess what I found? My hero, in my dorm room, hanging from the light fixture."

Obviously, I was stunned by what Hunter had said but also completely confused as to how it had anything to do with me. Mostly, I was bound and determined to stay in the moment and get out of that bathroom any which way I could.

"Why are you telling me this?" I asked.

"I'm telling you this, Mrs. LaForge, because that retired navy captain my mother was seeing at the time . . . the same man who got her pregnant and took my father away from me . . . was Charles Jackson LaForge."

Charles Jackson LaForge! I thought. *Garry's father?* I was stupefied. I couldn't believe it. I didn't *want* to believe it. I wondered if Garry knew such a thing! I was sure he didn't. Suddenly, I understood what this was all about. Hunter Rayburn was seeking vengeance, and everything he'd done over the past year had been planned, from getting Brooke Walker pregnant, to "accidentally" bumping into Garry and me at the Officer's Club, to "unknowingly" meeting my girlfriends. It was a setup. Hunter was getting back at C.J. And he was doing it through Garry.

You better believe I was scared, but there was no way I was going to let my voice give me away. "Hunter, I have nothing else to say to you, except call off the jets so Garry can finish the show." I made a move towards the exit, but Hunter stepped in front of me. That's when I realized he'd probably locked the bathroom door. (I mean, no line to the bathroom at a Garry LaForge concert is one thing, but no one coming *into* the bathroom is quite another.)

"The jets *are* a nice distraction, aren't they?" he said, gripping my shoulders.

"Let go of me." I tried to pull away. He pushed me up against the wall, pressing his entire body against mine. My brain shifted into panic mode. I could hardly move, *and* he was smashing my abdomen. 5'-5", 115 was certainly no match for 6'-4", 220.

"Are you going to make this pleasurable for yourself, or difficult?" he said, reaching a hand up my inner thigh.

I turned my head away lest he see the tears welling up in my eyes. That's when I noticed the fire alarm on the wall to my left. Slightly out of reach but my only hope. I stretched my arm along the wall as far as I could, until my fingertips touched the cold metal. Somehow, I managed, with all my strength, to pull the alarm.

It was loud, ear-piercing loud, and completely surprised Hunter.

The sprinkler system immediately rained down on us.

"You are one tough cookie, aren't you, Nichole Marie?" he said right into my ear. Reaching over with one hand, he tried to push the lever back up, but it must have been jammed, so instead, he ripped open my shirt, pinned my wrists against the wall and locked his lips in on my chest. I knew exactly what he was doing . . . leaving a permanent reminder for Garry.

Meanwhile, behind that locked door, hidden bedlam ran its course—stomping, yelling, banging—a stampede of intoxication trying to exit the stadium. We heard knocking, then pounding, on the bathroom door.

"Security! Is anyone in there?—Somebody's locked in the bathroom!" A voice bellowed above the alarm, "Who's got the keys for this bathroom?"

Hunter looked down at the mark he'd made on my chest, then directly in my eyes, "When you see Garry, or better yet, when you see C.J., won't you give him my regards. And be sure to tell him, what goes around comes around."

He walked casually to the door, unlocked it, and quietly disappeared into the crowd.

Chapter 55

Wishin' I Was Somewhere Other Than Here

I, too, tried to silence the alarm but couldn't do it. (My hands were shaking so badly anyway.) Rather, I sank down to the floor and buried my crying eyes into my knees as the sprinklers continued to rain down on me.

It rained so hard I drowned.

Security finally came back and stuck their heads in the bathroom. "Ma'am," they yelled, "Ma'am, there's a possible fire in the stadium. You've got to exit right away." I looked up and nodded but couldn't pull myself from the cold concrete.

Above the penetrating alarm I heard Garry calling from the stage microphone, "Nichole! Where are you? Nichole? Would somebody please find Nichole! Reggie, I need you here immediately!"

The teenage security guy squatted down next to me. "Are you okay, Ma'am?"

"Would you tell Garry I'm okay," I said, getting to my feet.

"Garry who?" he asked.

"Garry LaForge," I said. He looked confused.

"I'm Nichole," I said, just as Garry called out my name once more.

The security kid looked stunned. He radioed his colleagues with his "heroic news" then grabbed my arm and pulled me through the exiting crowd. Much to my great dismay, he kept yelling out, "Out of our way, I've got Garry's Nichole here." Funny enough, though, it worked.

As the Miami fire department muscled their way through the crowd, I grabbed one of them by the arm. "There's no fire," I said. He looked as if he didn't believe me. I yelled in his ear, "There's no fire! I pulled the alarm. In the women's bathroom."

Apparently, that statement earned me a double escort backstage: mister teenage security guy *and* mister pissed-off fireman. I spotted Garry and ran toward him just as the fire alarm abruptly stopped. All that could be heard was my uncontrollable sobbing in his arms.

"Are you alright?"

I nodded my head. I couldn't talk. Thankfully, our families had gone outside.

"He was here, wasn't he?" Garry asked.

I nodded again.

"I know. I saw him on the video. What happened, Nik? Did he hurt you?"

"No, he didn't." I looked around at the 6 or 7 people standing near us. A wrinkled brow signaled my reluctance to discuss the matter in front of others.

"Would y'all give us a moment, please," Garry said.

Once they were out of earshot, I tried to explain between sobs and sniffling, "This is all some kind of payback, Garry."

He looked confused. "What? What are you talkin' about?"

I started from the beginning. "You know when you looked up at the video screen and you lost your words? I knew something was wrong; something other than the damn jets, so I decided to go backstage and see what was going on. Well, stupid me, I should have remembered the advice you gave me once about not using public bathrooms. Anyway, I had to go to the bathroom so bad and noticed there weren't any lines, so I ran in quickly and went pee. When I was standing at the sink washing my hands I looked in the mirror and saw

Hunter Rayburn *right* behind me. He point blank denied drugging me and even has this delusional idea that *I'm* the one who wants *him*."

I explained what Hunter told me about his mother and Garry's father. The accusation stunned Garry, as it had for me, but I'm sure his mistrust of Hunter Rayburn left him doubtful.

I straightened up enough that Garry noticed my ripped shirt and Hunter's personal tattoo just above my breast.

"What the hell did he do to you!"

"He locked the bathroom door and wouldn't let me leave," I said.

Reliving that moment in my head, I started sobbing again.

"He pressed me up . . . against the wall . . . really hard . . . against my stomach . . . and started to reach his hand up my skirt." I pointed to my chest. "He said this message is for you. And for C.J. He said to tell you, 'what goes around comes around.'"

Garry paused a moment to take it all in. "So what happened next?"

"I pulled the fire alarm and he left."

"Just left? Just like that?"

There was that vein on his neck again.

"You should see it out there, Garry. It's a sea of people. He just slipped away and was gone."

"Mother Fucking Asshole! —That's it, Nichole. This guy has gone waaay too far. I hate to do this to you, but you are either with me or standin' right next to Reggie until we can get this fucker behind bars."

I knew enough to keep my mouth shut at that point.

"Why the hell are you runnin' around by yourself anyway? This is *Miami* for Christ's sake, not fuckin' *Fairytale Shores!*"

Okay, so I deserved that insult, but I didn't deserve the humiliation of everyone within earshot hearing me get insulted!

The fireman wandered back our way, anxiously awaiting an explanation, of which we gave an abbreviated version. Once all was resolved, the fans were let back in, a laborious task, but, being the ever-jovial fun-loving people they are, they weren't bothered one bit by the delay.

Meanwhile, as Garry and I stood before the band and our families, explaining why I looked like hell, I couldn't help but notice C.J.'s jaw drop open, ever so slightly, at the mention of Hunter Rayburn's name. I knew C.J. owed me an explanation.

A unanimous vote banished me backstage to Reggie's watchful eye for the rest of the show. Garry loaned me his camp shirt and I spent my first full day as a married woman sitting on a stool in the wings where my husband could keep tabs on me.

In the meantime, Garry put in a call to Ronny regarding the misguided jets, and Ronny, our savior, somehow found a way to call off the dogs.

So, Garry got back on stage and all systems were go. Or as he later told me, "It was simply a matter of righting the ship." There was no way he'd let Hunter Rayburn take the wind out of his sails. He was more resolved than ever to give the crowd an unforgettable performance; and believe me, he didn't disappoint.

Chapter 56

Live a Lie and You Will Live to Regret It

Now normally Garry would have joined the band for a backstage blowout and a night of bars and clubs in celebration of a successful kick-off weekend. Not that night. We assembled our families back at the Ritz for a quick "conference" in our room regarding the day's events. Garry and I felt the need to convince our families of my safety, which was a feat, considering we weren't too sure about it ourselves.

After bidding everyone goodnight, Garry called room service and hopped in the shower. He said he was too tired to have a discussion with his dad but promised we'd settle the matter in the morning.

Several minutes later, a quiet knock startled me from my comatose state on the sofa.

"Garry? Garry, it's Dad," I heard from out in the hall.

I wearily donned my robe and invited C.J. in. (As curious as I was to hear what he had to say, I really just wanted that day to be over with.)

Ever the gentleman, C.J. stood until I motioned for him to sit down.

"Garry's in the shower. You probably want to wait 'til he gets out before you . . ." I searched for the right words.

"Do you know why I'm here?" he asked, his head hanging low.

"I believe I do."

It was difficult for me to envision C.J.—mild-mannered, somewhat shy, C.J.—cheating on Charlene. (I know, I know, I've been told all sorts of unsuspecting people are cheating on their spouses.)

Garry joined us while C.J. recited his sad confession. He claimed it was a "'sin" he'd committed nearly 20 years earlier, one of which he was sincerely ashamed. He said his affair with Macy Rayburn was fleeting—a short three months before he'd come to his senses and called the whole thing off.

"That's when Macy told me she was pregnant," C.J. said, somewhat embarrassed. "But quite honestly, I couldn't trust that the baby was mine. She'd been known to have many gentlemen friends."

"So what ever happened to Macy Rayburn? And the baby?" I asked.

"Macy's husband, Vice-Admiral John-Henry Rayburn, was assigned to a fleet out of Charleston, so she and their son, Hunter, moved with him to the east coast. I had offered to do what I could regardin' the baby, but she just up and left. I heard through the grapevine about John-Henry's suicide at The Academy and it was but a month after that I received word from Macy that she'd had a miscarriage. —That was the last I've ever seen or heard from her, or ever thought about her for that matter. Until tonight when you mentioned Hunter Rayburn's name. I want y'all to know that I'm absolutely sick knowin' my actions most likely caused this fiasco tonight."

I looked over at Garry for direction. I realized it wasn't my place to confront C.J., but I could tell that Garry would have no problem doing that on his own. You see, we'd never told C.J. and Charlene about the rape. As far as they knew, Garry and I were having an "oops" baby.

"Let me be the one to tell you, Dad, that your actions caused more than this little fiasco tonight. What you don't know is that your 'sin' from 20 years ago caused Hunter Rayburn to not only *stalk* my wife, but to *rape* my wife. In my house. In my very own bed! —Now I don't give a goddamn about your apologies to me, but you better be apologizin' to Nichole for the rest of your natural born life."

Garry's words echoed off the walls as C.J. took it all in.

Although the moment was awkward for me, I agreed with Garry. C.J. needed to know, and he *did* owe me an apology.

"Why didn't y'all tell me this before?" C.J. asked, looking distraught.

"Well you know now," Garry snapped back.

C.J. took my hands in his and looked me straight in the eye. "With all my heart, I am sorry, Nichole. I don't know why Hunter Rayburn is takin' this out on you. Lord knows, I should be the one sufferin' for my mistakes. Not you. And not Garry." He looked over at Garry. "I should be the one to confront Hunter."

Garry was adamant. "*I* will be the one to confront Hunter Rayburn, thank you. —And tell me Dad, does Mom know about your affair with Macy Rayburn?"

Actually, knowing Garry, that wasn't his only concern. Think about it. You've just found out from your father that years ago, when life was good and the sky was blue, he was busy cheating on your mother. What is it you'd want to know (other than the "why" of it all)? Personally, I'd want to know that my father had confessed to my mother and secondly, and perhaps, most importantly, that he was sincerely remorseful for what he'd done.

C.J. looked Garry right in the eye. "Yes, your mother knows. I couldn't live with myself for what I was doin' to Charlene and you kids. Although y'all were adults at the time, I realized what I was doin' to you was wrong. I am ashamed of my disloyalty. —I love your mother, Garry. I was never unfaithful to her before that and never have been since."

Garry rubbed his eyes and looked especially tired.

"What's got me worried right now is you and Mom's safety. Who's to say Rayburn won't show up on your doorstep when y'all get home? God knows why he hasn't already. —I'll have Reggie stop by your room in the mornin' —'cause right now I want to be alone. "

C.J. stood up to leave. "I made a mistake and I hope you can find it in your heart to forgive me. It's my own damn fault and I'll do anything I can to make up for the pain I've caused you two."

Garry could find no forgiveness in his heart that very moment, so I walked alone with C.J. to the door and gave him a hug.

* * *

Garry took some time to contemplate out on the balcony. I'm not sure what he was thinking. As for myself, my body found its way back to the sofa, but my mind was a million miles away.

He was just hanging up the phone when he joined me. "Thanks Ronny. I appreciate it."

"I'm havin' Ronny email over Hunter's military photo and information so it can be distributed to security at all the shows. I'm also havin' him look into the jet maneuvers that took place this afternoon. Hopefully we can get some sort of retribution on that front. As for the other 'maneuvers' that occurred today . . ." Garry grew wearier by the moment. "This guy is slick, Nikki. He flies under the radar all the time. I haven't figured out what to do. Yet."

"Well," I said, "I know I don't want to live in fear every moment, but I also don't want to have security attached to me 24 hours a day."

"At this point, my dear, you have no choice. Walkin' around by yourself doesn't seem to be workin' too well for ya, now does it?"

We were both quiet, Garry for smoldering, me for submitting.

"I thought Hunter Rayburn was off in some 'classified location.'" I said.

"He may be out of the country, but don't forget, it's a holiday weekend, and the guy has access to any plane any time he wants."

"Are you still convinced he's in Cuba?" I asked.

"Oh, he's in Cuba. This I know for sure."

I sat up and looked over at Garry.

He put his feet up on the coffee table, took a swig of his beer and flipped on the TV, completely ignoring me.

I knew he had a plan hidden up his shirtsleeve. "You're going back there, aren't you?" I said. It wasn't a question, really, more of a factual statement.

"You better believe it," he replied—to no one but himself.

* * *

Irate. I was absolutely irate. With anything that moved. Animate, in-animate, it didn't matter. But I was exhausted too . . . which was very fortunate for my father.

Chapter 57

Stranded on a Sandbar

F rom that moment forward, Matthew Mulligan, otherwise known as "Muggs," was assigned to regard my everlasting safety. It was a foreign concept to me, inviting a stranger into my private world, but I really had no choice. Reggie brought Muggs over in the morning. On one hand, I was displeased with the whole follow-me-around idea, but on the other hand, knowing Muggs was a former Navy Seal and martial arts guru gave me some level of comfort. Okay, the fact that he was a blonde, blue-eyed, all-American guy was a big bonus too. A beefy Jamaican like Reggie would have stood out in Oakwood Shores like Anita Bryant at a Jimmy Buffett concert.

Reluctantly, Garry et al. were moving onward to Atlanta. As for me, I'd be spending a two week honeymoon playing tour guide to my parents in Key West.

And so, feeling sorry for myself, I drove south in the Corvette with my mom, Muggs, and my dad following close behind. Adding to my frustration, Garry said to me as he left, "You realize I won't make it back to Oakwood Shores for the 4th.

I knew perfectly well what he meant. He meant to say he'd be spending the 4th of July in Cuba.

"Please, Garry, just promise me you'll take Reggie with you. That's all I'm asking."

"I can't make that promise, Nik. But I will promise you I'll call just as soon as I have a noose around Rayburn's neck."

The tears began to well in my eyes. (At 10 weeks pregnant, every little thing set me off.) We kissed goodbye . . . and I brooded the entire drive home.

Chapter 58

This is No Camelot

T he following month, from Atlanta to Boston, Garry "did the coast." We talked constantly, and although unspoken, his 4th of July plans were a forbidden subject. And wouldn't you know it, my anxiety regarding Garry's Cuban crusade had once again kidnapped my ability to eat. (The only good news was that by 15 weeks my morning sickness had subsided . . . oh yeah, and pregnancy was working wonders on my complexion.) Going back to Oakwood Shores was an obvious choice for me. There, I could fill my time with friends and my head with design. The last thing I needed was to end up back in the hospital.

Muggs and I arrived in Oakwood Shores just in time for the 4th of July weekend. Meanwhile, Garry was finishing up a show in Boston and *would have* been meeting me there. (*But wait, I wasn't going to think about that!*) I happen to love the 4th of July in Oakwood Shores. I have enough vivid memories of block parties, Plaza carnivals, downtown parades, and M80 mischief to last a lifetime. Needless to say, it was good to be home, although it was hotter than the hinges of hell, and I could have done without the 90% humidity. The first thing I did at our newly renovated house was turn on the air conditioning and flop into bed, mentally exhausted.

"Nichole?" Muggs called in my bedroom door. "I'm famished. Do y'all have some take-out menus in the house?"

"In the kitchen, last drawer on the left . . . at least they used to be."

"Are you goin' to join me? I happen to know you haven't eaten all day."

"I'm okay, Muggs, thanks." (As much as I resented the idea of having Muggs around, he really *was* a great guy. He knew when to butt in and when to mind his own business. I realize now, that it must have been trying for him, a single guy dealing with a hormonally imbalanced pregnant woman.)

Muggs came in the room and stood next to the bed. "Far be it from me to dig into your personal life, but if you don't start eatin', I'm going to have to stand guard at your hospital bed. I mean it. I know you're worryin' about Garry, but just between you and me, I happen to know that Reggie will be with them the entire weekend. And Reggie won't let anything terrible happen."

"Them? Who's *them*?"

"See, now you got me tellin' you things I shouldn't. But if you really must know, 'them' is Garry and Josh."

"Thanks for trying to make me feel better, Muggs, but it's not working. And no, I'm still not hungry."

For those who are curious, this is what I was doing while lying there in bed, waiting for the air conditioner to offer me deliverance: You know when you're sitting on an airplane by yourself and you start to feel some turbulence? (Not that little shaky turbulence, but the kind of turbulence that sends the flight attendants running for the toilet.) And your mind starts to go through all sorts of "what if" scenarios . . . *Oh my God, this is it. Any moment now we're going to drop thousands of feet then take a nose dive straight for the ground. Everything's going to happen so fast; those oxygen masks will drop out, people will be screaming. Will I have time to say a prayer? Will my life pass before my eyes? How many rows away is the emergency exit? Should I try to go for that one or the one in back? Will I be one of the survivors?* And it's usually about this point when you catch yourself getting carried away and have to shake your head and make yourself stop. I'm sure you've done that, right? Well, *that's* what I was doing in bed that afternoon regarding Garry's trip to Cuba, or should I say, that's what I was trying *NOT* to do.

* * *

Saturday morning the 3rd.

With a reprieve from the humidity, Muggs and I ventured out for a long walk around Lakeland. Festivities were set up and ready to go at Main Beach and across the way at Lakeland Center: food booths, games, carnival rides, bands, and the ever-popular outdoor beer garden. As luck would have it, the parade was in full swing. In fact, we arrived just in time to catch the Lawn Chair Dad's Marching Brigade (complete with dego t-shirts and black socks—my favorite.) I needed that smile more than ever.

The evening plan was to get together with friends at the Lakeland Festival then walk over to Jessica's house and watch the fireworks over the lake. I was particularly glad to have something to occupy my mind . . . I hadn't heard from Garry at all, and hoped to God I wouldn't have to find a way to bail my husband out of a Cuban jail.

Why *hadn't* he called? That question plagued me all day long. Actually, that question was the same one on Jessica's mind when she stopped by.

"Nik, do you know what Josh is up to this weekend? He'd talked about coming to Oakwood Shores for the 4th of July. He said Garry was coming too, but I didn't hear from him. He said he'd call me." (Now I'm sure this came as quite a shock to Jessica. Let's face it, all her life she's had a man waiting for her on every corner.) "Is there someone else in the picture? You'd tell me if you knew something, wouldn't you?" (*Sure I would. At least I think I would. Wouldn't I? Oh hell—maybe I wouldn't.*)

"Of course I'd tell you. And no, there isn't anyone else. In fact, the only people in Josh's life this 4th of July weekend are Garry and Reggie."

I couldn't take it any longer. If I didn't release that pressure valve, I knew I was going to explode. I told her about the three-man operation allegedly going on as we spoke. And although I'd solemnly promised not to divulge Muggs' true identity, I had to tell her the truth. As the saying goes, "in time of war, the first casualty is truth" . . . and I had a sinking feeling Garry was at war.

* * *

Everyone who's anyone in Oakwood Shores attends The Lakeland Festival (even my parent's 83 year old, half-blind, chain-smoking neighbor) and that evening was no exception. Muggs, for his part, cursed and complained when he saw the crowded venue. Nonetheless, he followed obediently as The Girls of Oakwood Shores and I mingled with old friends and acquaintances, including that old boyfriend again, Patrick Kelly. It was a mini reunion of sorts. Of course, everyone brought up the one topic I did not care to discuss. "He had a show in Boston," was my standard reply. To which they would respond, "We can't wait to see him perform in Chicago at the end of the month!"

Walking into the beer garden, introducing "Cousin Muggs" to my friends, I was completely oblivious of the newest addition to the entryway, a metal detector. As I casually strolled through, Muggs had no choice but to follow. He got half-way through when the alarm went off, which it did for most people who'd forgotten their keys or cell phones or such in their pockets. Security pulled him aside, and he looked me in the eye, as if to say, *I just fucked up*. Too late, they'd found his gun. Before we knew it, a swarm of police surrounded Muggs, not to mention the entire beer garden looking over at us.

"He's from Alabama," I whispered loudly to the onlookers, as if that explained the gun. (I actually saw them shaking their Midwestern heads in recognition.)

Fortunately, Muggs had his business license and permit with him, so it was duly sorted out.—So much for discreet.

* * *

Before we knew it, dusk was upon us. Like a troop of scouts, a whole pack of us hiked the three blocks over to Jessica's house on the lake.

"Hey, Nik, wait up," I heard someone call out. I turned to see Patrick running to catch up with me.

"Listen," he whispered in my ear, "is there a chance we can talk alone?" He referred to Muggs' constant presence.

Eager to hear what he had to say, I walked over to Muggs and asked if there was any way he could give me five or ten minutes alone. Muggs gave me a stern look. "I'm not lettin' y'all out of my sight, though."

I kissed him on the cheek. "I wouldn't expect otherwise."

People were setting up watch along the shoreline, but we found a quiet spot to sit under a tree. "So what's the deal with Garry's cousin?" Patrick asked. "He seems overly attached to you. And why the hell does he carry a gun around with him?"

"He's protective, that's all," I said, pulling blades of grass so as to have something to do with my hands.

"So tell me, Nik, just how serious are you and Garry?"

It surprised me to know that he hadn't heard about the wedding, but mostly, I was curious to see where the conversation was leading.

Without giving me a chance to reply, he continued, "Remember the last time we sat together at the beach?"

"Clearly," I said, thinking of seven years earlier, a beautiful June evening out on the end of a pier . . . Patrick broke up with me. (I cried. I said foolish things.—I wished I hadn't done that. Oh well. Youth begets folly, doesn't it?)

Again, I opened my mouth to speak, but Patrick was on a roll. "I've been thinking lately about what a mistake I made back then. Jesus, has it really been seven years?"

Hold on there, Mister, could you repeat that? I was laughing too loud inside to hear you! I could hardly believe my ears. But I knew from past experience that when Patrick Kelly has a few drinks in him, all sorts of half-truths and lies spill from his mouth.

"Sometimes it seems like a million years ago," I said. "Other times it seems like just yesterday."

"Do you ever think what would have happened to us had we gone ahead with our plans for the future?"

"Well—I guess we would have been married now for a couple years, huh?"

"But do you ever think about it? I mean *really* think about it?" he asked.

"Patrick," I said, dumping my pile of grass and looking him square in the eye, "there was a time when I was haunted by *it* each and every day. I realize now that our lives were so simple back then. Things have definitely gotten more complex. You can't even imagine how complex. Anyway, you know me; I'm not one to live in the past. In reality, I should be *thanking* you for the last time we sat together at the beach."

Patrick smiled and said, "You never answered my original question, though."

"Which was?"

"About you and Garry."

"Oh." I raised my left hand to show him my rings. "I guess this would answer your question, wouldn't it?"

He was stunned (and a little embarrassed too, I think). "I had no idea," he said, looking at my rings. "How could I have missed *that*?" Realizing there were *two* rings on my finger, he said, "Wait a minute. Are you . . .?"

"Married," I answered. (Thought I'd leave out the pregnant part.)

Silence filled our little corner of the world, but only for a moment . . . the first fireworks exploded right over our heads. But it wasn't the sound of the fireworks that caused me to jump to my feet. The sound I heard was growing louder and louder. It was *Southern Cross*, flying low over the west end of the lake. It was Garry! He was trying to land, but the fireworks and all the boats were thwarting his plans. He flew low again and I turned around to look at Muggs . . .

But he was gone!

Chapter 59

Some Kind of Lunatic

M y heart sank to the pit of my stomach. I knew Muggs would *never* leave me, and I also knew that the only explanation for his disappearance had to be Hunter Rayburn. I was sure of it. In a split second, that familiar feeling of dread closed in on me.

"Something's wrong, Patrick. I know it."

"Muggs?" I called out. "Muggs! Where are you?" Throngs of spectators shushed me as I disturbed their patriotic moment, yet Muggs failed to answer my cries. I tripped over people in my search, the darkness impenetrable. I felt like a five year old who'd lost her mother in the grocery store. (Since I'm on the subject of losing people, allow me to quickly digress. I promise, it's quick . . . Once, when I was in Kindergarten, a girl in my class invited me to go over to her house after school. I wasn't quite sure how one went about arranging a playdate, so I decided to take matters into my own hands. I merrily got off the bus at her stop instead of mine. Little did I know, my classmate was a five year old latchkey kid. Once inside her house, she began telling me all sorts of stories about vampires, mummies, and the Holy Ghost. Thank God I had the presence of mind to call home and tell my mother what was going on. Unfortunately, I had no idea where I was. I'm pretty sure I was in tears, and I'm absolutely sure my mother was freaking out. It didn't take me long to leave the little girl's house and start walking in the direction I thought was home. At the same time my mother had gotten in her car and was driving around looking for me. Yes, in the end, the two of us had a tearful reunion, but the round-about point I'm trying to make here is that the terror, the fright, the dread that my mother must have gone through that afternoon was the same terror, fright, and dread that I was going through when I couldn't find Muggs. After all, he was the lifeline to my Titanic existence.—And that rope had just slipped through my hands.)

"Oh my God," I said to myself, "he's here." My heart pounded with fear, pulsating in my ears.

Patrick was thoroughly confused. "*Who's* here?"

I was in a frenzied state, looking every which way. "Hunter Rayburn."

"Nichole. Are you okay? What's going on?"

"It's complicated, Patrick."

"Try me."

"Okay, here's the short version," I said, grabbing his hand. "Hunter Rayburn is the bad guy, and he's here. Muggs is my bodyguard, and he's missing. And that plane trying to land is Garry."

Patrick was taking it all in and didn't quite capture the urgency of it all.

"Muggs! Muggs!" I called. There was no sign of him anywhere. "We need to get to over to Jessica's right away," I said.

I tried Garry on his cell as we ran over to Jessica's, but Lady Luck was not on my side.

We raced through Jessica's front door (a front door that's never locked), and I was immediately seized by a side cramp. I stood, doubled over in pain, hyperventilating, when Sarah stepped out of the bathroom.

"Nichole. What's the matter? Are you okay?" she asked.

"Do you know who *Hunter Rayburn* is?" Patrick asked.

"Hunter! Why? Is *Hunter Rayburn* here?!"

I nodded my head.

"Oh my God!" she replied. "Let me go get the girls!" And off she raced to the backyard.

Within moments, my girlfriends encircled us.

"I'm sure I should call the police about Muggs, shouldn't I?" I asked, after having told them what happened.

The three guys sitting at the kitchen table getting high looked at me like I was out of my mind.

I could hear Garry far off in the distance, circling the lake.

"Maybe I better wait 'til Garry lands," I said.

"So what do we do now?" Jessica asked, fear in her voice.

"Lock all the doors," Melanie said.

"What if he's already inside!" Amanda added.

That was enough to cause us to take two steps closer to Patrick.

"Well whoever this Hunter Rayburn guy is, he's got some kind of voodoo over everyone," Patrick commented.

Freaked out by the thought of Hunter lying in wait somewhere inside the house, we all agreed that outside would be a better choice.

For me, the fireworks were endless. I paced the length of the pier, surrounded by friends, watching Garry fly in the distance. So many thoughts raced through my brain, *Is Muggs okay and why was he so easily overcome? How does Garry know that Hunter Rayburn is in Oakwood Shores? Why can't I reach Garry on his cell phone?*

I tried to relax, I really did (I even used the Lamaze breathing I'd learned from Allison), but I couldn't. Eventually, I heard, faintly, over at Main Beach, the band starting in on the "1812 Overture" and knew that the end was in sight . . . the end of the fireworks, that is.

Chapter 60

Flyin' Low Not Like All the Rest

N o sooner had the last ash left the sky than Garry came in low again. I knew it would be a difficult landing with all the boats anchored at the buoy line, and I can tell you, he had quite an audience. I stood, paralyzed . . . held my breath . . . He did it! Resounding applause erupted around the lake, and I breathed a secret sigh of relief. I also started to cry. (I told you I was hormonal.)

To my disappointment, Garry taxied west toward our house. (For some reason, I assumed he'd know I was at Jessica's and would motor right over, jump out, take me in his arms, and everything would be okay.) I tried him again on his cell then called the house and left a message. Just as I did that, a thought occurred to me. I needed to contact my parents. They'd most likely be watching the fireworks somewhere along the lake, and I just prayed to God Hunter Rayburn would leave them out of his lunatic plot. I left them a message to call me on my cell, that I had reason to believe Hunter was in town, and that Garry was on his way in. Of course, I didn't mention anything about Muggs' disappearance. I didn't think they'd find much comfort in knowing that my trusted (not to mention obscenely paid) self-defense expert had just been kidnapped.

Now. What to do. What to do. I needed to get to my house and see Garry as soon as possible. And find Muggs! *God damnit.* I thought, *why isn't Garry calling me?*

Don't ask me why, but it never occurred to me to call Josh or Marty, or even Reggie for that matter. I suppose if you ever find yourself in such a panicked state, you wouldn't be thinking straight either.

I sure as hell wasn't about to walk the half-mile back to my house alone, in the pitch dark, with a psycho lurking in the bushes. And since everyone had parked over at the festival, the only means of transportation available was an old scooter left in Jessica's garage, a remnant from high school days. Patrick, by fault of being male (and available), became my escort, so I hopped on back for the one-minute ride home. As we sped along Lake Avenue, our single cylinder engine buzzing, an unmistakable noise was growing louder overhead . . . *Could it be . . . a fighter jet?* You bet it was, and it was barreling in on us!

"What is that?" Patrick yelled in my ear.

(Now some of you may live in places like Southern California or D.C. or Pensacola where fighter jets roaring overhead are an everyday occurrence. Believe me when I say that people in Oakwood Shores, Illinois are mystified by such a sight.)

"*That* sounds like an F/18."

Quickly, Patrick cut over toward my house. With no lights on inside, we parked the scooter in the driveway and ran around back. There was *Southern Cross,* bobbing up and down at the end of the pier. My instincts told me to run towards the plane, but a fighter jet making another deafening pass over the lake stopped me dead in my tracks.

"Here it comes again," I called to Patrick.

He yelled back, "I've never seen a jet fly so low . . . and *holy shit* . . . it's coming in upside down!"

Chapter 61

The Last Line

My breath literally caught in my throat. Sure enough, the F/18 was flying the distress maneuver we'd witnessed while on base. Ronny's voice rang out loud and clear in my brain, "It's a signal to people on the ground that there's a problem with another aircraft. It means clear the area immediately and get help."

A shiver traveled the length of my spine. I turned to Patrick, "It's a warning," I said.

"What do you mean, 'a warning?'" he asked.

"It means clear the area immediately and get help."

"You're *absolutely right*, Miss Nichole."

I practically jumped into Patrick's arms.—There stood Hunter Rayburn, within arm's length, *GQ* hair wild and unkempt, clothes tattered, eyes beady and savage. "I see there's a new man in your life, Nichole. I'm sure Garry wouldn't be too happy about that. As a matter of fact, I'm not too pleased about it myself." He nodded toward Patrick. "Have you told him you're a married woman now? Does he know you're pregnant?—With *my* child?"

Patrick looked at me momentarily as if to say, *You're what?* Then innocently enough started in, "Listen, I don't know what the hell you want, but we're leaving."

Hunter just laughed as he pulled a gun from his waistband and dangled it against his thigh. "Y'all aren't goin' anywhere." He said it so smoothly, so casually, as if he were the Principal and we'd just been caught trying to ditch school. Truthfully, I found that more unsettling than if he were to press the cold steel of his gun directly against my head.

Patrick instantly felt the gravity of the situation. "What is it you want?" he snapped.

"Why don't you ask your girlfriend here? She and I seem to be playing quite the game of cat and mouse." Then he looked at me with the most sinister gaze. "I have some unfinished business with you, Nichole. The LaForge Family fucked up my father's life *and* my life, and now it's time for me to fuck up theirs.—Payback's a bitch, isn't it?"

I was petrified. Absolutely, positively petrified. Rape, heck, that was nothing. Torture, murder . . . at that point I believed Hunter Rayburn was capable of *anything*.

He went on, "I happen to know F/18s do *not* normally fly distress over Oakwood Shores, my dear, so someone must have called in the Cavalry. Looks like you and I need to hightail it out of here." He glanced over at *Southern Cross*.

I was glued to Patrick, shaking like a live wire and void of my usual spiteful remarks. That pistol dangling next to Hunter's thigh had a choke hold on me.

I needed to bide some time.

"What did you do with Garry?" I demanded. "And where's Muggs?"

Hunter looked annoyed. "Who the fuck is *Muggs*?"

Now I was really confused.

Suddenly "Tropicana Jam" sang out its merry tune from my back pocket. (Believe me, the irony of it was not lost on me.)

"Don't even *think* about it," Hunter growled as I inadvertently reached to answer it.

Not more than a moment passed when it rang once again.

"Looks like somebody really wants to talk to you. I'm sure it's not Garry, though, seeing as I've got his cell phone right here." And, sure enough, he pulled Garry's phone out of his pocket.

Oh my God, I thought, *what did he do to Garry?*

"Funny how Garry's always one step behind me, isn't it?" he mocked.

"Try two steps behind you, asshole," came a voice out of the darkness. And there stood Garry in a navy flight suit, planted firmly behind Hunter with a gun pointed directly at his head!

"Put the gun down before I blow your fuckin' brains out!" Garry raged through clenched teeth. "And if you don't think I'll do it, you can be sure the Navy's 'Distinguished Pistol Shot' will be glad to."

Hunter's eyes darted to the left where Ronny stood in uniform, barrel of his gun pointed directly at Hunter.

"Don't think I won't do it Rayburn," Ronny called out.

"Drop, the gun," Garry said slowly, each word angrier than the last.

No one moved. I think Hunter was contemplating his fate. As for me, I stood so close to Patrick the sweat was dripping from his body onto mine, and I was having difficulty breathing. That is, until my dad arrived! (Then I stopped breathing altogether.)

"Nichole? Nichole?" he called out as he walked around back.

A layer of dread was added to the already sick feeling I had in the pit of my stomach. *Good God. Like things aren't messy enough already!*

Keeping eyes *and* gun on Hunter, Garry held out his hand to stop my dad. "Gino, don't come any closer! Let us handle this." My dad froze, mid-step—and to my surprise, didn't say another word.

Hunter used the distraction as an opportunity to grab me, abruptly, one arm tightly around my throat, the other, pointing his gun at my stomach! I remember desperately blinking tears out of my eyes, convinced it was the last time I'd see Garry or my unborn baby.

Slowly, step-by-step, Garry eased himself right up to Hunter until his gun practically touched his skull. Very firmly, yet with complete control, Garry demanded, "Last chance, mother fucker. Drop the gun. Now!"

Hunter looked over again at Ronny. Realizing he had no chance, he tightened his vise on my neck and whispered in my ear, loud enough for Garry to hear, "Fucking you was such sweet revenge."

Seething with fury, Garry grabbed that sucker by the throat and ripped the gun from his hand. A split second later he laid Hunter flat on the ground with a bloody, broken nose. "Come near Nichole again, and I'll fuckin' kill you." Then, with all his might, he gave Hunter a direct kick to the balls that left him curled up and crying like a baby. Ronny then yanked him to his feet and handcuffed him.

Garry took me in his arms. "You okay?" he asked.

I was shaking uncontrollably. My whole body shuddered, and I couldn't stop. "I'm okay now," I said, although I still hadn't exhaled. I looked over at Patrick, sitting on the lawn, visibly shaken. "How are *you*?" I asked him.

"Like you, I'm okay. *Now*."

Garry offered his hand to Patrick and pulled him up. "Thanks," he said, patting him on the back.

"Thanks? I didn't do a thing," Patrick replied.

Garry interrupted, "The way I see it, you were the one standin' by Nichole's side when I arrived. To me, that's worth a thousand thanks."

Now you're probably asking yourself, *What the hell* (or 'heck' or 'fuck' . . . depends who you are) *happened to Muggs?* Believe me, I was just as baffled as you are. "We need to find Muggs," I said. And just as I did, the Lakeland Police schlepped around back with my mom.

I could hear Ronny talking with the officers. "I've got Shore Patrol five minutes out. Lieutenant-Commander Rayburn will be taken into immediate naval custody and we'll work out the details later. Right now I've got two jets I need to get back to Key West ASAP. I appreciate your cooperation, officers." Ronny was extremely directive and as any good Commander would, took charge of the situation.

Sure enough, two naval officers arrived within minutes—one in flight uniform, the other, a Shore Patrolman. (Remember Lieutenant Barnes from the gate at Key West Naval Air Facility? Well, *he* was the Shore Patrolman!)

"I told you I'd be glad to help y'all out if you ever needed anything. I *knew* we had a few delinquents on base, and to tell ya the truth, I had a feelin' this Rayburn fella was a bit shady from the get go." Lieutenant Barnes was clearly swollen with pride.

Hunter denied knowing anything about Muggs or his whereabouts, even when Officer Barnes jogged his memory with his billy club.

"Ronny, I just can't thank you enough," I said with a big hug and a kiss on the cheek. "You're always saving me from naval officers, aren't you?"

Ronny laughed, thinking back I'm sure, to that day at the Officer's Club. "Nichole, I'm desperately trying to prove to you that not all naval officers are degenerates."

Garry gave Ronny an enormous bear hug. "You know I always wanted to fly shotgun with you, Ronny. But next time, let's make it under different circumstances."

Chapter 62

Simply Complicated

R onny said goodbye, Hunter was taken away, and we were left to deal with "Barney Fife" and his crew. We were gathered inside, filling out a missing person's report, when the most alarming banging came at the front door. (I tell you, my nerves at that point were shot. If I hadn't been pregnant, I would have downed a stiff drink right then and there—either that or a Valium.) Garry ran over to the front door, opened it cautiously, and discovered Muggs on the porch, blindfolded and gagged with both his hands and feet bound. There was also a note pinned to his sleeve.

"Jesus Christ, Mulligan, you look like sheep shit in a shallow pond!" Garry said, pulling Muggs to his feet.

"What happened?" I asked, once the duct tape was painfully torn off.

"You mean, besides being knocked out, bound, and gagged for the past hour?" Muggs was clearly embarrassed.

Garry read the note to himself.

"Who was it?" I asked. "It couldn't have been Rayburn. He was flying Garry's plane when you disappeared."

"I never saw 'em," Muggs said. "They took me from behind. Blindfolded me and locked me in a car."

Garry read aloud:

> "Sorry for the inconvenience . . .
> Understand that we needed to ensure
> Hunter Rayburn's presence here today.
> It served us both well.
> Dan Walker"

It was clear to Garry, Muggs, and me . . . Brooke Walker's reach was far and wide.

Thankfully, Muggs' pride was the only thing hurt, and Hunter Rayburn was finally out of our lives. As for the Walkers, they'd get *their* piece of Hunter any which way they could.

Well I don't know about you, but confusion hung in the room like a thick fog. I asked Garry to start from the beginning.

"Well, let's see. This mornin' I woke up in Boston, at least I think I did. It was so long ago.—Jake flew Reggie, Josh, and me down to Key West in *Global Escort,* and then we took *Southern Cross* west toward Cuba."

"Wait a minute," I asked. "You were just thrown out of Cuba. How did you expect to land there again?"

"Rayburn wasn't in Guantanamo Bay, my dear. I knew he was hidin' out in Havana."

"Ok. So how were you going to land in *Havana* without permission?"

"Every aviator knows that Cuba assists pilots who experience sudden emergencies. Well, we three *fishermen* just happened to experience a timely emergency while flyin' directly over José Marti International," Garry said with a wink. "They cleared us into Cuban airspace and told us to land immediately. Now Nichole knows I always carry a swag box in the back of the plane, filled with all sorts of CD's, hats and t-shirts for such occasions. Well, let's just say the Cubans are no foreigners to the idea of free trade. I shamelessly bartered for my liberty while Reggie and Josh occupied themselves with the plane's mysterious mechanical problem. The only trouble is, I came up empty-handed.

"So he *wasn't* in Havana after all?" I asked.

"Oh no, he was there, alright. I missed him by a couple hours, that's all. Actually, I was told I wasn't the first to come lookin' for him today."

"So the Navy was finally tracking him down!" my dad eagerly added.

(A former Navy man himself, and experiencing patriotic disappointment over the whole Hunter Rayburn thing, my dad had been rooting, all along, for the Navy to redeem itself.)

"No, no, Gino, it wasn't the Navy lookin' for Rayburn."

"The Walkers," I said.

"This is so perplexing," said my mom. "Who are the Walkers?"

"Nikki's right. It *was* the Walkers. Seems my ex-girlfriend's family is lookin' for Rayburn regardin' a paternity matter."

"So then what?" I asked impatiently.

"Well, our engine trouble inexplicably corrected itself, so we flew back to Key West to regroup. I landed at *Montrume's* to refuel and figure out what to do next, and guess who we ran into?"

"Hunter Rayburn?" I ventured.

"No. Brooke Walker's brother, Dan. He and another guy had, in fact, been tryin' to track down Rayburn, who'd never shown up for his court-ordered DNA testin' on Friday. There we were, the five of us sittin' around speculatin' where on earth Hunter Rayburn had gone to when all of the sudden, there goes *Southern Cross* off in the distance—and headin' north! I knew straight away who it was, and I had a hunch where he was goin'. That's when I decided to track Ronny down. I figured I needed to get to Oakwood Shores as soon as possible, and I don't know anybody else who can get from A to B faster than *he* can, nor anybody who can cut through the bureaucratic bullshit it was gonna take to get a fighter jet up to Illinois. 'The Powers That Be' required us to bring along a Shore Patrolman; that's why we took two jets. They flew the distress signal while Ronny and I flew directly to the airport. But, I was hopin' like hell we'd make it here sooner."

"And it would have worked, too," I said, "if only you were five or ten minutes earlier."

"So what's the reasoning behind Muggs' disappearance?" Patrick asked.

"You see, the Walkers had a vested interest in findin' Rayburn, and they knew Nichole would lead them to him, so to speak. They also realized Muggs needed to be out of the picture in order for that to happen. Unfortunately, they got here before we did and used Nichole as their bait."

"And unfortunately, Patrick, you got drug into this God-awful mess," I said apologetically.

The Lakeland Police, who had been listening intently, trying their best to follow the story, threw up their arms and called it a closed case.

"The moment I turned around and saw Muggs was gone, I knew Hunter Rayburn had to be involved. And I really thought it was you in *Southern Cross*, Garry.—So why *didn't* you call me somewhere along the way?" I complained.

"Well, first of all, you saw who had my phone. And second of all, I didn't want to scare you. I promised myself I wasn't goin' to burden you with the details of my bounty hunt. And remember, I told you I'd call just as soon as Rayburn was taken care of. Besides, I knew you were in good hands." Garry grinned and patted Muggs on the shoulder.

"Well, we're just glad it's all over with," my dad added.

"Not as glad as I am," I said.

My mom stood up. "Garry, you look dog-tired. We should let you get to bed."

* * *

Upstairs, Garry flopped down on the bed. From the bathroom I called out, "I don't care if it's Hunter Rayburn who brought you here, I'm just so glad you are."

But Garry was already asleep, flight suit and all, by the time I even got out of the bathroom. I knew he must have had a hell of a day flying from Boston to Key West to Havana, then back to Key West and on to Oakwood Shores, so I slid quietly into bed, pulled up the blanket, and cuddled close. For the past month I'd gone to sleep in a cold and empty bed. I can't begin to explain the contentment I felt at having

Garry by my side. I breathed in his scent and used all of my self-control to keep from waking him. I fell asleep to the sounds of fireworks in the distance and Garry's heartbeat in my ear.

Chapter 63

When the Dust Had Finally Settled

I ndependence Day . . . my independence day. Garry at home. Hunter Rayburn off to The Brig. A healthy baby on the way. I couldn't help but think, *Life's good on my boat.*

* * *

We never truly realize how stressed we are until the tension subsides and everything is back to normal. That morning, sleep, which had eluded me for months, had returned to my bed, breathing came easier, and a raw emptiness in the pit of my stomach reminded me that I was now eating for two.

The sun was brightly gleaming through the french doors. Garry had already showered and stood on the balcony in his boxers, talking with Muggs down below. I snuck up behind him, put my arms around his waist, and buried my cheek in his sturdy back.

"Hey. Good mornin' billfish. How'd you sleep?"

"Me? I slept great. How about *you*? You're the one who needs sleep," I said.

"You're right. I do. Let's go back to bed." Garry pulled me inside and slipped my camisole over my head.

"Is that a belly I'm beginnin' to see there?" He smiled and rubbed his hand over my growing abdomen.

I opened my mouth to reply, but he put his finger to my lips. "We'll talk about that later, but *first,* you and I have some important catchin' up to do."

And so, we made love like it was the first time, savoring every moment. Slow and unhurried. I wanted to soak Garry in. It'd been a long month without him, and I knew he'd be back on the road in the blink of an eye. That morning Garry was *all mine*. I wasn't ready to give him back to the fans yet.

"I don't want you to go," I whispered.

* * *

Garry and I lounged on the deck in the morning sunshine, eagerly gobbling up the omelets he'd made.

"So what's next, Mr. Rich and Famous?" I asked.

Garry smiled with his big dimples. (He gets a kick out of it when I call him that.) "Cincinnati, my love. Nobody misses Cincy. Are you game?"

"The thought's been crossing my mind," I said.

"Not 'til tomorrow though. Today is all ours. What do y'all do here in Oakwood Shores on the 4th of July?"

"Well. So far you've got it right," I said. "First we make love, then you make breakfast for your wife, then we hang out on the lake all day, and finally, we make love one more time before the day is done."

"Sounds like my kind of 4th of July."

Amen.

Chapter 64

Our Lives Change Like the Weather

H ard to believe it's been over a year since Garry and I first met that Halloween night. (Actually, it's hard to believe coconut shell bras and shark fin hats have become a normal part of my life.) Things definitely have changed since then. I guess you might say I certainly got the action I was looking for. In fact, there's never a dull moment around here. Allison is pregnant again . . . Melanie and Jessica have moved down to Key West . . . Brooke Walker and I belong to the same playgroup . . . Macy Rayburn made an appearance in our lives. . . . and last we heard, Hunter Rayburn is still in The Brig. But I can tell you about those things later.

I'm sure it's occurred to you that I'm no longer a typical Midwestern girl, languishing in quiet desperation at the end of the commuter line. As you're well aware, this year gone by ain't been a piece of cake. But, despite it all, or maybe I should say *because* of it all, I've come to learn a lot about the inner workings of Nichole Bocelli. I've learned to trust my instincts, to stop worrying for every little detail. I've learned that control is not always a good thing . . . that the future is uncertain, no matter how we slice it, and that the past is the past—dead and gone. I've discovered that it's far better to live in the NOW (or as my good friend Jimmy Buffett keeps telling me, "Breathe in, breathe out, move on"). I've come to understand the importance of friendship .. . that our friends (girlfriends, in my case) are the glue that holds us together when life gets tough. I've also learned the importance of valuing myself. I don't know about you, but before I met Garry, I thought of my life as merely "common" in the face of celebrity; when in fact, I discovered most celebrities are just down-to-earth, small-town people like you and like me . . . and that every single one of us, from street sweeper to bank owner, to 24 year old architect, has something worthwhile to contribute.

Overall, I like to think I've grown into a wiser and more mature woman this past year. After all, they say that trouble brings experience and experience brings wisdom. And knowing who you are, isn't that *true* wisdom? Isn't that what life's all about? I believe Mr. Marley said it best, "Don't gain the world and lose your soul, wisdom is better than silver or gold."

So, what am *I* up to lately, you ask? Well, I'm working hard being mom to an adorable baby (who has the most wonderful dimpled smile) and doing my best to keep Garry on the straight and narrow path.

It's true, being married to a rock star seems to have it's up and downs, but if I can just watch out for that boom, then any direction he blows'll be fine.

Care to know what's goin' on in our lives?
Be sure to catch Nichole's latest account of our adventures at:

www.lisamottolahudon.com